DATE DUE			
6-22			
9-11			
10-27			
5-18			
8-4-08			
1-31-11			

<·> The Pipestone Quest

Also by Don Coldsmith

The Pipestone Quest

A Novel

Don Coldsmith

University of Oklahoma Press : Norman

A Novel in the Spanish Bit Saga
Time Period: late 1700s

All of the characters in this book are fictitious, and any resemblance to actual persons, living or dead, is purely coincidental.

Library of Congress Cataloging-in-Publication Data

Coldsmith, Don, 1926–
    The pipestone quest : a novel / Don Coldsmith.
        p.   cm.
    "A novel in the Spanish bit saga"—T.p. verso.
    ISBN 0-8061-3612-X (alk. paper)
        1. Indians of North America—Fiction. 2. Great Plains—Fiction.
    I. Title.

PS3553.O445P57 2004
813'.54—dc22

                                                              2003063415

The paper in this book meets the guidelines for permanence and durability of the Committee on Production Guidelines for Book Longevity of the Council on Library Resources, Inc. ∞

1 2 3 4 5 6 7 8 9 10

<⋅>Introduction

Most people have seen, or at least are aware, of the reddish stone from which many American Indian artifacts are carved, especially pipes with a ceremonial or religious function. This special material is almost sacred in its usage and in its "spirit." It is called "pipestone" by the Native cultures and "catlinite" by geologists, after George Catlin, artist and explorer, who first called it to the attention of the world. It is known to every North American Native culture, over three hundred in all, yet has only one source. All of the red catlinite pipestone comes from the "Pipestone Quarry" in what is now Minnesota. It became so sacred to all that even traditional enemies honored its function. The area of its source became a haven against violence.

DON COLDSMITH

<> The Pipestone Quest

<> 1

It was an unusually fine morning in the Moon of Growing, called "May" by the white man. The tallgrass prairie was lush and green, still damp from morning dew. Sun Boy had thrust his flaming torch above Earth's rim only a short while ago. The People were still straggling up from the river, where they had performed their daily ritual cleansing baths to start the day.

The camp, including the lodges of some forty or fifty families, the Southern Band of the People, spread across the prairie near the river. The horses, herded by some of the young men in a meadow downstream, numbered in hundreds.

The day was warming. A pair of hawks perched in a giant cottonwood near their lodge of sticks, preening and waiting for the rising air currents. They would ride these in circles high into the sky. From there, their keen vision would allow them to locate game with which to feed the four hungry nestlings in the old tree.

On a low hill to the south of the camp stood three young men, each holding the reins of a sleek, well-muscled horse. Beaver and his friend Wants a Horse were almost the same age, and had known each other since before they could remember. Wants a Horse was so called because of his fascination with his father's buffalo-runners.

He had been a capable horseman by the age of nine, very aggressive in his racing and in other competitions.

Beaver, however, was less aggressive, more quiet and sensitive. His name resulted from his two big permanent front teeth that came in during his seventh summer.

"You look like a beaver!" his friend Horse had giggled. And the name stuck.

Beaver admired his friend's ability to compete, but suffered a major handicap himself. When he had beaten someone at a race or wrestling or swimming, he found he felt sympathetic for the loser. Too much, maybe.

"He would not feel sad for you!" Horse often teased. "Enjoy your win!"

"I *do!*" insisted Beaver. "But still my heart is heavy for him . . . Not for you today, though. I'm going to beat you!"

"Not on your best day!" laughed his friend. "Now, to that tree and back?"

Horse pointed to a small lone tree, a few bowshots to the south.

"*Around* the tree and back," specified Beaver. "Will you start us and judge the winner, Turtle?"

The third young man, enjoying his friends' good-natured banter, agreed.

"Now," he instructed, "you both start behind this line."

He drew a mark on the ground, and continued.

"To the tree and around it, back here. The horse to cross the line first wins."

"The nose or the tail?" joked Wants a Horse. "My horse is much longer."

"The nose, then," instructed Turtle. "Now, I will walk out a few steps and drop this stone. That starts the race, but don't run over me. I'll stand still until you pass."

Turtle had selected a smooth stone the size of a goose egg, and now walked a few steps toward the distant tree, then stopped and turned.

"Ready?"

The two horses, sensing the race, fidgeted and strained against their rawhide war bridles.

There was quite a difference between the two. Beaver's mount was his pride and joy, a roan filly sired by one of the best stallions owned by his father, Finds His Arrow. She was an attractive blue, slender in build but sleek, and wiry.

The animal on which Wants a Horse sat was a large, well-muscled stallion, a favorite buffalo runner of the young man's father.

"Wait!" called Beaver. "Which direction around the tree? I don't want to run into you coming around the other way!"

The horses were becoming unmanageable in their excitement.

"Right to left!" yelled Turtle. "Now *go!*" He dropped the rock, and as the two horses swept past him, he trotted back to his finish line and turned to watch the race.

Beaver's roan took a slight lead for the first few strides. Her small frame and quickness provided an advantage as the larger animal lumbered into motion. In only a short distance, however, the longer stride of the big spotted stallion allowed him to surge ahead.

Both horses were excited, the whites of their eyes showing, straining every muscle. Each animal wore only a girth around the rib cage, to be used by the rider to hold on if necessary. Neither rider sought to do so, at least, not yet.

Beaver felt the warmth of the animal under him, and the slippery sweat, already bursting forth from the excitement of the contest, as well as the exertion. He gently eased the pressure of the war bridle to the left as they approached the tree. He must be careful not to swing too wide.

The big stallion was easily three lengths ahead when he thundered past the tree and his rider tried to turn. Wants a Horse attempted to make the change in direction, but the animal was interested only in running.

Meanwhile, Beaver kneed the roan as close to the tree as he dared, to make the turn. His left knee and calf scraped the trunk as they brushed past. He caught a glimpse of his friend's stallion, fighting the rein as they executed a much wider turn, wasting the space of a few heartbeats.

Even as Beaver urged the mare back into the spring for the finish line, he heard the pounding hooves of the spotted stallion behind them. He loosened the rein and leaned forward over the blue roan's neck, flattening himself over the withers to lessen the wind of their passing.

The hoofbeats of the stallion were closer now. From the corner of his right eye, he could dimly recognize the shape of the big animal's head drawing abreast. He did not turn to look, knowing he could not afford the risk of any distraction. Ahead, above the roan's flattened ears, he could see their friend Turtle, standing astride the left end of the finish line, ready to call the winner as they swept past.

Beaver wasn't certain. He had been busy urging the last bit of speed possible from his mare, paying attention not to the other horse and rider, but to the finish line. He reined in, gently at first, as they slowed and circled back toward Turtle, who was jumping excitedly and yelling, pointing to Beaver and the blue roan.

Wants a Horse, riding a bigger loop to slow his mount, circled back to the starting point.

"You win," he admitted sheepishly. "But you couldn't on a straight-away run."

"That's right," panted Beaver, trying to catch his breath. "Of course not. I had to use the quickness of the turn."

"Clever!" admitted Wants a Horse, a bit disgruntled. "Another race?"

"Not today," Beaver answered. "But see, I do not feel sorrow!"

All three laughed, and Turtle spoke.

"The trader will be unpacking. I'll maybe see you there."

"Ah, yes, I forgot," said Wants a Horse. "Well, we can race later."

The three mounted and rode back toward the camp at a walk. The main activity of the day would be the visitor from elsewhere. That was always entertaining.

⟨ ⟩

Beaver watched intently as the trader unrolled his packs and began to spread his wares on the blanket.

The coming of a trader to the camp of the People was sure to create a few days of fun and excitement. Traders fascinated Beaver. He could not imagine the places they had been and the sights they had seen. Of course he did not believe all the stories some of them told. The tales of places where boiling water spurted up out of the ground in spouts much higher than a man, and several times a day, were obviously exaggeration. Yet the trader who told that had also insisted that in the same area there were puddles of paint of all colors along the ground. It could be used, the trader said, though it was difficult, because it, too, was boiling hot. The man had lost all credibility when he claimed to have caught trout in a cold stream and cooked them in a boiling hot spring a few steps away. It was no matter about the fish, anyway. The People did not normally eat fish, preferring buffalo or other red meat. Even dog, in a hard season, was a delicacy compared to the white, watery flesh of a fish.

This trader today, however, was known to the People. He called on them nearly every season, when he could. He was Arapaho, known for their trading, sometimes even called the Trader People. This one, simply called "Trader," had a cheerful and friendly manner, necessary to his vocation.

A trader must get along with everyone to be successful. By the nature of his work, he deals with people who are enemies of each other. He himself must be honest and above suspicion, remaining neutral in all the disputes among his customers. This, in turn, gives him a certain amount of immunity. If an honest trader comes to harm, the word finds its way around. Soon, the reputation of those responsible will spread, and no trader will visit. And, the trader is needed. He supplies commodities available nowhere else. This was becoming more apparent all the time. White trappers and fur traders had been encountered frequently in the past few years.

That was good, in a way. It had given easier access to metal knives and tools, and to the thundersticks that were becoming popular among some of the prairie tribes. Not too much so among the Elk-dog People. The thunderstick was not much good in a buffalo hunt, because it carried only one shot. Reloading on a galloping horse was virtually impossible. Most hunters used a lance or a bow. For a lone hunter, of course, it was a different matter. One man could easily stalk his quarry on foot to within reach of the leaden ball that could strike it down. But some of the older men still preferred the bow . . . An arrow leaves a better blood trail than a bullet to follow a wounded animal, some claimed. But one thing was certain, powder and lead must be obtained from traders, either at the trading posts of the white man, or from a traveling Indian trader, such as this Arapaho.

It was a respected profession, dating back into antiquity. Traders were usually accomplished linguists, because of the necessity of communication in bartering. The old men said that the ancient hand-sign talk had been developed by traders to fill this need. There were even rumors that far to the East, a language had been developed just for trade . . . The "Eastern trade talk," a mix of many tongues, it was said.

But all of this was of no concern to young Beaver, now in his seventeenth summer. He and his friends were interested only in the fact that here was someone from outside their close-knit band, the Southern Band of the People. The trader would have new stories, maybe, and surely items for trade that would be interesting to see, and maybe to handle, with appropriate permission. He had arrived late on the previous day, and announced that there would be trading in the morning. He and his wife had set up their camp, after a polite social call at the lodge of Far Thunder, the band chief. That was only proper courtesy.

There had been, of course, the usual social gathering and story fire that attended the presence of an outsider. The trader would carry news; maybe, even, some new stories, gathered from far-away tribes and nations.

It had been so, and in fact this man, whose word could be trusted, had actually verified some of the wild tales they had heard from the trader who had stopped last season. It was true, he insisted, about the boiling springs and paint pots.

<>

Now, the next morning, the trader was preparing for the day's activity. He had opened a couple of packs and artfully arranged his wares in attractive patterns on a couple of blankets.

Curious members of the Southern Band began to gather, mostly curious youngsters, so far. But, as the People returned, a few at a time, from their morning dip at the stream, they began to saunter over to see the trader's offerings.

Snakewater, the medicine woman, approached with a greeting.

"*Osiyo*," said the old woman.

She spoke in her own tongue.

"You are Cherokee?" asked the trader in surprise.

"Yes. The 'Real People.' But now, this is my home. Elk-dog, 'The People.'"

"Ah, I remember!" observed the trader's wife. "You had just joined them the last time we traded with the Elk-dog People. It was at the Sun Dance, no? And you are a holy woman?"

"The Sun Dance, yes," Snakewater agreed. "Holy woman? Not really. I do a little medicine, that's all."

"Of course," said the trader.

Among the Elk-dog People, one who does have the powers of the spirit must deny it, to avoid the false pride that would weaken the gift.

The conversation was in the tongue of the People, quite familiar to the trader and his wife.

"Good morning, Grandmother," said Beaver respectfully. "Snakewater is one of us now," he added, turning to the trader.

"Yes, I remember, now," the trader mused. "There was an accident at the Sun Dance, no? The buffalo at the medicine lodge fell?"

"That is true," said Snakewater curtly. "Let us not speak of it."

Beaver remembered it well. There had been much talk and speculation. A woman had been killed when the effigy collapsed.

An outsider, someone from the medicine woman's past. It had been considered an event brought on by the evil of the woman who was killed. One of those things not to be questioned. It was meant to be, and the less talk of it, the better. Hence, Snakewater's dismissal of the subject.

The trader, accustomed to dealing with a broad range of customs, quickly saw the need to change the subject. It was an event which involved things of the spirit, and among any of the various peoples with whom he dwelt, such things should not be questioned.

"I have some good things for trade today," said the trader, deftly changing the subject. "Some new metal needles . . . Knives, mirrors . . . Ah! Glass beads, much easier than quill-work . . . Thread to sew them with."

The old woman nodded, not really interested.

"Do you need a pipe, Mother?" the man persisted.

Enticingly, he took out a well-tanned buckskin case and untied the drawstring at its mouth. Slowly, he drew forth the pipe. There was nothing really unusual about it. Its stem, as long as his forearm, was carved and painted and adorned with two small circlets of fur . . . *White* fur, probably that of the winter weasel. A single feather hung near its mouthpiece.

The bowl of the pipe was most important. Beaver took a quick breath, startled at his own reaction. He had seen many pipes, and this one, while an excellent example of the stone-worker's art, had nothing unusual to call attention to it. But it reached out to him in spirit. The highly polished surface of the red stone seemed to come alive with a radiant glow.

Beaver was fascinated, hypnotized by the object. There was a feeling that he had suddenly approached a new part of his life, and that nothing would ever be quite the same again.

2

Beaver sought out his uncle to talk about the stone pipe he had seen.

"Uncle" was a term of respect among the People, used when addressing any older adult male. In this case, it was a blood relationship, because Grasshopper was the younger brother of Beaver's mother, Antelope Woman. It was the custom for a maternal uncle to take a major responsibility in the upbringing of a young man. This may have accounted, in part, for the use of the term "Uncle" as a mark of respect for any male older than one's self.

"Uncle," he began, "I have had a strange thing happen."

Grasshopper shifted his position against his willow backrest, uncrossed his long legs and recrossed one over the other. He took a puff from his pipe and blew a thin wreath of bluish smoke into the air, watching it drift and disappear.

"What was it, Beaver?" he asked seriously.

Beaver had always been full of questions, since the time he was old enough to use words to ask. Grasshopper's was a challenging responsibility, trying to answer such questions. Usually enjoyable, sometimes frustrating. The boy was serious and thoughtful, respectful of others, with a keen sense of humor, yet had a powerful feeling for loyalty and responsibility. Grasshopper knew that Beaver was only satisfied with the most complete answers. Now, nearly a man, some of Beaver's questions and problems demanded the best of his uncle's thoughts and advice.

"You know the trader is here?" asked Beaver.

"Of course."

Grasshopper puffed his pipe again.

"He has a pipe, Uncle . . . One of red stone."

"Yes . . . You want to buy it? What have you to trade?"

"No, no . . . Not that . . . Well, maybe. But it seemed to call out to me. Not to buy it, but to *think* about it. To feel its spirit, maybe."

Grasshopper nodded solemnly. It could be so, he thought.

"Did you handle it?"

"No, no. I only looked."

"Did you ask about it?"

"No. It . . . Well, it seemed important. I felt the need to know more. I should have asked . . ."

"No, no, Beaver. There must have been a reason to feel so. The trader does offer this pipe for trade?"

"I suppose so . . . It was on the trade blanket with other things."

Grasshopper nodded again.

"So, it is not a personal thing, it seems . . . The trader should be glad to have you look at it."

"I . . . I suppose. I did not ask."

"Hmm . . . Probably expensive, no?"

There was a glint of humor in Grasshopper's eye.

"Maybe so. I did not think of that, Uncle."

Grasshopper knocked the ash from his own pipe into his palm and tossed it on the ground as he rose, tucking the pipe in a bag hanging on the tripod in front of his lodge.

"Let's go look", he said.

"A very fine pipe," beamed the trader, extending it toward Grasshopper almost ceremoniously.

"No . . . This young man wants to see it," Grasshopper said, nodding toward Beaver.

"Oh . . . Of course," said the man nervously.

Beaver took the pipe carefully, holding it with both hands, one near the mouthpiece, the other near the stone bowl.

The trader apparently saw the reverence with which the young man handled the object, and began to relax, entering into the importance of the moment.

"Feel the stone of the bowl," he urged.

Beaver complied, carefully cupping a palm around the smoothly rubbed stone. It was warm, pleasant . . . Comforting, somehow.

"Its spirit is good," said Beaver in awe. "I can feel its importance."

The trader smiled.

"Yes . . . Probably the finest pipe I have ever had."

This was an obvious exaggeration, of course.

"What makes this one different?" asked Grasshopper. "There are many pipes made of the red pipestone. Several men here in our band have them."

"That is true. The pipestone itself brings its spirit. The workmanship and pride in the carving and polishing, too, I suppose. The design . . . Some are more artful than others, more graceful, as a deer is more graceful than a bear cub, no? But the spirit is in the stone, and this one is special. Notice its smooth texture, its even color. Then, add the skill of the finest workmanship. It helps the spirit express itself, does it not?"

The trader was reaching toward the peak of his sales effort.

"Where is such stone found?" asked Beaver. "Is it found near our country?"

"Ah, no," chuckled the trader. "Some that is similar, and useful. Pipes are made from it, yes. But this is a strange thing: all of the stone such as that in this pipe, the red pipestone, with *this* spirit, comes from only one place."

"Really?" asked Grasshopper in amazement. "You have been there?"

"No, no!" The trader chuckled. "Maybe I will go there some day. But, look at my wares, here . . ." He spread his hands to demonstrate dozens of small objects on the blankets. "Arrow points . . . Look at all the colors! Blue-gray flint from your own area, here. Good quality, of course. But there," he pointed, "white from far to the West. Red and pink from other places. Yellowish or tan from farther East. Over there, the black shiny points . . . That is *not* flint. A white man told me it is like their glass. It takes a very sharp edge. Makes good knives."

"But," said Beaver, puzzled, "what has that to do with the pipestone?"

"Nothing! I only wanted to show you that most things can be found in many different places. A trader travels. He picks up things in trade. I even have some shells of creatures that live in the salty 'Big Water' many moons' travel to the West . . . Others from the South, the *Tejas* coast. Most things are found in many places, in different forms and kinds. But this," he pointed to the pipe's bowl again, "this red pipestone all comes from the same quarry."

"Where is it?" asked Beaver, handing the pipe back to the trader.

"Far to the north," said the other. "But, are you not interested in this fine pipe?"

He asked without much enthusiasm. It was apparent that a young man of only a few winters would not be able to afford such an item.

"No, Uncle, I have nothing of such value to trade," said Beaver, slightly embarrassed.

"I understand," nodded the trader. "Some day, maybe."

"Maybe. But I would ask . . . What is the source of this stone's power?"

"Who knows?" the trader shrugged. "What is the source of *any* power, the medicine of *anything* of the spirit? Some say it is all one . . . For my people, the Arapaho, it is all part of the 'Great Mystery.' Life, living and dying, the changing of seasons, new generations of grass and buffalo . . . All one mystery, maybe, but with many parts."

"Maybe," suggested Grasshopper, "you should talk with White Buffalo about these things."

"White Buffalo?" the trader interjected. "Your holy man, is he not? Yes, that would be good. His is the medicine of the buffalo? I remember him. It is good. And, may our trails cross again. How are you called?"

"Beaver."

"Ah . . . Yes, of course," said the trader, with a smile.

It was a handy name for now, and Beaver hoped that before too many seasons he would earn his adult name with deeds that would prove his manhood. That would be good, to be able to shed the name that called attention to his prominent teeth.

Beaver and Grasshopper strolled along the stream, no particular goal in mind.

"Yes, Beaver . . . Maybe White Buffalo can be of help in this. You should ask him, tell him of your feeling for the stone. Another thought . . . Snakewater, the medicine woman. Maybe she would know of this."

"But Snakewater is not of the People, Uncle."

"Yes, that is true. That is *why* you should ask her. The red stone is important to the People, and as the trader said, to *his* people. Is it, then, important to *all* people? Cheyenne, Kenza, Osage? Snakewater could tell you whether it is to *her* people, the Cherokees. That would tell you more of its importance, no?"

"Yes . . . That is true. I will ask her."

"Good! I am made to think she is very wise, Beaver. It is said that she talks to the Little People."

"*Aiee!* Her Little People, or ours?"

"I don't know. Maybe you'd better ask her about it."

"You are joking, no?" asked Beaver. "About the Little People?"

"Well, maybe. But their Little People are more important to them than ours to us. It would be interesting to know."

There was a glint of mischief in Grasshopper's eye again.

"I am not asking Snakewater about Little People!" said Beaver firmly. "But I will, about the pipestone."

3

As he headed back toward the lodge of his parents, Beaver saw the Cherokee medicine woman. She was again looking over the wares of the trader, visiting with him as she did so. Here were two people who had traveled widely, and had experienced a broad variety of events. They must have much in common to talk about, thought Beaver.

He drew near, waiting for a pause in the conversation so that he would not interrupt the talk of his elders. Soon there was a pause, and the trader looked up.

"Ah!" he said. "Beaver, is it not? You came back about the pipe?"

It is always flattering to have a stranger remember one's name, and the young man's heart responded warmly.

"Not now," he smiled. "I would speak with the grandmother, here."

"Me?" asked Snakewater, pretending to be overly surprised. "I have nothing to trade!"

Beaver knew she was teasing him.

There had been a time, long ago, when Snakewater's attitude was that of a bitter old woman, defiant against the world. Beaver had never known her in that light, for she had begun to change before she came to become a member of Far Thunder's band. Now, she was beloved by both children and adults, for her stories as well as her skills with healing potions and ceremonies.

"Maybe you do have something to trade, Grandmother. I seek advice."

The old woman smiled.

"That is free," she teased, "and probably worth the cost."

"No, no. I am serious. My uncle suggested that I might talk to you."

"Your uncle . . . Let me think . . . Grasshopper, is it not?"

"That is true."

"*Okeh*," she said, reverting to a word of her own tongue. "Let us walk . . ."

They strolled a little distance from the trader's display for a moment, and then Beaver spoke.

"I do not know how to start, Grandmother . . ."

"At the beginning, maybe?"

"Don't tease. I am serious."

"I know. Go ahead, Beaver."

"Well, the trader spoke of a pipe. You saw it, maybe," he began.

"Yes. A beautiful thing. You are trying to buy it?"

"No, no. That is far beyond me, Grandmother. But I am curious about it."

"How so?"

"It is hard to say. I felt that it called out to me."

"How so? 'Buy me'?"

"No, not that way! A thing of the spirit."

Snakewater's face was dead serious now. She nodded, waiting.

"It was a warm, good feeling."

"Not threatening, then?"

"No, no! The opposite."

"Ah! That is good. But, you have seen pipes before. How is this different?"

"I'm not sure, Grandmother. It seemed not to be the *pipe*, but the stone itself. That of which the bowl is made."

"The red pipestone, no? But you have seen that before, too."

"Not quite like this. The trader let me hold it. The bowl fit in the palm of my hand. It was warm and alive, and, well, its spirit was good. It called to me . . ."

"You said that before. 'It called.' Called to go somewhere, do something?"

"No. Not that I could tell."

"Maybe it is meant that you wait."

"For what?"

"For more information. Sometimes we are meant to do something. Something important, maybe. Sometimes we are meant to wait. When it is time, you will know."

"Thank you, Grandmother."

"One more thing. Have you spoken to White Buffalo?"

"No. Grasshopper spoke of that, but of you, also. I just saw you first."

"It is good. But you should see your own holy man. His medicine is good, too, but different from mine. You have heard the saying, maybe, 'There are many paths to the top of the mountain, but they all lead to the top of the mountain', no?"

"Yes. But I do not see *any* path."

"Ah, you will, Beaver, I am made to think it will be shown to you."

"But how?"

"Who knows? When it happens, you will have no doubt. But keep your head open, ready to listen. And, do go and talk to your holy man."

"Thank you, Grandmother. I will."

Clouds were drifting in, and a light breeze from the south had now shifted to the north. There seemed to be a good possibility of a summer storm before evening. It was expected at this time of year. Rain Maker would march across the prairie, pounding his mighty thunder-drum and hurling his spears of fire. Beaver glanced toward the west, from which direction Rain Maker usually came at this season. A dark cloud bank on the horizon a day's travel away told him that he had a little time. It would be evening before the rain struck. He headed toward the lodge of White Buffalo.

People were beginning to move things into the lodges before the expected storm arrived. There was no hurry. There would be plenty of time, but most of the lodge covers had been rolled up to allow the cooling south breezes to blow through the dwellings. It would take a little time to roll the skirts down and peg them to the ground and to the base of each lodge pole.

As he approached the lodge of White Buffalo, Beaver saw that the old man and his wife had already pegged down the lodge cover, and carried their willow back rests inside. The thought occurred to him that long years of experience had taught them much about the prediction of Rain Maker's behavior. But, there should still be ample time to inquire briefly before heading home.

He shook the deer-hoof rattle that hung over the doorway of the tepee, calling out as he did so.

"It is Beaver, son of Finds His Arrow, Uncle. May I speak with you?"

There was stirring inside the lodge, and a woman lifted the doorskin and looked out.

"What do you want?"

It was not a challenge, and the tone of Buffalo's wife was not unpleasant. It was merely an inquiry.

"I am called Beaver," the nervous young man began. "I have questions about things of the spirit, and was told by Grasshopper, my uncle, to ask White Buffalo."

He decided not to mention that he had seen Snakewater first. The holy man might be offended.

There was more movement inside and a deep voice called, "Come in!"

The woman held back the doorskin, and stepped aside. Beaver stooped to enter, and rose to his full height inside the lodge. It took a moment for his eyes to become accustomed to the dim interior.

Buffalo's wife had apparently just started a small fire in the central firepit. It was not needed for warmth, and in summer most of the cooking was done outside. Now, however, a blaze of some sort was needed purely for light.

The lodge was much like any other, except larger, and in some ways, more ornate. An older couple, of course, with their children in their own lodges, would still have more possessions than a young couple just starting a home. It was also the function of White Buffalo to keep the Story Skins, the pictographic history of the Southern Band of the People. Beaver wondered where they might be stored. Probably in the pile of baggage to the left of the entrance, piled there hurriedly in the haste to prepare for the storm.

White Buffalo sat on a pile of robes directly opposite the entrance, and motioned to the visitor.

"Come, sit," he offered, pointing to a place on his right.

Beaver was flattered. To the right of the host was a place of honor; thus, he was being accepted as a man, not as a child. Now, the tempo of the conversation would be determined by the old man, who simply sat and smoked for a while.

Beaver tried to think of what he knew of this man. "White Buffalo" was both his name and his office, as custodian of a white robe, one of the most sacred objects of the People. It was handed down from generation to generation, to the one selected to hold the office and the responsibility. Usually it had been a father-to-son legacy, but not always. Once, according to legend, the white robe had been destroyed by an unqualified impostor, and the band had fallen on evil times. It had required a vision quest, and a newly ordained White Buffalo as holy man, for good fortune to return to the People. That had been a generation or two ago.

Beaver now recognized, with his improving vision in the dim lodge, that behind the medicine man there hung a light-colored robe . . . The legendary white buffalo skin.

"Beautiful, is it not?" asked the holy man.

"Yes . . ." was all Beaver could think to say.

He had seen the robe used ceremonially sometimes, but never at this close a distance. He still could not see it well in the dimness of the closed lodge.

As he studied it, he saw another object hanging over the white robe. It was made of metal, but decorated with bits of fur and a single eagle feather. He had seen it before, too, worn by the holy man in ceremonies.

White Buffalo saw that gaze, too, and spoke again.

"Yes, that is the bit worn by the First Horse. It was ridden by Heads Off, the foreigner who became one of us."

Beaver had heard the story many times, but only now had he come to realize its importance. And here he was, sitting in the lodge of this all-important holy man, the custodian of their heritage. He felt embarrassed and unworthy, and for a moment, thought of jumping to his feet to run away. Maybe it had been a mistake to even come here, so pretentiously.

But now, White Buffalo was speaking.

"What is it that you come to ask me?"

Where to start? There was so much that he wanted to say, to ask about, to tell, to try to explain how he felt. The story poured forth as Beaver attempted to interpret and describe his emotions.

The expression on the face of White Buffalo did not change as he listened. It remained flat and emotionless, his eyes focused on some distant thought as the youth talked.

Finally, Beaver paused, not quite sure whether he had said enough, or too much, or if it had actually made any sense at all.

Buffalo puffed his pipe for a moment.

"You have told no one of this?"

"My uncle, Grasshopper, who suggested that I talk to you."

The old man nodded. "No one else?"

"I . . . Yes . . . My uncle also said I might talk to Snakewater, the medicine woman. I happened to see her first, at the trader's camp."

Beaver paused, wondering if he had been wrong to speak of this. Maybe, even, wrong in the eyes of White Buffalo to have talked with Snakewater at all. Especially, *before* he sought the counsel of the holy man.

"Never mind," assured Buffalo. "The medicine of the woman is different, but in no conflict with mine. And what did the woman say?"

"Only that I must watch for some sign, to tell me what I need to do."
Buffalo nodded seriously.

"As I would have told you, had you come to me first."

There was only the slightest trace of sarcasm, a gentle reminder.

"What does this mean, Uncle?" blurted Beaver.

The old man shrugged and spread his hands helplessly.

"It is no matter what it means to *me*. What does it mean to *you*?"

"But I don't know. That is why I come to you."

"Yes . . . And you still have no answers. Is it not so?"

Beaver nodded.

"Beaver," said the old man, frowning a little, "you are impatient. When it is time, it will be shown to you."

"But *how*?"

"I don't know. It is *your* mystery."

"I don't understand, Uncle."

"Of course . . . Beaver, if you still think you need to understand, you have missed the message. Many things are not meant to be understood, no?"

"So, what must I do?"

"Nothing, maybe. Wait. Have you taken a vision quest?"

"No. Should I do so?"

"Ah, you have answered your own question! If you have any doubt, it is not time. So, wait."

"Wait for what? The answer to the spirit of the stone, or for the call to a vision quest?"

"Truly you are impatient, Beaver. I don't know. It is to be your quest. Either one, or both. Maybe for you, they are the same. You search for meaning, and maybe there is no meaning. Some things just happen, maybe, like the sunrise."

"But that has meaning, Uncle."

"Yes, but meaning that maybe we are not meant to understand entirely. Some say we will find more understanding on the Other Side, but this does not make me eager to die to find out. That, too, happens when it is time. When it is time, you will be shown."

Beaver was not entirely happy with this interpretation.

"Snakewater told me much the same."

There was a slight smile on the face of the old man, a twinkle in his eye.

"Yes. Our medicines are different, but in many ways, alike."

The advice from both individuals whose counsel he had sought was the same . . . *Wait. You will be shown, when it is time.*

He sought out his uncle again, and informed him about both interviews.

Grasshopper listened thoughtfully, nodding occasionally.

"It is good!" he said finally. "The same advice from both. No need for a decision, until you know more."

"So, I wait, then?"

Grasshopper nodded. "What else can you do? Sing your songs of prayer: Morning Song, the Song for Fire, maybe. Yes, that would be good. Perform your devotions."

"I do that, Uncle. I had not thought of the Song for Fire, though."

"Maybe it's worth a try. Don't expect too much, though."

<>

There is a time in the growing-up of any young person, when it seems that his parents know nothing . . . They have never been young, they have no sense of humor, and are, of course, completely unaware of the important things which are occurring around them, the new discoveries that improve life. It is easy for a young person to scorn the thoughts of mere parents, because their generation has no imagination or insight.

This, maybe, became the reason for the tradition among the People that a young man's teacher be not a parent, but another . . . Hence, the Uncle.

That evening, Beaver chose to ride to a spot he had found before, well out of sight of the camp. He told his parents only that he would be back a little later.

Beaver's parents watched him ride out of the camp and around the shoulder of the hill.

"Does he seek his vision?" asked his mother.

"I think not," assured Finds His Arrow. "Our son would have told us, if he intended to be gone that long, would he not?"

"I hope so."

"Besides, he is very close to your brother. Grasshopper would know, and would tell us. And, to undertake a vision quest, Beaver would need to inform Far Thunder of his absence, no?"

"I suppose so . . . But he is so young!"

Finds His Arrow laughed.

"About my age when I started to court you!" he teased.

"Yes," she chuckled. "Maybe that is what worries me. And, he took a blanket."

"Of course. He may need it for warmth. But I expect him back before morning."

⟨⟩

Beaver carried very little. The blanket, a few strips of dried meat, in case he became hungry, his bow and arrows, and a small bag with his pipe, tobacco, and a fire striker. It was not a ceremonial pipe, but a small one used for social smokes. Any smoke, of course, has significance.

He reached the spot where he planned to build his fire as Sun Boy retreated toward the West, painting the sky with his brilliant colors as he went.

Beaver picketed his horse and began to gather dead sticks from the trees along the stream. A big fallen cottonwood, its trunk silver-gray in the fading sunset, furnished ample fuel.

He had pondered as to how he should kindle this important fire. There were several options: old-fashioned fire sticks, the flint and steel, or more modern matches from the trader. These had been found unreliable when damp. He had even considered carrying a few coals in a gourd full of ashes, but rejected that. This important fire should be a new one, born for this occasion. He settled on the flint and steel to produce his spark, the quickest reliable means.

He caught the spark on a scrap of charred cloth from his pouch, and breathed it into a larger glow. He wrapped it loosely in a handful of dry grass and blew on it gently, then harder, until it burst into flame.

The fire is a symbolic thing, a statement that may go back to the first man who ever controlled it. *Here, I intend to stay, for now. This is my camp, my home, my place.* It allowed man to claim a small territory, even though temporarily, against the terrors of the night. They may have been physical and real, dangerous predators in search of prey; or worse, the menacing *spirits* which prowl the darkness. For good or evil, it might still be advisable to acknowledge the presence of such spirits, by announcing one's presence. *I am here. I will remain for now.*

Beaver sang the Song for Fire as the cheerful orange flames, the color of Sun Boy's evening paints, curled up and around his little pile of kindling. He tossed a pinch of tobacco, known to please the spirits, into the flame. This would indicate to them that his heart was right. A little sage, at the edge of the growing fire . . . He took handfuls of the sage smoke and rubbed it over his face and shoulders to purify his person in the eyes of the spirits.

He sang the Song for Fire again, and added a few sticks before he sat down nearby to watch and wait and think. He did not want to build it up too big, like the fire of a white man. That was a widely enjoyed joke. Most white men built a blistering fire, so big that they could not come near enough to warm themselves. Any of the Native peoples would build a small fire and hover near it, enjoying the warmth. The exceptions among whites were the occasional trappers who had learned the Indian ways and found them good.

All of these things flitted through the mind of young Beaver as he sat, waiting. For what, he did not know. In his mind, this ritual repetition of the Song for Fire did have a purpose. It was a statement, not only *I am here*, but *I am ready. I am waiting.* He knew,

<· >5

Beaver thought that he must have dozed off, because something had changed. He didn't know what, but the fire had burned down to a patch of sunset-colored embers, which shimmered and writhed slowly, fanned by the changing currents of the light summer breeze. It was easy to visualize it as a living thing, placed there as a kaleidoscope by which he might receive information. Different parts of the picture would sparkle and then fade, as if time had become accelerated, or possibly meaningless.

It was said by the old men that one may see faces in the embers of a good fire . . . Faces which call up memories of the past, of the present, and maybe the future. Beaver had to admit that he saw nothing of the sort. He was fascinated by the slow, rhythmic motion of the writhing patterns, but he saw no meaning. The thought crossed his mind that maybe life itself is like that . . . Much activity but little meaning. He was surprised at himself for such thoughts, and for being so serious about it. He tried to detach himself from such philosophic pondering, and to concentrate on the familiar night sounds . . . The cry of a whippoorwill in the heavy growth of the oaks along the stream. The call of *Kookooskoos*, the great hunting owl, from farther away, and the answer of its mate, nearer at hand.

of course, that probably nothing would happen. The sort of help that he needed can seldom if ever be summoned. It must be sought, and the willingness to accept an answer must be apparent. Also, the willingness to accept *no* answer. In a sense, though, is not a prayer always answered? Sometimes, the *answer* is "no."

He was impatient, but finally was able to calm himself enough to sit still and watch the suggestion of motion in the shimmering glow of the embers. He began to see patterns and fanciful shapes in the white-hot coals. He added another stick, and new flames pushed back the darkness again, the shadows retreating from the light. He found it enchanting, both the darkness and the light, and he waited.

A distant coyote chortled at the night sky, sounding like a whole family of the creatures. Beaver had never understood how that was possible.

Something caught his attention and he turned to look. In the east, behind him, the moon was rising, its rim the color of the embers and of the sunset. Odd, he had never thought of that before.

The moon was a little past full, so it was rising quite some time after dark. It was large, but lop-sided rather than a full circle. He did not attach any importance to these facts. He simply practiced his powers of observation and attention to detail. Grasshopper had impressed his pupil with this necessity since before he could remember: *The danger lies in that which you do not see.*

He watched for a while, as the Seven Hunters made their way in their mighty circle around the Real-star, the one which never moves. He had once been told by a trader that the same constellation was called the "Big Dipper" by white men.

"What is a 'dipper'?" he had asked.

"Like a big spoon," the man had explained, through a bit of difficulty with language and hand signs. "Like a gourd, maybe, with a long part for a handle."

"Ah! Of course!" Beaver had grasped the idea.

Now he thought of it again. Yes, it could be a drinking gourd. He had also heard that to some, the same seven stars represent a bear. That, he could not quite visualize. To Beaver, it would probably always be the Seven Hunters. Just for practice, he sought out the dim star that represents a dog that accompanies the second hunter in the line. *Yes . . . The dog still follows him*, thought Beaver. Some things never change.

He took a deep breath and expelled it in a long sigh. What was he doing here? It was a pleasant night, but no more. Yet what could he have expected? This was not a vision quest.

You are impatient. The words of White Buffalo came back to him.

True, he had felt that something significant was about to happen. He had been pleased to notice that the colors of the sunset, the embers of his fire, and the rising moon were all the same. Maybe he had gained some insight, and in doing so, had come closer to being ready for . . . for whatever was to come. There are nights that are filled with excitement, and the feeling that something important is about to happen. A person hates to retire to bed, because he might miss something. This had not been one of those nights, as beautiful and relaxing as it had been. But it was good to be alone with the night sounds, to have a little while to think, apart from the constant activity of the camp. It occurred to him that maybe the evening *had* helped to make him ready for *something*. Nothing much could happen, in the realm of the spirit, until all was ready in his own heart. There was a lesson here, if he could find it, he was sure. Maybe, even, simply to relax and be receptive rather than too eager.

Smiling to himself, he rose to prepare to go back. Maybe he wouldn't even tell his uncle of his evening's experience. Grasshopper would only tell him to be patient, and to listen for guidance. Beaver was tired of that advice.

He was in the process of extinguishing the last embers of his fire by emptying his bladder on them, when his horse, waiting patiently, gave an odd snort. Beaver turned to look, as best he could, to see the cause of the horse's snort.

A horseman learns to interpret the talk of his animal. He cannot come to speak such a tongue, but he can come to understand it. Simple sounds from the lips of a horse may take on meaning and express feeling. Boredom, hunger, affection, such as a mare for her foal, sometimes just a soft greeting, or occasionally, alarm. A good horseman comes to understand this talk, and in this moment, the interpretation of the animal's soft snort might be critical. Though Beaver was distracted by the stream from his freely flowing bladder, he tried to concentrate on the quality of the sound he'd heard as he finished and quickly readjusted his loincloth.

It had not really been a snort of alarm, more like one of surprise. Yet the quality of the brief sound had been unusual. Every horseman, every human who works around animals, knows that they see and hear things not made available to mere humans. Theirs is a special contact with the spirit-world, kept from Man in his present lifetime.

What horseman, riding alone, has not had the experience of having his mount shy suddenly away from a spot where there is *nothing*, staring at empty space? Sometimes curiously, sometimes with alarm, maybe even trembling in what seems to be terror. Dogs and cats behave in similar ways occasionally, but the horse is possibly the most sensitive of domestic animals to things of the spirit world. It may be essential to look and listen to the horse's reaction.

Beaver turned to study the attitude and position of his mare. She was a five-year-old, his pride and joy, blue roan, and sired by one of his father's best buffalo runners. One front foot was white, to the pastern, and a slender strip of white ran from between the eyes nearly to the nostrils. His father had given her to young Beaver when she was born . . . His first horse. He had named her Blue, and he knew her well.

"What is it, Blue?" he asked now. "You heard something?"

The answer was a few soft syllables of horse talk, similar to that with which a mare comforts her foal. *It is all right, but be alert.*

Her stance, however, was slightly tense. She stood, staring at a space between them and the rising moon. Her ears were pricked sharply, points directed stiffly upward and almost pointing together, while her large intelligent eyes focused on something unseen by Beaver. He felt a prickling sensation at the back of his neck.

"Is somebody out there?" he called softly.

Instantly, he knew it was a stupid question. Anyone who wished him harm would not answer. And, if some of his friends were playing tricks, they wouldn't either. He thought that unlikely, but not impossible. That theory was reinforced by what he thought might be a very soft, snickering laugh from the darkness.

He was about to call out. Wants a Horse was the likeliest culprit, but at that moment Blue spoke again. She was looking directly toward the lop-sided moon, and her murmuring voice was reassuring. *Look! There!*

Beaver looked, and saw nothing. Then for an instant, something passed across the brightness of the moon's face. A wisp of cloud, maybe, he tried to convince himself with only partial success. Blue's eyes were still fastened on the apparition, or entity, or whatever it may have been. He could visualize a form that walked upright, on two legs. Or was it? Maybe only a patch of fog. Yes, surely . . . Fog or cloud at greater distance.

The form seemed to dissolve, now. Blue resumed grazing, and Beaver found himself feeling foolish. He shrugged the experience aside, and began to stir the ashes of his fire with a stick to be certain there were no embers.

Yet, he had a hard time denying what he thought he had seen—a small but very human-appearing figure, less than half his own height.

As if to reinforce this thought, he heard again the soft giggle in the darkness. It was rather unnerving that the sound was answered by a soft whicker from Blue.

<· ·>**6**

The Little People . . .

Beaver tried to think of everything he had ever heard about the Little People. They had been mentioned by someone not long ago. Who was it and what had brought up the subject? Something about Snakewater . . . Someone had said, "She talks to the Little People." He couldn't remember who had said it. There was so much going on in his life just now, so much to think about it made his head hurt.

But Snakewater had been good to him, lending advice and counsel. Maybe she could tell him more. He had, somehow, the idea that there are some risks involved, even in talking about the Little People. He had never wondered much about it. There had been some suggestion that there are many kinds of Little People. As many, perhaps, as there are tribes and nations of humans. Probably as many differences, as each tribe must have its own stories of the Little People, just as they have different stories of Creation. He also thought it possible that maybe no one knows very much about the Little People. He could recall very few stories about them. *Maybe they don't like to be talked about*, he thought.

He was slightly embarrassed to ask Grasshopper about it, so he elected to inquire directly to Snakewater. He approached the medicine woman's small lodge, close to that of the band chieftain. The family of Far Thunder had virtually adopted the Cherokee "grandmother" and helped with the erection of her lodge each time the band moved.

Beaver rattled the deer hooves and announced himself.

"Grandmother, it is Beaver. May I speak with you?"

There was the sound of movement in the lodge, and she drew the doorskin aside.

"Come in,"

Beaver stooped and entered. His first impression, after entering the dimness, was of the smell. Hanging from strings on the lodge poles were dozens of bunches and bundles of drying herbs. This mix of odors, vaguely familiar but exotic and somehow exciting, made him think that he had been here before. Yet he knew otherwise.

He did not know how to begin, and finally Snakewater broke the silence.

"About your quest?" she suggested.

"Oh! No . . . I think not, Grandmother. Something else."

"Sit," the old woman said, pointing to a backrest chair, and seating herself on a pile of robes.

Beaver took a deep breath.

"I would ask about the Little People."

She gave him a sharp look, one that indicated alarm.

"Stop!" she said. "Say no more until I have spoken."

Beaver nodded, his heart pounding.

"Now," the old woman began, "I don't know why you want to know, or why you ask me. But first, are we talking of the Cherokee Little People, or of yours? They are different, you know."

He nodded and started to speak, but she stopped him again.

"Let me go on," she said seriously. "There are things you must know. Among my people, one who sees a Little Person must never say so. To do so would betray their trust, and that person would die."

"But how would he know whether that was what he had seen?" asked Beaver. "What would the Little Person look like?"

"Stop! How would I know? How would anyone know, unless they had seen one? And they could never tell, is it not so?"

"So, no one can ever tell whether anyone has seen one? Maybe no one has?"

"That is possible," she said cautiously. "But we still don't know. Are we talking of your Little People, or mine?"

"I don't know, Grandmother," he admitted.

"Then, I assume you have seen or heard something . . . No, don't even say yes or no! Let me tell you of the Cherokee Little People. I know less about yours, but I am made to think that Little People are not so common among your people."

Beaver nodded, and she continued, phrasing her remarks carefully.

"Now, if anyone ever saw one of the Little People—mine, that is—I would suppose that they would appear like small Cherokees, no?"

He nodded, entranced, and she went on.

"It is said," Snakewater began cautiously, "that our Little People are of three kinds: The Rock People, Laurel People, and Dogwood People. They are named for the places they live, among rocky places, or in a laurel thicket. That is a plant not found here in your prairie country, and dogwood, though the dogwood there is different than prairie dogwood. But, no matter. Let me go on.

"Rock People do not relate well to humans. They usually stay invisible, but may toss rocks to frighten people away from their dwellings. In caves, maybe. They are not very nice. Some say they steal children, but I am made to think that is only to frighten children so they behave well.

"Now Laurel People are filled with mischief. They like jokes and are silly. They might play tricks on you, and they have a sense of humor. Dogwood People do, too, but they are more serious. They have responsibilities."

"What sort of responsibilities?" asked Beaver.

"I am coming to that. I am thinking that maybe most of our Little People, Cherokee, that is, are the Dogwood People. They are said to have several abilities not readily available to humans. They know where important plants grow, those whose medicine is good . . . Or bad, I suppose. The qualities of *all* plants."

Beaver glanced at the hanging bundles overhead, and he wondered how the medicine woman knew how to find them. But she hurried on, pretending not to notice.

"They have two more usual pursuits, however . . . Duties or assignments, in a way. They protect unsupervised children, and help to keep them safe. There could be much danger to a child playing alone, no?"

He nodded. *Is this why a lone child often has an unseen playmate whom he calls by name?* he wondered.

"And the other?" he asked.

"The Little People are responsible for looking after lost articles. Did you ever find something that appeared to belong to somebody else?"

"Yes. A knife, once, in the woods."

"Ah! It was in possession of the Little People. You kept it?"

"Yes . . ."

"You should have held it up so any could see, and made an announcement: 'Hey, Little People! I am taking the knife!'"

"But I didn't. I kept the knife, and nothing has happened."

"Ah, yes! You did not *know*, so you were not responsible. But now that you do know, it would be best to make the announcement. Just do as I said: '*Hey, Little People* . . .'"

"I will do it, Grandmother. But I wish to know more."

She studied him for a moment, and then smiled.

"Ah, don't we all? Young man, there is always more to know, and many things that are not meant to be known. We spoke some of this before, did we not?"

"Only a little, Grandmother."

"Yes . . . But, now tell me what you know of *your* Little People. That might be of help."

"I . . . I am made to think that my people don't find them as important as yours, Grandmother. We talk about them mostly in children's stories. They are fond of mischief."

Snakewater chuckled. "Yes, ours too. But no real harm, as long as we respect their ways. What else?"

"I don't remember much more about them. They can help or hurt. Maybe I should ask my uncle if he knows more."

"That is good. Grasshopper will know more than you or I, about *your* Little People."

She paused for a moment and then spoke again.

"Beaver, there is a thing I do not understand. Why did you come to *me* about your Little People? Why not to your uncle first?"

He thought for a moment, then spoke.

"I'm not sure, Grandmother. Maybe because you were helpful to me about the pipestone. Maybe, because someone had said of you, 'she talks to the Little People.' I don't know."

There was a look of concern on the face of the old woman, and she appeared to be choosing her words very carefully.

"Let us be sure where we are in this talk, Beaver. You have heard it said, 'she talks to Little People.' But cannot *anyone* talk to Little People? One may talk to a tree, a rock, the sky, or a bird. That is not to say that there will come an answer, no? So, 'she talks to Little People' means nothing. I talk to the stream . . . Sometimes, I talk to myself. I seldom answer, though. People would think that strange."

She was smiling now, but then became serious.

"You must also realize, Beaver, that to say I *talk* to Little People does not mean that I have *seen* them. When your people sing prayer songs, they talk and sing to spirits that are unseen. As we have said, many things are not meant to be understood."

It was apparent that the conversation was at an end. Beaver rose and thanked her, and she held the doorskin aside for him.

"Talk to your uncle," she advised in parting. "Maybe to White Buffalo, too."

She watched him thread his way among the lodges, and spoke softly.

"*There* is a strange one . . . Curious, but maybe wise beyond his years. Are you there, Lumpy? Yes, I thought so. Don't mess with his mind, *okeh*? *What*? Oh, that's what this is about, then. Ah, I wish you hadn't shown yourself. Sometimes you try my patience. Stop it, it isn't funny."

She reentered her lodge, still talking. There was no one to see her, but if there had been, she would have appeared to be talking to herself. If anyone had heard her next statement, spoken to the apparently empty lodge, they would have suspected that maybe she was crazy.

"Damn it, Lumpy, come on out! You know how it irritates me when we're talking and you stay invisible. And you had to show yourself to Beaver!"

There was a soft giggle behind the backrest.

<＜ ＞7

Grasshopper was vague.

"I don't know, Beaver, I never thought much about the Little People. The medicine woman was of no help?"

"Of some help, yes," answered Beaver. "Snakewater told me much, of *her* Little People. Much more is known of them, maybe, than of ours. Did you know, if one of her people sees a Little Person, and *tells* of it, he *dies*?"

"*Aiee*! But, you know, none of *our* people would probably tell. It would be a private and personal thing, like one's spirit guide, no?"

"Yes, but, Uncle, one may tell of that . . . 'My guide is Coyote' or Bear or whoever."

"True. Yet few tell the circumstances in which the guide came to them. Is it not so?"

Beaver nodded. "Maybe."

Grasshopper studied the young man for a few moments, and then spoke, slowly.

"I am made to think, Beaver, that there is a reason for your asking these things. No, don't interrupt . . . I don't want to know. Maybe it would be good to ask White Buffalo, though his medicine has little to do with Little People. It is plain, though, that when it is time, you will learn some answers."

He paused and chuckled.

"Or maybe not. There are some things best unanswered, because they are not meant to be understood. Is it not so?"

Beaver nodded, not quite convinced.

"Snakewater said the same thing."

"Ah! See, that is good!"

<>

The next few days were frustrating. For a youth, time passes slowly, and he is impatient to move on to greater things. The wait is difficult, for he does not realize that to be forced to wait is in itself a learning process. The passage of time is a great teacher, unappreciated at the moment.

Beaver carried out his minor tasks around the lodge, bringing some wood and buffalo chips for his mother's cooking fire. He spent a while grooming and playing with his blue mare, and then went swimming with his friend Wants a Horse and some of the other young men. But his heart was not really in it. For some reason, the rough and tumble antics of the others seemed childish and foolish.

"What's the matter, Beaver?" Horse finally asked. "You sick?"

"No . . . Just thinking," said Beaver casually. "Maybe I'll take a vision quest this season."

"Have you decided when?" asked Horse seriously.

"Oh, no . . . I'm just thinking about it."

Wants a Horse nodded. One does not probe or pry about anything so personal as a quest.

"It is good," he said.

He turned away to plunge into the clear water of the stream's deep pool. The conversation was at an end.

<>

Beaver was not even sure what his questions were. It had begun with his strange fascination with the red stone of the pipes, but he was now distracted. At times he thought he must have imagined the glimpse of a short human-like figure silhouetted against the rising moon. He tried to thrust the very idea aside, but it kept bobbing up again, like a stick tossed into a still stream.

I did see something, he assured himself. It may have been a coyote or a deer, even a turkey or two . . . Though turkeys would have been roosting for the night in one of the big oaks along the river, most likely.

<>

He woke in the night, vaguely aware that he had been dreaming. The dream itself was vague. In fact, it was already gone, and he could not even remember any of its substance. All that was left of it was an idea . . . a thought. Maybe someone or some spirit-being had given it to him during the dream. Maybe it had been born in his own mind. It did not matter. The thought was there, in the strange way thoughts are born during sleep, and problems solved. But just now, his attention was attracted to the thought that had wakened him.

As he sought advice, he had completely overlooked a valuable source of information. There was, in this very camp, a man who could offer valuable information about the pipestone that had so affected his thinking. The man was a respected holy man, advanced in years, experienced and wise. His very name should have suggested to Beaver that he inquire. *Pipe Bearer.* Maybe he had been distracted by the vision or illusion of the little person. However it had happened, he now realized that his quest lay somehow in the red stone of the pipes. But, what was the connection?

Pipe Bearer should be able to help. As he now thought about it, Beaver was irritated that he had not recognized this opportunity before. He seemed to recall now that there was some sort of quest involved in Pipe Bearer's younger days. Had the man not made a quest himself, far to the north? Maybe, even, Pipe Bearer bore that very name because of such events. But before he approached such a man, Beaver needed more information.

8

Beaver's heart beat wildly as he rattled the deer hooves hanging at the door of Pipe Bearer's lodge. It was pure coincidence that the lodge of Pipe Bearer and Otter Woman sat on the opposite side of nearly any camp the Southern Band made as they moved. In a camp of more than forty extended families, some would be closer friends than others. It was not that Pipe Bearer was withdrawn or reclusive. He and his family merely lived in another part of the camp. Beaver could recognize the man by sight, but the families were simply not close.

The weather was warm, but a little windy, and most of the lodge covers were rolled down to the ground today. At the lodge of Pipe Bearer the doorskin was also closed, and Beaver was hesitant to disturb the occupants. But it was mid-morning. It should be an acceptable time. Even so, Beaver was uneasy as he called out.

"Pipe Bearer? I am Beaver. May I come in?"

There was a sound of movement inside the lodge, and a woman lifted the doorskin to beckon him inside.

Pipe Bearer was seated opposite the door, across the fire pit. There was no fire, for with the warm weather, there was no need to heat the lodge, and most cooking took place outside.

The old man scanned the visitor quickly head to foot.

"Yes, young man. What is it?"

"Uncle, may I speak with you?"

Pipe Bearer took a puff of his pipe and blew out a little cloud of fragrant smoke.

"You already have!" observed the medicine man.

His eyes twinkled with quiet humor, though his facial expression remained stern.

"That is true," agreed Beaver, caught off-guard and a bit confused. The very dignity of the man was imposing, making all other matters seem small. Beaver took a deep breath.

"Uncle," he said, "I wish to learn."

The eyes of Pipe Bearer widened for a moment, and then resumed their amused yet distant expression. He took another puff on his pipe.

"Why do you ask me?"

"Because you are wise, Uncle. Yours are gifts of the spirit."

The old man studied him for a little while, apparently approving of what he saw.

"A good answer," he finally agreed. "Sit down, boy. How are you called?"

"Beaver."

"Yes . . . Son of Finds His Arrow and Antelope Woman, no?"

"That is true."

"Tell me more about why you ask of these things."

Beaver blurted out the whole story of his strange reaction to the warmth of the pipestone, and his attempt to be alone to think, and to search for a vision. He stopped short of telling of what he thought he had seen in the moonlight.

Pipe Bearer studied him as he talked, nodding occasionally. Finally, Beaver paused, feeling a little foolish, knowing that he had not expressed himself well.

"And where," asked Pipe Bearer, "does all this take us?"

"I . . . I don't know . . ."

"Good!"

"Good?" asked the startled Beaver.

"Yes!" affirmed the holy man. "There are many who will not admit they don't know. It is a wise young man who realizes such a thing. And, you hope to *learn*."

"Well, yes . . ."

"And that is good. However, some things are not meant to be known. Others not to be understood. Still others, to be accepted and experienced, but not told to others. Do you understand what I am saying?"

"Not entirely, Uncle . . ."

"Good! We are making progress, then!" The old man smiled.

"But then, what must I do?"

Pipe Bearer spread his hands helplessly as if in question.

"I can't tell you that. Mostly wait, it seems. When it is time, you will know."

This seemed much like some of the previous advice he had received, and he was somewhat frustrated. Yet, from this man, it seemed reassuring.

Now he spoke again, almost gently and with a smile.

"I know it is hard to be told to wait and see," he admitted. "Especially at your age. But it is a part of growing up. One of the harder parts, really. Don't worry about it. It will come. I am made to think that your heart is good, Beaver. It will come."

The tone of his voice and the expression on his face seemed to reflect approval, but Beaver was too tense to notice. He took a long breath.

"Uncle, I am made to think I need to go on a quest."

"It is good," said Pipe Bearer.

He puffed his pipe, waiting to hear more.

"I am not sure where to begin," Beaver said finally.

Crinkles of humor turned to lines like crows' feet at the corners of the old man's eyes.

"Maybe at the beginning?" he suggested.

Now Beaver was completely rattled. He felt like a fool. He should not have come.

Pipe Bearer smiled.

"Be at ease, son," he advised. "I understand. Have I not felt the same, long ago? About the quest, I mean."

Beaver reddened, but was grateful. Of course, that was his purpose in being here . . . To inquire about the factors that had called this man on a quest to the north country.

"Yes, that is it. Your quest . . ."

"Ah, yes. I was little older than you, Beaver. We were married, Otter Woman and I . . . Are you married?"

"No."

"That makes no difference to your quest. But Otter and I went together to seek the answers to my questions."

"About the pipestone?" asked Beaver.

"Pipestone? No, it had nothing to do with that."

There was complete confusion on the faces of all three. Somehow they were not communicating.

Outside, there were sounds of someone approaching the lodge, and the rattle of an armful of sticks, tossed to the ground near the cooking fire outside.

Otter Woman rose and spoke briefly.

"I'll go help her."

Pipe Bearer nodded, and Otter Woman slipped out.

"Plum Flower, my second wife," he explained. "Like a sister to Otter."

Beaver was confused. Why should this matter to him?

"I don't understand, Uncle."

The crows' feet crinkled again around the eyes of Pipe Bearer.

"Few men do, Beaver. Understand women, that is. But, Plum Flower was part of the quest."

"I thought . . . Your name, Uncle? 'Pipe Bearer.' Was that not part of the quest?"

"No, no! That had nothing to do with it." He appeared puzzled. "I already had that name. I had protected my father's medicine pipe from destruction. But no matter."

"Then what brought about your quest?"

"Oh, that was about a horse. A foal of my mare appeared to be wearing a medicine hat. Strange markings. This led me north. That Otter and I found Plum Flower was maybe part of it, maybe just a coincidence. But again, are there really any coincidences?"

Beaver was confused.

"But . . . What about the horse?"

"Oh, yes. That, too. Sometimes a quest has more than one meaning. But some things are meant to remain a mystery, no?"

He changed the subject.

"But, what of *your* quest, Beaver? What did you wish to ask?"

Beaver sighed deeply.

"Well, Uncle, I am made to think it is connected with the red stone of the pipes. I seem to be drawn to it. I need to know more, to understand its warmth and its power."

"Yes, its spirit is powerful, no?" observed Pipe Bearer. "You know that it comes from only one place?"

"I was told that by a trader. You have been there?"

"No, no. Only heard about it."

This was not going well. Beaver was dejected.

"You have had visions of this place?" asked Pipe Bearer.

"No. Nothing like that. I just feel an excitement when I touch the red stone of the pipe, a feeling that I want to know more. I thought maybe you could tell me."

"No. I regret that I cannot. My heart is heavy for you. But, your quest seems clear."

"How so, Uncle?"

"You must go there. To the Pipestone Quarry."

"*That* is the meaning of my feelings?"

"I am made to think so. Only you can know for sure. You will be given the information you need. Listen for your guide."

"Thank you, Uncle."

Beaver started to rise, and then paused. It was apparent that he must wait for such information to be given to him, but he had another question.

"Uncle . . . This is another thing. Do you know of the Little People?"

There was a long silence in which the old man seemed lost in thought.

"Which Little People?" he asked cautiously.

"Any . . . I talked with Snakewater, the medicine doctor, about those of her people."

"Ah, yes . . . Cherokee, no?"

"Yes, Uncle. Their Little People are much different than those of the People. And, more important."

"That is true."

"What of the Little People of the northern tribes?" Beaver asked. "Do you know of them?"

"Not much. They, too, have different kinds of little people. Some are dangerous."

"To whom?"

"That depends. Some are allies . . . The Absaroka, for instance, 'Crows,' the white man calls them. Their Little People ride into battle with them. In one of their stories, their Little People tear the hearts out of the enemy's horses."

"*Aiee*! You mean *really* or only in spirit, the heart to fight?"

"That, I don't know, Beaver. I wondered at the time, but I heard this from a storyteller, and there might have been a language problem, even with hand signs."

Beaver nodded.

"You said other tribes are different?"

"Oh, yes. Some tribe has Little People who live in the water, and sometimes come out. They're dangerous, I guess . . . Steal children, maybe, I am made to think. Ah, Beaver, I don't remember. It was long ago, and we were thinking of other things, you know. But, why do you ask about the Little People?"

He paused for a moment, and then spoke again, slowly and cautiously.

"You have seen something? A vision, maybe . . . No, don't answer!"

The latter remark carried a sense of urgency.

Beaver was confused. He longed to tell the old man everything he could, even about the little figure that had crossed the face of the moon. It would have made him much more confident if he could share that with someone. But in the back of his mind was the warning of old Snakewater. Among her people, one who sees a Little Person and tells of it will die.

For that matter, had he actually seen the small figure against the rising moon? He was not completely certain now, but it had seemed so real. Assuming for a moment that he *had* seen it, whose Little Person might it have been?

Yet on this point, he was becoming even more confused. If someone of another tribe chanced to see one of her Cherokee Little People, would he, too, be doomed? Or could an outsider even see such a being? Or, could it be that the death sentence did not apply to an outsider unless he *believed* in his heart that it would happen? How much risk, then, should one be prepared to take in talking to others about it?

Now his thinking had come full circle, and he was wondering why he had assumed that what he had seen was connected to Snakewater and her Little People. Could it not have been a little person of his own, the Elk-dog People? Or even someone else's . . . There must have been people of many different tribes and nations whose feet had crisscrossed this grassland through the centuries. Quite possibly, Little People of any of these could have remained behind. At least, he thought so. Who knows the character of any Little People? As beings associated with things of the spirit, they would probably be immortal, but who could be sure?

It was not reassuring that old Pipe Bearer had suddenly closed down the conversation. And the way he had done so . . . *Don't answer!* Clearly, a thought had struck him that had come as a warning.

"Uncle, I . . ." began Beaver, but the old man held up a hand to stop him.

"Beaver," he said seriously, "there are many things of many tribes that are intended to remain mysteries. Life, death, things of the spirit, the seeking of one's guide . . . Some differences among different people, which makes it more interesting, of course, but eventually it boils down to the same mystery. Arapahoes call it 'The Great Mystery,' which is as good a description as any, maybe. A person could spend his whole lifetime worrying and wondering. But since we can never really know anyway, it seems unwise to worry about it. Now, for you, it seems certain that you are being drawn on a quest, and that is good. If you understood it, you would not need the quest, so for now, listen and watch, for any hints. You do know some things about it already: You are to go north, and some of it is about the red pipestone."

"But when? How?"

Pipe Bearer was of no further help. He merely shrugged and began to relight his pipe. It was apparent that the interview was ended.

"Thank you, Uncle," said Beaver as he rose and stooped to slip past the doorskin into the windy day outside.

9

Grasshopper was interested in the recounting of his conversation with Pipe Bearer, but rather noncommittal.

"Yes, I'd heard his second wife was Lakota. I was a small child when that happened."

"He, too, said to wait for guidance," said Beaver. "Maybe that's all I can do."

"That is true, Beaver. Sometimes the only thing to do is nothing."

<>

It was that night that the dream occurred. He was running. Not away from danger. There are dreams like that, where the dreamer is pursued, and frantically attempting to escape from some unseen, unknown pursuer. Fear of the unknown is maybe the worst fear of all. This was not like that. Neither was he running *toward* something. There seemed to be no definite goal. It was as if running itself was the goal. He ran, glorying in the strength of his young manhood, the long strides falling behind him one after another. It was good to draw the fresh air of the rolling grassland into his lungs and exhale it again with each deep breath.

He loped through an encampment of scattered lodges, and people looked up, smiled, and waved. He was moving much faster than he could have in reality, and this proved to be an inspiration, a thrill of achievement.

As he settled into a steady pace, again in open prairie, he began to notice a few more details. He was running north. He could tell that from the lodges he had just passed. Their doorways had faced to his right, to the east, as doorways and smoke holes always must in a tepee. Otherwise, the smoke will not draw properly.

It was morning, because the rising sun fell on his right shoulder. He felt thrilled as he realized that he could reason such things even as he dreamed. It struck him as amusing that now he could objectively tell himself *yes, it is a dream, a night-vision, but within it I can think and reason and observe.* This discovery was exhilarating. *Maybe this is it . . . My vision . . . The answer to my quest!*

He knew better. It could not be this easy, but somehow he was sure there was a connection. This vision must be the way, the means to learn what he needed.

He leaped across a stream that snaked its way through the grassy prairie. It was a leap that he never could have managed in reality. He virtually soared . . . At least twice the distance that he could have traversed in the real world. Or was *this* the real world, and the one with all the limitation and pain, all the *problems* . . . Was *that* the unreality?

With that idea in mind, he thought again about the way he had jumped across the stream, now far behind him. How far *could* he have jumped in this strange detached existence in which he found himself? He considered as he ran. Maybe he could try.

There was a hill ahead. In the real world, maybe a day's travel. In this accelerated existence, it was approaching rapidly. There was little time to think about it. He could not see the landscape beyond the hill yet, but before he reached it, he knew that he must make the try. He increased his speed a little. He did not feel he was moving fast at all. The effortless lope was like the easy canter of a well-gaited horse, running without the pounding exertion and sweat of a race.

Even the slight rise of the slope ahead presented no extra effort. He did push just a little as he neared the crest. Not that he felt a need, just that if one were to try to fly, there must be some effort required. He reached the top of the ridge and had no time to study the rolling prairie beyond before he jumped, arms spread wide like those of the eagle. Then, he was flying . . .

He looked down on the vast expanse of grassland, the scattered bands of buffalo and antelope, and it was good. A motion to his left caught his attention, and he turned his head slightly to look. An eagle soared majestically, on a parallel course.

"Good day to you, grandfather," said Beaver.

"And to you," answered the eagle.

There seemed to be no motion of the creature's beak. No sound at all, maybe. It was as if he could read the greeting in the very thoughts of the great bird.

I am inside his head! The young man marveled. *I can think his thoughts.*

The bird wheeled away in a long sweep to the west, and the thoughts which Beaver believed he could access faded. They were replaced by a darker mood, an ominous feeling like that of death nearby. He glanced around. Just to his right and a little above him soared a vulture, wings motionless as it rode the rising air currents in a great circle. The bird was near enough for him to see a small, beady eye, set in the pebbly red skin of the naked head. Somehow the mood of the creature was reflected in that brief glance. It was a dour, cynical outlook on the world and all in it. *Some day!* the dark glance seemed to say. By contrast, the look of the eagle's eye had been majestic, yet not without respect. Possibly, a trace of good-humored understanding and even a hint of recognition for a fellow traveler. Not dark, like this.

Beaver realized, of course, that such feelings and observations were quite ridiculous. After all, this was only a dream, was it not?

No sooner had that thought struck him, than he started to fall. It was as if, by conceding that it was impossible for him to be flying, it became so in actual fact.

Frantically, he flapped his arms. He had not been moving them until now, but merely spreading them stiffly like the wings of the soaring birds. That was all it had taken beyond the running start. But the admission of his limitations had somehow destroyed the power that had kept him soaring. He plummeted toward the earth, reduced to a panic as the ground rushed up at him. He screamed . . .

"What is it, Beaver?"

The voice was that of his mother, half roused from the bed she shared with his father across the lodge. The fire was dying, but the reddish glow made it possible to see objects dimly.

"What? Oh! I . . . It is nothing, Mother. I thought . . . *Aiee*, a dream! I was falling . . ."

She chuckled. "You have landed now?"

"It seems so."

"Good. Go back to sleep."

<>

He lay a long time, staring at the small patch of starry sky that could be seen through the smoke hole. A dream . . .

Dreams are not unusual. Some are frightening, some silly, some so pleasurable that the dreamer hates to waken. Among some cultures, dreams are critical, telling events to come, and providing guidance for decisions. Maybe, both.

Among the People, they were considered important. *Some* dreams, anyway. Can anyone say which dream carries the power and importance of a vision, and which merely reflects the influences of one's life? A dream that deals with improbable unrealities may be seen, years later, to have been quite significant.

<>

Beaver's parents said little about the disturbance of their sleep during the night, beyond his father's tongue-in-cheek remark, "Sleep well, Beaver?" The boy mumbled an answer and slipped out of the lodge, to look for Grasshopper.

"Uncle!" he blurted. "I have had a dream."

Grasshopper held up a hand for caution.

"Not so fast, Beaver. Do you mean a *vision*?"

"I . . . I don't know. It was like nothing I've had before. I was flying . . ."

"Stop! You don't need to tell me, Beaver, if you think you should not."

"No, I *want* to tell it, Uncle."

"It is good, then. Go ahead. But we need a more private place. Let us walk."

He turned and sauntered away, and Beaver fell in step.

Well outside the camp, Beaver began to relate his dream. He told of running, faster than the wind, of his extraordinary physical feats, and at last, his ability to fly.

"To *fly*?" asked Grasshopper, surprised.

"Yes, Uncle. I was soaring with an eagle, and we spoke. Then, a vulture."

"You talked to him, too?"

"No. I did not like Buzzard's thoughts."

"You were inside his head?"

"Well, yes. I did not want to go there. But Eagle, yes, I felt better with him."

"What did he say?"

"Nothing, really. This was not as if we talked out loud, Uncle. I must have said 'good day' or something, but I don't remember whether it was out loud. Maybe just the exchange of thoughts. It was very strange."

"Ah! And very different, no?"

"That is true."

Grasshopper was silent a few moments, apparently lost in thought. Finally Beaver, impatient for an answer, spoke again.

"I was traveling north."

"When you were running?"

"Yes. Flying, too. It was morning."

"Ah! How did you know?"

Quickly, Beaver explained the orientation of the lodges and the sun on his right shoulder.

"Good!" said Grasshopper. "You noticed things. So, they must have meaning."

"But, *what*?"

"Hmm . . ."

Grasshopper seemed lost in thought for a little while, and then began to speak, slowly and seriously.

"I am made to think," he began, "that this vision tells of the future. You have wondered what you were to do. It would seem that you are to travel north. You found it pleasant?"

"Oh, yes. Beautiful. But, I was *flying*."

His uncle nodded.

"Yes, running also. Same direction, no?"

"I think so."

"*Okeh*!"

Grasshopper used a word that the People had begun to adopt from its common usage by old Snakewater, the Cherokee medicine doctor. *Okeh* could be used to imply agreement or satisfaction or merely to indicate "it is good."

"Now, Beaver," he went on, "you were doing things that would not be possible in this life, running faster, jumping, *flying*?"

"That is true."

"Then this must mean you will be successful in your quest."

"This means a quest?"

"Yes, to the north. Probably to answer your questions about the pipestone."

"But that wasn't in the dream."

"I know. Yet you were traveling. Flying. This means success."

"I *fell*!"

"Yes, but was that not after you began to doubt?"

"Well, there were the dark thoughts of the Buzzard."

"Just a warning, I am made to think. Danger. Of course, the world is filled with dangers. Maybe it is only a warning to be careful."

"Are you sure of these things, Uncle?"

Grasshopper smiled. "Of course not. How could *I* be sure of *your* vision? But you have felt that something was about to happen. I am made to think it has. You have been given a quest. You could talk to White Buffalo about it, if you like, but it seems plain. And oh, yes! Do you not think that Eagle is your guide?"

Oddly, that had not even occurred to Beaver. In the next moments his spirit sank. How stupid could a young man be? Not to recognize one's own guide. His heart was heavy over this.

But good, for his vision.

$<\cdot>$ 10

Beaver did decide to consult with White Buffalo again. He had felt the power of the old man's medicine during the brief time they had spoken. There could be no harm in asking.

$<>$

"Uncle, I have dreamed."

The old man looked at him quizzically, as if seeing him for the first time. It was apparent that White Buffalo was more interested than before, taking his visitor more seriously. His gaze seemed to probe, questioning, looking for something.

"A vision?" he asked.

"Maybe, Uncle. A dream. It seemed different, somehow."

The holy man nodded thoughtfully, drew in and puffed out a small cloud of smoke from his pipe, and spoke again.

"How?"

Beaver was at a loss for a moment.

"Maybe more clear. I remember it more easily than some."

"It is good. You need not tell me of it, though."

"But I would be honored to do so, Uncle."

White Buffalo nodded again. "Go ahead."

The young man told of his dream-vision, of running, flying, communing with the eagle, and finally, falling.

"Hmm . . ." mused the other, eyes half closed.

"Was this only a dream?" Beaver asked impatiently. "Or, are you made to think that I am being called to a quest?"

"It seems so . . . Ah! I will cast the bones! I had not thought of that."

"The 'bones'?"

"Yes. They have not been called upon for a long time. I had almost forgotten about them."

He rummaged among the odds and ends of personal possessions lying near the outer skirt of the tepee. In winter, this area would be behind the lodge lining, in the storage area that need not be heated. Most of the People did not bother with hanging the lining skirt in summer. It would only be in the way if the wife decided to roll up the lodge cover to allow a breeze to cool the dwelling.

"Ah! Here it is . . ."

He sat down, untied the thongs and unrolled the skin bundle to reveal a boxlike container of rawhide the size of a man's fist. The medicine man shook it lightly, rattling the small objects inside as if to assure himself of the contents. Then he set it aside and turned his attention to the skin in which it had been wrapped. It was a soft-tanned buckskin, and as he spread and smoothed it on the floor, Beaver could see that it was heavily decorated with symbols and geometric designs. Four of these obviously represented the four directions. White Buffalo rotated the skin as he spread it, matching the symbol for the sun to the doorway of the lodge, facing east. He took a pinch of tobacco from his pouch and tossed it into the fire.

"To let the spirits know what we're doing," he explained. "Its smoke is pleasant to them."

He added another pinch of dried herbs from each of two other small pouches, and watched the smoke rise, fanning it gently toward the spread skin on the floor with a wave of his hand.

"Sage and sweetgrass."

Beaver nodded, understanding. He had never seen this ceremony before, but was aware of its serious nature.

The old man now began a singsong chant, holding the boxlike cup and waving it slowly over the skin. Then, with a sweep of his arm, he tossed the contents across its surface. The chanting stopped abruptly as he did so. A dozen or more oddly shaped bits of bone, carved wood, and stone came alive for a moment as they jumped and skittered across the surface of the skin. The colors of the pebbles were startling in their variety. So were the carved shapes of bone and wood. The small objects scattered for only a moment, like the covey-rise of a band of quail, and then came to rest.

White Buffalo grunted with satisfaction, nodded, and leaned over the skin to examine the results. He mumbled softly to himself as he examined the positions of the various objects on the skin. Beaver now saw that these were symbolic forms. The wood and bone fetishes were carved to represent animals, birds, a fish, a snake . . . The stones were mostly in the natural shapes carved by eons of running water in a stream bed. A couple were of the gray-blue soapstone common to the region, carved by human hands, but there was one which especially caught his attention. It was a bird fetish, with a hooked beak and half-spread wings. He had noticed it as the "bones" scattered, and now looked more closely. It was now on the far side of the skin from him, almost off the edge, the head pointing north. An eagle . . . And now he noticed that it was not a carved and painted wooden image, as he had first thought. It was made of red pipestone, smoothed and polished.

White Buffalo was still studying the pattern of the tossed objects, mumbling to himself.

"Hmm . . . Yes . . . But . . . No, there . . . *Aiee!*"

Beaver longed to ask questions, but felt it not appropriate.

"Maybe . . ." pondered the old man.

He leaned over to point at some of the objects on the skin, touching a few with apparent curiosity.

"Very interesting!" he said at last. "Beaver, there are some curious things here. Some, I do not understand. There are contradictions.

Again, as we've said, some things are not meant to be understood. But this is like none I have ever seen. Some success, some danger, success and failure both, in a closely related mix. But your guide is strong."

Beaver was puzzled.

"Then," he asked cautiously, "I am called to a quest?"

White Buffalo appeared surprised.

"Of course. I thought you knew that. Yes. You are called north."

He pointed to the eagle fetish of red stone, almost at the northernmost edge of the painted skin.

"See? Your guide points the way."

"Then the eagle . . . My guide?"

"I am made to think so. Now, be ready. Listen. Your call may come in any number of ways. But, it will be soon."

He began to gather the scattered fetishes, returning them to the cup. It was plain to Beaver that the ceremony and the interview were over.

"It is good," he told the medicine man. "I am grateful to you, Uncle."

⟨ ⟩

Now, what? He spoke to Grasshopper again, explaining the casting of the bones.

"I have never seen that done," said his uncle. "I am made to think that it was more common in the old days."

"Maybe so," said Beaver. "It seemed to me much like the plum-stones game."

Grasshopper laughed. Gambling with plum stones was a common winter pastime. The plums that grow along the streams in the prairie were gathered by the People for food in season. The seeds, or stones, could be used for beads or ornaments, or for the gambling game. Naturally yellow in color, each stone would be marked with red paint on one side. Three or five or seven stones, any odd number, would be rolled on a smooth surface, and scored; red or yellow side up, relating to the player's call.

"Do you mean to say," Grasshopper asked, still amused, "that your quest can be compared to a gamble?"

Beaver had not thought along exactly those lines, but he paused to think about it now.

Is life itself not a gamble? he mused.

<>**11**

Where to start? Wait for more guidance? He had to think about it. What more did he need? He had to keep in mind the seasons of the year. In the north, autumn would arrive sooner, and travel would become more difficult, he supposed. But how soon? A few days? A moon? Pipe Bearer would know, maybe, having spent a season or two with his wife's people, the Lakotas. Yet it did not seem appropriate to bother such a distinguished elder with such questions. He should have talked further with the Trader, whose occupation required knowledge of travel. But of course, at the time the Trader had camped with them, the idea of a quest had not yet materialized.

Things were now happening too fast. The Trader had visited in the Moon of Growing, called May by the white man. The band would soon move to meet the other bands of the People for the annual Sun Dance, in the Moon of Roses, the white man's June. That occasion itself required only five days, but there must be preparation, as well as social interaction with friends and relatives of other bands. This would consist not only of visiting, but games and contests and stories and gambling, festivities to be enjoyed by all. The entire gathering might last half a moon or more.

"Where is the Sun Dance to be?" Beaver asked his father.

"You have forgotten?" asked Finds His Arrow with a smile.

"Maybe so. I was much younger then," said Beaver.

Both his parents laughed.

"That is true," his mother admitted. "Our Beaver has grown up in this past year, Arrow. I hate to see this."

"But I must, sometime!" protested Beaver.

"Yes, I know," said Antelope Woman, somewhat sadly. "Our lodge will be quiet."

She and Finds His Arrow had produced three children. The first, a promising young man, had been killed in an accident on his first buffalo hunt. A wounded bull had gored the young hunter's horse with its dying effort, throwing the rider to the ground beneath a sea of hooves and horns.

Their next child was a girl, a beautiful child with large soft eyes and a mischievous sense of humor. Laughing Gull was now grown and settled in her own lodge, even now expecting a child.

It had been several seasons before Antelope Woman had been able to conceive again. She had nearly given up hope of another child, when she found herself pregnant again, with the boy now known as Beaver. She was now past her moon-time cycling, and she knew that there would be no more chances. Maybe she could console herself as Beaver left the nest, with thoughts of a grandchild in Gull's lodge.

"It is the way of things," her husband consoled. "A young bird must leave the nest sometime."

"I know."

"I will be back, Mother."

"Yes, I know," she said quickly. "But you have grown up so fast."

It did not seem so to Beaver, but he decided to change the subject.

"So . . . Where is the Sun Dance?"

Finds His Arrow laughed.

"Back to that? Sycamore River, downstream from Medicine Rock!"

"Ah, yes, I remember, now."

Medicine Rock. A place known for its close association with the spirits. Many young men of the People had chosen the cliff above the river as a spot to seek their vision quest, during or just after the Sun Dance. But the Sun Dance was held in a different site each summer for the convenience of each of the far-flung bands. It had been several years since Medicine Rock, in the territory of the Southern Band, was chosen.

"Will you seek a vision while we are there, Beaver?" asked his mother.

He did not know quite how to answer. He felt he had already had his vision, pointing his course of action. But there would surely be no harm in communion with the spirits of the Rock, since the People would be in the area anyway.

"Maybe so," he said cautiously. "I don't know yet, Mother."

In the back of his mind lingered the thought that maybe it would be better to start *before* the Sun Dance, to leave from their present camp. It would put him into the northern regions considerably earlier in the season, maybe simplifying the decision as to where to winter.

It was that very day that Far Thunder, the band chieftain, gave the customary three days' notice prior to the move. The People immediately began to pack.

⟨⟩

Now Beaver was confronted with a real decision. He could travel with the People to Medicine Rock, participate in the prayers and supplication of the important ceremonies, possibly even go on to Medicine Rock for a period of fasting. Then, start on his quest, as the big encampment began to break up, and the various bands began to go their separate ways. That had some appeal to it. The Sycamore River and Medicine Rock were northwest of their present camp anyway. He would be traveling, at least partially, in the right direction.

Another option . . . He could, when the band broke camp, head directly north, following the Real-star. In that way, he could spend half a moon on his quest instead of at the Sun Dance. This would give him many extra autumn days to make such decisions as where to winter or when to start home, whichever proved appropriate at the time. Since he did not know the seasons in the area where he might find himself in the Moon of Falling Leaves, this could be an important advantage.

⟨⟩

He still had not decided when the morning came to break camp. Among the People, the basic philosophy had always been that what is intended to happen, will happen. Likewise, *when*. In such an atmosphere, there is little sense of urgency. So, as the big lodge of his parents came down, Beaver helped with the work of folding and rolling the cover, and laying out the poles. Several pairs would be used for the pole-drags to transport the lodge cover and all of their baggage.

He began to have some feelings of guilt, wondering who would help with their moves during his absence. He shook such thoughts aside as best he could. He realized that everyone must eventually leave home, to strike out on his own. Well, he could travel with them a few days, and then decide.

⟨⟩

Beaver was honored to be allowed to ride as one of the outriders some distance from the main column. There were always a couple of riders well in advance of the party and several along the flanks, as well as a rear guard, behind the huge horse herd. Beaver had acted as a horse herder last season, but this was a great step toward manhood, to be chosen as a scout. "Wolves," such scouts were called, an analogy to the gray wolves that traveled with the buffalo herds. Constantly circling, the gray predators were on the watch for any weak or sick animal, or an unsupervised calf. But the "wolf" outriders were for protection. It was an inside joke, generations old.

⟨⟩

On the third day of travel they camped at a large, clear spring. It gushed out of a shallow cavern beneath a shelf of limestone in a hillside. It was apparent that others had camped here, probably for centuries. A place with good water in the vastness of the rolling grasslands would be known to all travelers, just as an oasis in the desert is known to the camel caravans. The Big Spring had been a stopping place to the People since before memory. It was also known to others of the prairie nomads, and to all who traveled through the area. There are wandering trails through the tallgrass region, established through the centuries by hooves, padded claws, and moccasinned feet. All of these lead to watering places which have become camp sites.

In this case, there was a crossing of two trails at Big Spring. The one on which the People traveled ran southeast to northwest, wandering along paths of least resistance. The second approached the spring from almost due south, and meandered on to the north, bending slightly eastward to avoid a rocky hillside with a caprock of gray limestone.

One of the wolves rode back to the approaching column to inform them that a trader camped at the spring.

"Not the one who visited our camp earlier," he explained. "This is another one."

It was good. This might provide an interesting evening.

"Is he anyone we know?" someone asked.

"I think not, Uncle," replied the scout. "I have never seen them before."

"Them?"

"Yes. He has a wife and a daughter. A young girl!"

"*Aiee!* How old?" asked Wants a Horse.

"I don't know, Horse. About your age, maybe."

There were hoots and teasing looks directed at Wants a Horse.

"Is she pretty?" asked someone.

"Ugly as mud!" said the scout. "It spoiled my need for food."

There was general laughter.

"Sorry, Horse."

The scout wheeled his mount and rode back to resume his assignment.

<>

It was well toward dark when Beaver encountered his friend. The cooking fires were beginning to blossom along the shallow ravine.

"A good day?" asked Wants a Horse.

"Yes, good."

Horse had been helping to herd the horses, trading off with other young men, but had been with his parents when the scout had brought the news of the trader.

"You heard about the trader?" asked Beaver. "His daughter?"

"Yes . . . Ugly as mud, no?"

Beaver roared with laughter.

"Spotted Snake said that?

"Wh . . . What?"

"Horse, this is the most beautiful girl I have ever seen! Snake was teasing you!"

< >12

As it turned out, none of the outriders spoke truth. It was all a joke on Wants a Horse.

True, there was a trader, and the trader did indeed have a wife and a daughter. The daughter, however, was not exactly a candidate for courtship by Wants a Horse or anyone else. She was only a few moons old.

The trader was a personable young man, as traders must be. He had not previously been in contact with the People, and was pleased with this opportunity. He had some new stories, of course, and the People decided to camp with him for a day before moving on. His pretty young wife nursed her owl-eyed infant with obvious pride.

They had spent the winter with Cheyennes, the husband related. He asked many questions about the People, their customs and their Sun Dance.

"We plan to go on northward this season," he explained. "But your Sun Dance seems a good occasion to trade. Would that be permitted?"

"Of course," answered Far Thunder. "It is a time of visiting and contests and gambling. All the bands of the People will be there."

"How many?"

"Six . . . No, seven, now. Our 'Lost Band' has returned."

"Lost Band?"

"A long story. Later, maybe."

"It is good. But, I am made to think that we should go on to the north this season. Maybe next year. Where will your People gather then? Same place?"

"No, no. Another place, nearer one of the other bands. It will be decided at this gathering."

"Of course. Where do you winter?"

"To the southeast of here. Our Eastern band winters in the forests . . . *Miss-oor-ie*."

"You are the Eastern band?"

"No!" Far Thunder was emphatic. The Eastern band was noted for foolishness. "We are the *Southern* band, the band with wisdom. We had the first horses in the plains!"

"Ah, I see," said the visitor, though it was apparent that he did not. "Maybe we could winter with one of your bands and attend your Sun Dance next season?"

"A good thought. How are you called, again?"

"Ah, I may not have said. Usually, just 'that trader'."

Both chuckled.

"That is common with traders," observed Far Thunder.

"Yes, but we do have names sometimes. Mine might as well be 'trader.' I am 'Trades His Moccasins.' When I was a boy I once traded all day and ended with my own moccasins. But I had made some good trades."

Both laughed.

⟨⟩

Beaver, who had been listening, smiled to himself. Here might be an opportunity. He could possibly make himself useful to the trader's family. The wife was occupied with a small baby, and the trader could probably use some help with his displays, as well as with an occasional hunt for fresh meat. And the family's direction of travel was to the north, as suggested by Beaver's vision. It seemed logical. Well, he could watch the trading for a day, become better acquainted, and then approach the subject. Meanwhile, he'd ask Grasshopper's opinion.

<>

"A good plan!" his uncle agreed. "Has the trader been there before?"

"I am made to think so," said Beaver. "The way he talked of his trip. But I have not yet talked to him."

"You would miss the Sun Dance?"

Beaver paused. "Yes, but, maybe I am called to this."

"That must be your decision."

"I know."

<>

There was little time. Both the People and the trader would move on early tomorrow, in different directions. Beaver did not yet have any idea whether the trader would even consider what he had in mind.

He loitered around the trader's display, but at a little distance, waiting for a chance to talk. Finally the stream of people looking to trade began to dwindle. Beaver strolled over, and waited while a woman bargained for some glass beads, a small knife, and a metal awl. Another, a steel fire-striker.

"I lost mine when we spilled a pack in crossing a stream," she explained. "I felt around in the rocks, but couldn't find it."

That trade completed, with the exchange of a beaded pendant, the woman moved on, and the trader looked toward Beaver.

"You seem very serious," he said pleasantly. "You seek something special, no?"

"No, not exactly, Uncle. I do not seek a trade, really. I am thinking of a quest."

"A vision quest?"

The trader looked puzzled.

"Maybe. I am not sure."

"But what has that to do with me?"

"Nothing, maybe. But I am made to think that I am called to the north. You have been there?"

"Some . . ." There was a twinkle in his eye. "North is a big place."

"Yes, I know, Uncle. That is why I ask. I am drawn toward the red pipestone."

"Ah! I begin to understand. The Pipestone Quarry? The red stone all comes from one place, you know."

"So I have heard," agreed Beaver.

"A very powerful place," the man went on. "Its spirit is so strong that there is an understanding there. No one may fight another there."

"Even enemies?"

"That is true. If one is there, and an enemy approaches, they may speak, but not fight."

"And everyone knows this?"

"All in that area. Anybody who is there to procure the red stone must be allowed to do so, and to depart in peace."

"You are going there now?"

"Yes, that area. Maybe not exactly there. Trading is better where there are more people, you know. A large camp or a town of Growers. But . . . I . . . How are you called?"

"Forgive me, Uncle. I am Beaver, son of Finds His Arrow. I was thinking . . . If we both are traveling north, maybe I could be of use to you. Help with your packs, your camps. Your woman has a small baby, and it needs attention frequently, no?"

Beaver glanced at the woman, who responded with a shy smile. She spoke to her husband in a tongue that Beaver did not understand. The trader listened, and turned back to the young man.

"My wife, Cactus Flower, understands enough of your tongue to know what you spoke about, but she has some questions. Just a moment."

He turned back to talk in their own tongue. Then he turned to Beaver again.

"Flower thinks that you could be of help to us. How many are your years, Beaver?"

"Sixteen."

"You have no wife?"

Beaver was caught off guard.

"Uh . . . No!" he stammered.

He had not expected such a question. He had, of course, with the surge of manhood that had spurred his growth and changed his voice felt attracted to girls in a far different way than before. Some were good friends. But, those his own age had begun to show the transition to womanhood a year or two before the change occurred in their male counterparts. Consequently, young women of the age of Beaver and his friend Horse were being courted by males a year or two older than them. It has always been so, maybe to provide better protection for the mothers of the next generation.

"It is good," said the trader. "Flower only wondered if there would be another woman to help. You do not object to helping with what might be seen as a woman's work?"

"Work is work," Beaver said, "no matter who does it."

The woman laughed, indicating that she might have a pretty good grasp of his language, and spoke briefly to her husband.

Trades His Moccasins chuckled and explained.

"Flower says that you have been raised by a very good mother."

"I have been made to think so," Beaver agreed.

"Then, it seems to be agreed," said the trader. "At least, we can try it. It is my plan to leave in the morning. You will be ready?"

It was not really a question.

There was much to do before the day's end. Beaver would travel light, riding his blue roan mare. He had few possessions, which could all be rolled into a parfleche pack and added to the load of one of the pack animals.

Goodbyes were a trifle more complicated.

"You are *what*?" asked Wants a Horse. "*Aiee*, you are trying to fool me again!"

"No, no, Horse. I am really going with the trader. I will help him, and he will teach me about the country I will see, about my quest."

"Ah, your quest! Then that *was* a vision?"

"Maybe so."

"How do your parents see this?"

"As I do, pretty much. I have been called to do this."

"I will miss you, Beaver."

"And I will miss you and Turtle and Snake. But I will be back probably this autumn, or surely next season."

<>

It was difficult for his mother, but she had resigned herself, long ago. It must happen sometime, that the fledging leaves the nest. She stood a long time, watching the departing figures grow smaller in the distance, tears welling up in her eyes.

His father was proud, and Grasshopper, who had been in the know since the beginning, was not surprised at all.

<> 13

The trader and his wife were quite young, not much older than Beaver and his friends, as it turned out.

"My parents are traders," Trades His Moccasins explained. "I grew up this way. But I married two summers ago. Cactus Flower and I met when we traded with her people. We both were children then. My parents and I returned every year or two, and our friendship grew. It still grows."

The young mother smiled, slightly embarrassed.

"It did not prove efficient to travel together, two families of traders . . . There is not enough trade to do so. So, we are on our own. This is the second summer," Trades His Moccasins continued.

"You have seen your parents?" asked Beaver.

"Oh, yes. We wintered together. But my father trades to the west this season, while we go north. There is plenty of room for trade. We will meet again for the winter, with the people of Cactus Flower, my wife. They are Cheyenne, Southern."

"There are northern Cheyennes too, then?"

"Oh, yes. There are also northern and southern Arapaho. My own, the 'Trader People.'"

The trader casually made the two-hand sign for "trader," which also indicated "Arapaho."

"Which people of the north will you seek trade with?" asked Beaver.

"Anybody with goods to trade. Anything I can sell or trade again for something better."

It was apparent that Trades His Moccasins was a man who enjoyed his vocation.

"What people will we see, then?" asked Beaver.

The trader shrugged.

"Who knows? They all move around a lot, as your people do. Except for growers. They must plant crops. Even so, some of them . . . Well, the Pawnees! They live in towns, in lodges half buried, but they hunt, too. After the second hoeing of their corn. *Big* buffalo hunts!"

"Yes, we know the Pawnees. Our Northern Band trades with them. They fight, sometimes."

"Oh, yes, of course. You know their ways. Different, but interesting, no?"

"That is true."

"You know about their god, Morning Star, how they find a bride for him, so that he will make the corn grow?"

"I have heard. A virgin, is it not?"

"Ah, yes, but not one of their own! A virgin stolen from their neighbors."

"*Aiee!* I had not heard that. The girl is sacrificed, no?"

"Yes. She is taught. Several moons' training. It is an honor, to be the chosen bride."

"Huh! Some honor!" Cactus Flower voiced her opinion in Beaver's tongue to join the conversation.

"But Flower, she goes willingly, it is said. It is their way," answered her husband. "*Their* problem."

"My husband," the girl said firmly, "I know that we must respect the beliefs of all tribes and nations. Especially, since we trade with them. No one has a right to question what the spirits have said to another, or to another tribe. There are things that are forbidden to some. Remember when we camped with the hunting party of Kiowas and Comanches? They are allies, no? But the Comanches had killed a bear cub, and were eating the meat. Their Kiowa hunting partners ate none, because it is forbidden to them."

"We ate some of the meat, Flower."

"Yes! Your people and mine may eat bears, no?"

"That is true. But what has that to do with Morning Star?"

"Nothing!" Flower's temper appeared to be rising. "Each tribe and nation has its own rules, that which is right and that which is forbidden."

"So, how can you question the Morning Star ceremony of the Pawnees?"

"*Because*," she almost hissed at him, "the chosen 'bride' has no choice. It is forced on her."

"But as I said, Flower, she climbs the scaffold willingly,"

"Were you there to see this?"

"Well, no . . ."

"So, you cannot say for sure, or whether she was drugged . . . Maybe, even, too proud to scream!"

"But it is *their* way, not ours to question."

Now, the voice of the young wife grew very soft, yet crackling with intensity as she spoke.

"My husband," she said sweetly, "look at this child in my arms, sleeping. Your daughter, and mine. When she becomes a woman, what if she were stolen to become a bride of this Morning Star? Would it still be only a problem for somebody else?"

Without waiting for an answer, she carefully laid the sleeping child on a blanket and rose.

"I go to empty my bladder," she said over her shoulder as she moved off into the darkness.

Neither of the men spoke as they watched her go.

Beaver was impressed at the manner in which a woman may express indignation by the way she walks. He had never thought about it before, but the same is true of many emotions. A woman, merely by her manner of moving, may reflect joy, despair, anger, frustration, sorrow, a flirtatious mood. He felt that he had been permitted to enter a previously unknown area of human knowledge. It was such a major discovery that he glanced at Trades His Moccasins to see his reaction.

The trader was staring at the figure now disappearing into the darkness. The expression on his face reflected some sadness and a trace of anger, but was mostly puzzled.

Beaver said nothing. It was a bit embarrassing to have been the only witness to such an exchange. He knew that husbands and wives are sometimes outspoken or critical. Some women, some men too, are known for their irritability and unpleasant dispositions. But this was the first he had seen of anything short of devotion to each other on the part of either of these young people. He still had no doubts about their love, and had already developed a vast respect for them. It had merely been a shock.

"I'm going to bed," Beaver said quietly, rising and heading toward his blankets.

There was a non-committal grunt in answer, but before the younger man reached the edge of the firelit circle, the trader spoke softly.

"She's right, Beaver."

Beaver was embarrassed and unsure, to have been exposed to the innermost hearts and souls of these two. He felt good about it, without being certain why. Only much later did he realize how much he had already learned from traveling with this intelligent pair of young lovers.

He lay awake a long time, watching the Seven Hunters wheel around their camp at the Real-star. He found the star representing the dog that follows the second hunter in the line. It was reassuring. A whippoorwill called from the oaks along the stream, and another answered from a timbered ravine.

He heard Cactus Flower return and begin to settle in for the night. The baby woke, and she put it to breast, talking softly. There were a few words exchanged between husband and wife, cautious and tentative.

Then he heard Flower's melodious chuckle, followed by quiet laughter from both, and Beaver smiled to himself. He felt much better as he drifted off to sleep.

<>

The next morning was foggy. Moisture hung in the air, and settled on everything like a heavy dew. It could be felt on the skin, clothing, and everything they touched. With the sun not visible, it was impossible to determine direction, so travel was out of the question.

"I'll find some wood," Beaver suggested as he started toward the creek. He had spotted a dead cottonwood before dark, and was certain that it would furnish fuel.

They spent the day there, rigging a lean-to shelter with one of the canvas tarpaulins used on the packs. The delay was no problem. It was a good opportunity for the horses and pack mule to graze.

The trader, skilled in travel, was well versed in such things.

"A horse has to spend half his time eating," he explained. "When you're traveling, if he doesn't get enough graze, he'll start to lose weight, lose strength, and we'd have to stop a few days to let him recover."

Beaver thought about it. Why hadn't he known that? Then it struck him: The People, though nomads, always traveled a few days, then stopped to camp for maybe a moon or two. Their horses were never under the sort of continuous work and travel for as long a period as those of the trader. The trader, however, paused every few days for a day or two of trade. During that time his horses would rest and graze, recovering from the days of travel. Beaver began to see that there was much that he could learn, and about many things.

<>

The sunset that evening was beautiful as the clouds cleared from the west.

"Sun Boy chooses his paints well tonight," observed Beaver.

"What?" asked Trades His Moccasins.

"Ah, a saying of ours. Sun Boy is one of our spirits."

"Oh, yes, I remember," said Moccasins. "Part of your Sun Dance, no? It is so with the prairie people, those who hunt the buffalo. Sun returns, which brings back the grass, which brings the buffalo."

Beaver nodded.

"That is true. In winter, Cold Maker comes from the north, and tries to blow out Sun Boy's torch. Sometimes, in the Moon of Long Nights, he nearly does. But then, Sun Boy makes and lights a new torch, and Cold Maker retreats back to his ice mountains to the north."

The trader nodded.

"Many stories are similar. The Moon of Snows, the Moon of Hunger, then the Awakening, that of the new year."

"Yes," Beaver agreed. "It is said that our people, before the horse, had very hard winters with little food. What we now call the Moon of Hunger was sometimes the Moon of Starvation."

"The same with many others. The white man starts his new year when the Sun begins to return, though."

"Even before the Moon of Awakening? Why do they do that?"

The trader shrugged.

"Who knows what a white man thinks?"

<>

The next day was clear, and they traveled on.

‹ · › 14

Beaver's reaction to the conversation between the trader and his wife was a mixture of amusement and approval. Among the People, a strong-hearted woman was highly regarded. Beaver had grown up listening to tales of heroic deeds by women of the People. An ancestor of his, Eagle Woman, had earned status as a warrior, dropping the "Woman" designation, and claimed the right to change her name to "Running Eagle." After the need for her leadership qualities in battle had subsided, she had married a fellow warrior and raised a family.

There was Pale Star, kidnapped as a child and carried far away from her family. As a grown woman she managed to return to the People. She had learned several languages, including the French tongue of her husband. This greatly helped the People in opening trade with the Spanish in the town of "Sennafay."

There were others, such as Bear's Rump, who had saved her husband's life shortly after they were married. The young hunter was being mauled by a bear, and she had, in desperation, grabbed his spear and thrust it with all her strength into the animal's exposed posterior. This, in defiance of the People's age-old prohibition against hunting bears. The startled animal had fled, roaring with pain, and was seen no more. The People, out of regard for her self-less bravery, had renamed her "Bear's Rump."

It was reassuring to find that a strong-hearted woman was also valued and respected among the trader's people and those of his wife. Beaver was finding that his regard for this energetic young couple was growing. He not only respected, but admired them. He envied their ability to speak several languages. It had not occurred to him before how useful that would be. As practical as it might be to use hand signs, there are times when a more complicated exchange might be called upon. He quietly resolved to try to learn at least a little of the trader's Arapaho tongue, and maybe some of the Cheyenne spoken by Cactus Flower. His major problem, he realized, would be to keep them separate. It would be easy to confuse the two under his present circumstances. Maybe it would be better to concentrate on Arapaho, the tongue of the Trader People. Yes, he decided, that was best.

Trades His Moccasins was pleased when Beaver stated his intention. "It is good!" he stated. "I have a suggestion: For now, let us speak only in Arapaho or in hand signs. You will learn more quickly, no?"

"That is true," Beaver said. "We start now?"

"Agreed!" answered Trades His Moccasins, in his own language.

Both men chuckled, and Cactus Flower smiled to herself. This should be interesting.

⟨⟩

There was no need for much conversation that evening, but the trader occasionally spoke, half-teasing his pupil, pushing the young man into an attempt or two to speak in Arapaho. With short statements, simple ideas, and the aid of hand signs, they managed to struggle through the evening without resorting to the language of Beaver's people. Cactus Flower, watching the young men, listened carefully, smiled a lot, and occasionally chuckled at the efforts of Beaver to wrap his tongue around the unfamiliar syllables.

When they retired to the blankets, Beaver found himself distracted with the excitement and challenge of the new activity. He lay awake, thinking, running new words through his mind and over his tongue, softly mouthing each syllable, half aloud. The trader and his wife were on the other side of the fire, under their blanket, the infant between them. He could hear the soft snores of Trades His Moccasins and the gentle breathing of the woman. Theirs appeared to be a good relationship, with much teasing and laughter. Beaver found himself hoping that when the time came for him to marry, his union would be as happy and comfortable as this one appeared to be.

This line of thought brought to mind some of the girls with whom he had grown up. The first to whom he had been attracted, even before he had begun to feel the stirring of manhood in his loins, had been Fox Woman. She was slightly older than he, and they were never more than acquaintances. She had matured early, at least three summers before Beaver began to sprout a few hairs on his lip and along his jaw. Still, he felt the frustrated jealousy of an adolescent male when Fox Woman married Little Shield, a respected warrior whose wife had died in birthing. They had since had two little ones of their own. Beaver now realized that there had never been any hope for him to establish a romantic relationship with Fox Woman. She had been hardly aware of his existence, in all probability. In fact, no one had ever known of the attraction Beaver had felt toward her. It amused him now, but was a little embarrassing.

The next young woman to whom he was powerfully attracted was nearly his own age. They were good friends in the years they spent together in the Rabbit Society, the instruction phase of learning among the People. Lizard, she was called. Lithe, sinuous, and quick, she was boyish in her activities. This had endeared her to Beaver, because she could compete on an equal basis with the throwing sticks, with a bow, and even in the games and races of the Rabbits. She could outrun most of the boys. There were jokes, when she began to show signs of womanhood, that Lizard could have any man she wanted, because she could catch him in a running pursuit and probably out-wrestle him.

But her sharp angles, long legs, and knobby knees soon evolved into shapely feminine bulges and softly rounded curves. Lizard became one of the most desirable women imaginable, not only to her friend Beaver, but to every male in the Southern Band. Once again Beaver, who had not yet completed the changes of adolescence, was deleted from the selection process. Lizard married a young man two years her senior. She did share her regrets with her friend, Beaver.

"I will miss you, my friend," she told him, smiling sadly.

But the smile was almost patronizing, and belied the message. She might as well have said "run along, little boy," thought Beaver. His heart was very heavy.

There had been no others to whom he was greatly attracted. He had managed to concentrate on the other activities of young manhood.

The hair on his lip and jaw had become heavier by that time. He had learned to pluck it clean as the other young men did, with clamshell tweezers. The process was annoyingly painful, but was cherished as one of the rites of passage . . . A matter of pride. He was aware that some of the white men who now trapped for furs and lived among the prairie tribes had special knives for cutting face hair rather than plucking it. "Shaving," of course, must be done much more often. It was no wonder that some of the whites who were heavily furred practiced neither method, but bore winter fur on their faces all year. He was aware that some women were repulsed by a bearded man, while others found facial hair quite erotic. He had heard his mother's friends gossiping about it, when he was not supposed to be listening.

For Beaver, who was not heavily furred, the choice was easy. He plucked the face-hair in the traditional way.

<>

He had watched the girls a season or two younger than he as they began to blossom into womanhood. But, they seemed childish and silly, and he had been unable to take them seriously. Especially, since he had been feeling this strange call to the North. Just now, he had no time for girls. This did not, however, prevent him from appreciating the strong relationship between the trader and his wife. That, he thought, was the sort of marriage he would hope for when the time came.

Finally he drifted off to sleep.

Some time later he awoke. He was not certain what had awakened him. He had been dreaming, but the dream had fled. There was not even a hint as to what its subject may have been.

The moon was rising, sending his thoughts wandering again. He looked around the camp site. The fire had burned low, and he thought of rising to feed it another stick or two. But there was no need. This season was warm and the cooking done for the evening. The campfire was mostly symbolic at this point, a statement to any spirits that might inhabit the area.

The thoughts of Beaver were far from such things, as he sleepily stared at the glowing coals. He tried to choose between the comfort of his blanket and the unnecessary attention to the fire. Even as he pondered, he dozed off again.

<>

The next time he woke, he had the unmistakable impression that some sound had roused him. But *what* sound? He listened. There was the soft chuckle of water over white gravel, from the shallows of the stream a few steps away, and the regular breathing of his companions. A little farther away he heard the odd hollow grinding noise made by a horse's chewing, like no other sound he knew. That was good. Horses, calmly feeding, indicated that all was well. If there were any unusual events in progress, the animals would be silent, listening, or talking among themselves in the soft mutter that a mare uses to speak to her foal. A frog sounded its watery, mournful cry, and the horses paused for only a moment before resuming their feeding.

The position of the moon told Beaver it had been some time ago that he had fallen asleep. His full bladder suggested the same thing.

Well, he could get up for that, and while out of his bed, toss a couple of sticks on the fire . . .

He rolled out, walked downstream a little way, and answered nature's call. As he readjusted his loincloth, he was again impressed with the fact that *something* was going on. It was not something that he saw or heard, but a vague and poorly defined feeling. And, oddly, it did not seem to be threatening.

Beaver retraced his steps and picked up a stick from the pile near the fire. He stirred the ashes a little and piled the few hot coals together, laying his stick across them. Then another stick. He blew gently, stimulating the dull coals to white heat. The new fuel began to smoke. There was no need, actually, to induce a flame, but it seemed a logical thing to do.

The sticks broke into flame, pushing the edge of the darkness back, forming a circle of light. For just a moment, maybe the space of a heartbeat, he thought he caught a glimpse of motion out of the corner of his eye. Then, it was gone into the darkness. The horses paused in their chewing. *Maybe just startled by the light*, he thought. They resumed feeding. *Maybe a raccoon or a possum*, but nothing seemed amiss.

Beaver returned to his blankets, and was soon asleep.

<·>

Back in the camp of the Southern band of the People, darkness had fallen, and the camp was quiet. Fires burned low. Snakewater sat in her lodge, talking. It was known that the old woman frequently talked to herself. The members of the band assumed it an amusing eccentricity. But is not one with a gift of the spirit assumed to be a bit strange? Such a medicine-doctor is in close contact and communication with the spirit world. Is it not possible that they would see and hear things not seen or heard by others? Maybe, even, that they might carry on conversations with unseen beings as a part of their medicine. It is not for others to question such a gift.

On this occasion, alone in her lodge, Snakewater would have appeared to any observer to be speaking to empty space. To a passerby, her muted voice could have been heard through the canvas wall of the tepee, though few words could have been distinguished. No response would have been apparent at all.

"What? Gone *with* him? Who is this friend of yours, Lumpy? I don't know her. Yes, I know there was no reason I should, but, damn it, Lumpy, I know. And I appreciate your loyalty, ever since I left Old Town. Yes, *we*, of course. But your friend . . . Has *she* been with us all along? Ah, I thought not. Just visiting you? But I haven't seen . . . Yes, I suppose not. I don't see *you* unless you choose to show yourself. Still, she likes to travel, you say? But why with young Beaver? Well, no, it had not occurred to me that some of *your* people might want to travel. Will she help him or bother him? Oh, that's good. Of course, I see that. It depends on *his* reaction. But she won't *hurt* him? Good. He may need some help. Now, let me get some sleep. The Sun Dance starts tomorrow."

<· >**15**

As they approached, it appeared to be an encampment much like that of Beaver's own people, but larger. The Southern Band of the People had never exceeded thirty or forty lodges. The village which lay before them as the trader's party topped the ridge must have consisted of at least a hundred lodges.

They were much like those of the People, with similar painted decorations on the covers. There was a minor difference in the shape of the door opening, but Beaver felt that inside, such a lodge would seem somewhat like that of his parents. A great many were of canvas rather than skins, he noticed. Most of the hunter tribes of the prairie were accepting the white man's canvas as a lighter, more easily handled material to replace the traditional buffalo skin lodge covers.

A village of this size must naturally have a great many horses. The animals were scattered across the prairie to the north and west, herded closely by young men. Beaver had spent many days and nights at this very task. He smiled to himself. Some things never change much, even with varying customs and languages. And, the problems of such a camp would be the same. Water would be needed for people and for horses, and grass for the latter. A bigger camp meant more horses. Grass would be eaten more quickly, and the herd must range farther. There would come a time when the grass around the camp for a half-day's travel would grow scarce. It would be time to move on.

There were still other factors in the decisions that the leaders of such a village must make. Some were purely practical, like that of the grass, but some were esthetic. Some related to both. A camp of a hundred lodges, each containing a family of several people, quickly translates into a population of at least four to five hundred. Add to the human population a few dogs for every lodge. In the hot summer days, the generation of large quantities of human and canine waste brought unpleasant odors and an abundance of flies. It was not only for esthetic reasons, but for the health of the People that they must move on. When the odors became enough to offend the senses of those in leadership positions, they would hold a council and decide on the day of departure, usually two or three days ahead.

This particular band had not been in their present camp site for very long, Beaver guessed. There seemed to be a good supply of lush spring growth to the grass, and the horse herds were fairly near at hand, grazing contentedly. They appeared well fed and healthy, and their coats were sleek and shiny. This camp must have strong leadership, he reasoned.

A number of dogs loped out to meet them with a chorus of barks and howls, followed by a group of five horsemen. Most of the riders were young, and their leader was a middle-aged warrior with a stern and capable visage. The five drew up in a line to confront the newcomers. Beaver felt nervous, but the trader reassured him.

"Just a welcome party," he said softly. "Ceremony. They know me."

Trader held his right hand aloft, palm forward, as he drew his horse to a halt a few paces away from the greeting delegation. Their leader returned the hand sign, the empty hand.

A simple motion or gesture carries much significance. This greeting ritual was familiar to Beaver, of course. He had seen it many times among his own people, and had used it in play and in greeting friends. The open, empty palm says much: *"I carry no weapon. I come in peace."*

The stern face of the warrior who served as leader of the delegation now broke into a smile, and he began to speak, still in hand signs.

Trader! It is good. Welcome to our camp.

The trader returned a similar message, also in signs, and introduced Beaver.

This is our helper for the season.

Beaver and the warrior exchanged nods, and the other signed again.

It is good. How are you called?

I am called Beaver.

The other nodded. *I am Blue Hawk*, he signed, in answer. He turned again to the trader, gesturing toward Cactus Flower and her infant.

You have a new child. Good.

Yes, we have. A girl.

Cactus Flower, a bit embarrassed by the attention but filled with pride, blushed.

You have some trade goods, too? signed Blue Hawk.

Of course!

Both men chuckled.

It is good! Come, camp with us.

Blue Hawk and his warriors turned their horses, flanking the travelers and forming an escort. As they moved on toward the camp, the escorts in turn were joined by a scatter of barking dogs and running children. The newcomers had been accepted as friends by the greeting party, and the news of the arrival of a trader spread quickly among the lodges. An exciting time, with stories and visiting and exchanged news.

<>

It was late in the day, however, and everyone knew there would be no trading today. The newcomers must pay a ritual visit to the lodge of the leader of this camp, requesting permission to trade. It was an accepted fact that such permission would be granted, barring unforeseen circumstances. Still it was a mark of politeness and respect to do so.

Some white men understood such need for custom and respect, others seemed not to. Beaver's mother had often voiced disgust at some of the latter. Had they never had parents, she wondered indignantly, to teach them manners?

In this case, the ritual was preordained. The visitors would pay their respects, the chieftain would give his approval to the trader's visit, and the visitors would make camp. As was the custom, a story fire was in order as darkness fell. Traders usually told not only stories of their own people, but those of other tribes and nations with whom they dealt. A camp of this size would also have at least one expert storyteller. It should be an interesting evening for everyone.

<>

The visitors were, of course, welcomed by the chief, and the expected story fire prepared. As the western sky began to blossom with colors of gold and purple and red, people began to gather.

"Sun Boy chooses his colors well tonight," remarked Beaver to Trades His Moccasins.

"Sun Boy? Yes, of course! One of the stories of your people. You must tell stories at the fire, Beaver."

"But, I am no storyteller," the young man protested.

The trader laughed.

"Everyone has stories," he observed. "Some tell them better than others, but your people have good ones. Tell your Creation story. Your Old Man, is it not, who sat on the log and tapped it with a drum-beater?"

"Yes, the Old Man of the Shadows," Beaver answered, "but Trader, I don't know . . ."

Trades His Moccasins stopped him with a wave of the hand.

"Don't worry. Tell it in your own tongue, and in hand signs. If it is not well understood, I will translate. But your people have good stories, no?"

"We have always thought so," Beaver agreed. "But there are many good stories."

"Of course. Someone once told me, a Cherokee I think, 'The World is filled with stories, which sometimes permit themselves to be told.' Is it not true?"

Beaver smiled.

"I will try," he agreed.

<>

Darkness had fallen. The fire blazed brightly, pushing back the blanket of night into scraps and puddles of shadow among the lodges. There had been welcoming speeches and introductions, and the storyteller of the encampment had recounted how his people entered the sunlight, swimming up through a lake from the underworld below.

Then the trader told of some of the ways of his people, and how at the end of this present lifetime, they go "over the hill" to a place inhabited by those who have lived before. Parents, grandparents, and friends from the lifetime call to him and welcome him and make him feel at home. It is a happy place. Sometimes, though, the friends and family who are still living want very much for him to stay with them. Then he may go back. This can happen more than once, the look over the hill and then the return.

"And oh, yes," Trades His Moccasins finished, "on the Other Side all are the same, whether they have been good or bad."

All are the same? signed one of the listeners.

"So we are taught," Trader answered, accompanying the words with hand gestures.

Then why should one be good? the young man signed.

"That he may please himself," Trader suggested.

"And that he please his *mother*!" called an old woman.

There was general laughter.

"Agreed," answered the trader. "He might have trouble indeed, but now, my friend here is of a different people than mine. Theirs is a good creation story."

He motioned for Beaver to rise. Embarrassed, the young man stood and clumsily began his story using hand signs and the tongue of the People.

"I will help him," Trades His Moccasins interjected. "If he needs it." There was a murmur of acceptance.

"I am no storyteller," Beaver began. "My people are sometimes called Elk-dog People because of the horse. A hair-faced stranger came, riding the First Horse . . . But that is not our Creation story."

There was a sympathetic chuckle around the circle, and he stumbled on.

"In stories of how people came into the world, many start with living under the ground. It is so with ours. In your own story, your people came by swimming up through the water of a lake. That was new to me. But, how my people came out . . ."

He paused nervously and took a deep breath.

"Somebody heard a drum beating, above, and tried to see from where it came. There was a tunnel with light at the end. First Man crawled through the tunnel and out into a world of bright sunlight. After his eyes stopped blinking, he looked around and saw an ugly old man sitting on a hollow log, astride, like this."

He demonstrated, using the hand sign for "man on a horse."

"This old man held a drum stick in his hand. Then he raised it and struck the log, and a woman crawled out. First Man recognized her as his wife, First Woman. Each time Old Man hit the cottonwood log, out came another of the People, and soon there was a small crowd. He continued . . . One after another . . ."

At this point in the story, it was customary to pause, and he did so. Nothing happened. Beaver began to panic. He had seen and heard this story many times, but always at this point someone asked a question. Now, there was only silence. Had he told the story incorrectly?

Just then, Trades His Moccasins spoke.

"Beaver," he said, "do they still come through the log?"

At the same time, he signed the same question.

Now Beaver recognized the situation, and why someone always asked. It was a joke on the listeners, and if none of them asked, one who knew the answer would do so. This restored his confidence.

"Sad to say, no," Beaver confessed. "A fat woman got stuck in the log, and no more could come out. *Aiee*, this is why we have always been a small tribe."

Now there was general laughter. Beaver began to gain a little confidence.

"Wait!" asked someone. "This 'old man' . . . He is your trickster, maybe?"

Beaver nodded.

"He is called 'Old Man of the Shadows.' He can help or hurt you, or play tricks."

"How is *your* trickster called?" asked the Trader.

"He is 'Old Man Coyote,'" answered their storyteller. "Everybody has a trickster, by different names."

"I am made to think," said the Trader, "that he is all the same, or nearly so. 'The Grandfather,' 'Old Man Coyote,' or just 'The Old Man.' 'The Great Rabbit,' in one place I visited. 'Saindi' to the Kiowas. But he is usually tall and thin, with long unbraided hair, a big nose. He is older than Creation, and can turn himself into a rock or a tree or a stream."

"Yes, yes," people were saying. "Is it not so?"

Trades His Moccasins smiled and laughed with his hosts, and Beaver was developing a new respect for this unusual man. He had become everyone's friend.

Trading would be good tomorrow.

<‹·›16

As expected, trade was good. A pleasant summer season, with warm sunny days and cool nights, put everyone in a comfortable and friendly mood, ideal for bartering. Ideal for any purpose, in fact, that called for human interaction.

This was a day that seemed to have been created to make life easier. Everyone was relaxed and apparently free from care. True, it was understood that soon they must move the camp. That would entail work and confusion and inconvenience. But not today . . . Today was a day to enjoy the weather, visiting with friends, gambling with the plum stones, and, of course, negotiating with the trader. If a person had nothing to trade, it was still amusing to watch others haggle over a desirable trade. And the goods carried by this man and his wife were of excellent quality.

Beaver assisted with the unpacking and display of the trade items. By this time he had seen the process several times, and was beginning to understand the techniques involved. He had noticed how Cactus Flower would help with a shrug, a gesture, or a sigh. She would watch a trade in progress, and shake her head in apparent disapproval, as if her husband's offer had been far too generous. Often, this caused a customer balancing on the edge of doubt to accept the trade before Trades His Moccasins could withdraw such a bargain.

"It is good to be an honest trader," Trades His Moccasins explained. "If I deal fairly, they will remember, and trading will be better next time. But if I cheat someone, he will remember it all his life."

"And," interjected Cactus Flower, "he will tell everyone he ever meets, no?"

⟨⟩

Beaver was learning much about the trader's profession, and was interested in learning more.

"How is it, Uncle, that you get the things you trade?"

"What do you mean, Beaver?"

"The trade goods. You offer knives, fire strikers, beads, maybe lead for bullets, powder for the guns, in exchange for furs, and sometimes things the women have sewn. Sometimes, arrow points, no?"

"I don't understand, Beaver. Yes, I trade almost anything. Somewhere, somebody wants it. I have only to find him. Or, her. But what is your question?"

"Ahh . . ." Beaver paused in confusion. "Where do you get the knives and the other white man's things, and where do you take the furs you have traded for?"

"Oh, I see! Several ways. There are white traders who stay in one place. They have a supply of metal tools, beads, 'trade goods,' canvas for lodge covers . . . Surely, your people visit them sometimes. You have canvas lodge covers."

"Of course. But what do *they* do with the furs?"

"Sell them to other whites, I suppose. Furs are good to wear. Beavers, I have heard, are used to make hats. I don't know how. I have seen such hats, and they don't look much like a beaver's fur. It was once, I am told, that there were gatherings each year, the time of awakening, I think. Everybody, white trappers as well as our people, would gather with the skins from the winter's trapping, and trade for several days. Maybe half a moon."

"*Aiee!* But my people do not trap very much, Uncle."

"Not as much as some," agreed Trades His Moccasins. "But you do stay in winter camp during trapping season. There are now traps made of metal, much easier to reset."

"Yes, we have seen these."

"The trader's purpose is to find who needs what, and where," Trades His Moccasins went on. "That is not always easy. And needs and wants might change. We must be ready to see the change, and to use it. This helps people get what they need, and, of course, helps the trader earn a living."

"Look, here is something," the trader went on. He drew out a small packet wrapped in buckskin. He unwrapped it to reveal a rather uninteresting lump of a dark brown substance, the size of a fist.

"What is it?" asked Beaver.

"It is called *chok-l-attel*. Here, taste it."

He shaved a morsel from the ball with his knife, and handed it to Beaver, who placed it on his tongue.

"It is bitter!"

"Yes. It comes from far to the south. Those who live there boil it with water to make a drink. Strong medicine, it is said. Good for lovers. I haven't needed it, but someone will, sometime."

"How is it that you have it?" asked Beaver.

"I took it in trade. I had heard of it, but had never seen it. There are many things from other places, Beaver. This makes the trader's life interesting."

"The whites brought this *chok-l-attel*?" asked Beaver, still confused.

"No, no. Whites had not many crops, I am told, until they came here. The growers say that whites had no potatoes, or beans, no corn, or pumpkins or tobacco; many other things. Maybe that's why they came. They had nothing good to eat!"

Both laughed.

"But now," the trader went on, "anything grown almost anywhere is carried everywhere by traders, along with the different colors of flint arrow points, and other goods. Anything available to any tribe can be traded to any other."

Beaver was learning much about a way of life completely unfamiliar to him, and finding it fascinating. Beneath all this valuable experience, however, was always the underlying purpose of his quest, that of the red pipestone and its mysterious power which seemed to beckon to him. There were times when he did not think about it for a while, as he busied around the usual camp chores of the travelers. But it was seldom far from his mind.

It returned forcibly when an old woman approached with a request to trade. She carried a buckskin pouch, and the manner in which she held it cradled in her cupped hands indicated that it held something of great importance to her. She spoke in the trader's tongue, which Beaver was beginning to learn. He could not follow the rapid exchange, but was fascinated when she withdrew a pipe to offer in trade. It had been stored in two pieces, bowl and stem separate, as commonly done. The sumac stem was decorated with beads and fur, but the bowl itself was an exquisite carving in the red stone of an eagle's head. It seemed alive. The eyes of the graven bird's head were small, polished black stones. It was almost as if they might blink at any moment.

The woman talked rapidly and with great emotion, and both the trader and his wife seemed to hang on every word. Beaver caught a reference to "husband" and "son," and several times, "dead." From these references, and from the attitude of Cactus Flower, it was apparently a sorrowful tale. It was also apparent to Beaver that Trades His Moccasins was not interested in trading for the pipe . . . A most uncharacteristic reaction.

"What is it?" Beaver asked quietly in his own language.

The trader waved him aside, and turned to the woman with a couple of further questions. A tear glistened in the eye of the old woman, and Beaver's curiosity was weighing heavily on him.

"What are they saying?" he asked Cactus Flower.

At last she turned to him, as the husband continued to haggle with the customer.

"It was her husband's pipe," Flower explained. "He was killed on a buffalo hunt, but did not take the eagle pipe with him to the Other Side. He had wanted their oldest son to have it, so it was not placed on the burial scaffold when he crossed over. The pipe was given to the son. Then he, too, was killed, soon after."

"How?" inquired Beaver.

That might make a difference. Could there be a connection?

"He was kicked by a horse."

This explained the trader's reluctance. The object, though very beautiful and valuable, had been associated with tragedy. Since it had not been given away before the warrior's death, it should have been placed on the funeral scaffold. To know that the father *wanted* his son to have the pipe was not enough. It should have been given as a gift, from the living to the living.

Beaver wondered if maybe the son had not been entirely honest. If he coveted the valuable object, he might have *said* that it had been given to him. That would cast a shadow over *his* ownership of the pipe. When it should have brought the young man favorable luck, he had suffered a tragic accident.

Regardless of interpretation, it was now an object associated with death and tragedy. It was apparent that the widow's circumstances were not good. Her garments were ragged and worn, she was thin and feeble. There was no man to hunt for her. Her sustenance probably depended on the generosity of others. It was ironic that her most valuable possession, the pipe, carried a curse that reduced its value to virtually nothing. It would not be good to own such a thing, yet it was all she had.

Beaver's heart was heavy for the woman. She probably suspected the bad influence of the pipe. Some would have concealed its terrible history, but she had told of it with perfect honesty, it appeared.

Trades His Moccasins must have been thinking along the same lines.

"How are you called, Mother?"

"I am Elk Woman."

The trader nodded.

"It is good. I like to know the names of those I trade with."

The old woman smiled at the kindness in his voice.

"So, we trade?" she asked.

"Ah, there is a problem, Mother. You have a beautiful pipe, here, but its story is not good. It carries sadness. Maybe it should have crossed to the Other Side with your husband."

"But he wanted our son to have it."

"Yes, so you said. Maybe it should have been placed on *his* scaffold.

"*Ah!* I did not think of that. Its value . . ."

"Yes, of course, Mother."

It was apparent that the woman had little else. The trader was trying hard to find a way to help her.

"Maybe," he said thoughtfully, "maybe you could find a way to put it on the scaffold of your son."

The wrinkled old face brightened, and then fell.

"But . . . Then, I would have nothing to trade."

Aiee, this is not a very wise woman, thought Beaver.

Maybe it was *she* who had hesitated to sacrifice the pipe because of its value.

"Look, Mother," the trader suggested, "tell me about your needs, what you want if we were to trade."

Quickly, Elk Woman pointed out a few objects of considerable value. A knife, a fire striker, beads, a small axe, an awl, needles . . . Things she could easily trade for staple foods and necessities. She had done some thinking on this.

"Now," said Trades His Moccasins, "these things are yours, on one condition. You must return the pipe to your son's burial scaffold. That should end your bad luck. And, tell no one. I cannot do this for everyone."

"You are *giving* her the trade goods?" asked the startled Cactus Flower in her own tongue.

"What can I do?" asked her husband. "She is in need, Flower."

"You are not taking her pipe in trade?"

"No, I am made to think it carries a curse. But, maybe she will find a way to return it to her son's burial scaffold."

Tears welled in Cactus Flower's eyes.

"What is it?" her husband inquired with concern.

She gave him a quick hug.

"My heart is good, my husband. I have a good man."

Trades His Moccasins was embarrassed.

"It was nothing, woman!"

"No, it was the sort of thing my man would do," Flower insisted. "But not too often!"

Beaver swallowed a lump in his throat as the old woman, with her own tears of gratitude, gathered the gifts of the trader. With profuse thanks, she backed away and departed.

"Now, will everybody expect free goods?" asked Beaver.

The others chuckled.

"Maybe," admitted the trader.

<>

It did not happen so, however. The plight of the old woman was well known in the encampment, and the generosity of the trader met with whole-hearted approval.

Rather than hurt the trading, it appeared to help. Such a kind person, they seemed to tell each other, would not cheat in a trade, would he?

Everyone in the encampment became aware of the trader's kindness almost immediately. It was a tradition among the people of the prairie to find ways to help those less fortunate. Among Beaver's own nation, there was a special ceremony intended to redistribute the wealth to some extent, and at the same time provide honor for loved ones.

The Gift Dance could be inserted into other ceremonies, usually the Warriors' Dance, or other celebrations under the supervision of one of the warrior societies. Beaver remembered well some of the occasions when he had seen it carried out.

⟨⟩

The warriors moved in rhythmic cadence to the drums and chanting. Their colorful capes fluttered in the breeze of their motion, and the single eagle feather in the top of each roached headdress twirled and spun as if it were a living thing.

Then a woman walked out among the dancers to confront her mate. She carried a beautifully beaded and decorated robe, which she ceremonially deposited at his feet to honor him. His skills, his warrior status, his dancing, ability as a hunter, perhaps even his skill as a husband, warming the robes of the marital bed. It was a statement: *In this way I bring honor and pride to my husband.*

The warrior, he who had been honored, stopped his dance and thrust his spear firmly into the ground at his feet. The drums and the chanting stopped, and all was still. He must stand so, until someone recognized and acknowledged the honor to this warrior. In effect, the wife had made a statement about her pride in her husband, but someone must agree and verify, by *accepting* the gift.

It was only a few moments until an old woman shuffled forward. Her garments were somewhat shabby but her posture still showed pride. She looked the motionless warrior straight in the eye, giving a smile and a nod. Then she bent to pick up the ceremonial gift. Without words she had indicated honor for the warrior by accepting the robe: *I, too, claim that this is a man who deserves honor. In his honor, I accept this gift.*

Such a custom might seem strange to other cultures, but among the People it had served well. A warrior might be honored by his family, as some do only after the death of the honoree. But among Beaver's people, one might be honored in this way while he still lived, so that he could experience it, and enjoy the respect of his community. In addition, there was the purpose of helping those less fortunate without causing them embarrassment.

⟨⟩

Beaver assumed that this tribe with whom they camped might have some similar custom as a means of redistributing necessities.

Yet, here was the old woman, obviously in need, who had only a single item, one of great value, with which to barter. The timing was probably wrong. It was not the season, maybe, for this tribe's version of the Gift Dance, and the woman had day-to-day needs. The hunters would stop by her lodge with a gift of meat sometimes, perhaps. But, she had no way to repay them. Her pride would trouble her. A woman whose husband had owned the eagle pipe had not lacked for much at one time. Here had been a lodge which reflected the wealth and status of the family. Then, she had lost her husband, and later her son. Nothing had been said about other children, so she may have had no one at all. And, as a last crushing misfortune, her only remaining possession of value possibly carried a curse. Despite the heaviness of heart on the part of her friends and neighbors, it could easily be felt that it would be too dangerous to associate closely with the woman.

The trader had made a great impression on the others of this camp by not taking advantage of an unfortunate old woman.

"You did well, my husband," said Cactus Flower later. "These people are pleased with your kindness, with your respect for the old woman. Still, do not do such an expensive act of kindness *too* often. That was a pipe of great value. But, I am proud."

<⋅>17

The encampment moved on two days later, and it was, in a way, a relief to be on the move again. Trades His Moccasins had conferred at length with the leaders of the camp, and learned much about the country ahead. They would travel together for a few days and then their paths would diverge, their companions moving farther to the west, while the trader veered eastward.

There were the usual problems with travel. At intervals a pack would slip, and it would be necessary to stop and repack one of the horses. Beaver did not recall so many problems when his own family was on the move. In thinking about it, however, he realized a difference. A family, moving with other families of the People, would be using one or more pole-drags behind horses. Lodge poles were used for this purpose, and small household items were stacked on the platform of the dragging poles. *Travois*, the pole-drag was often called now, because of the influence of the French fur trappers and traders. Many French words had entered the language of the People.

But a cargo of small items such as those carried by a trader must be packed in bundles and packs or in *parfleche* carriers. These packs in turn were tied on the backs of pack animals. This in itself was a special skill, and one at which Trades His Moccasins was an expert. Beaver had learned much about pack horses as he worked with the trader.

It was frustrating, then, when his knots slipped, and he had to endure the good-natured taunting of the trader. His ties, of which he had been gaining confidence, seemed to slip more often. Finally he asked about it.

"Am I doing something wrong?" he asked. "My packing will not stay tied."

The trader laughed.

"There are days like that," he said. "The spirits have a sense of humor, you know."

"So I have heard," answered Beaver. "I thought I was doing better!"

"And you are," the trader assured him. "It is sometimes this way. I have to admit, my own knots have been slipping."

"I had not noticed."

"Ah, yes. You were busy with your own, and I was not eager to point it out to you."

Both laughed, and then Trades His Moccasins became serious.

"I am made to think that it's the weather," he said thoughtfully.

"The *weather*?"

"Yes. Have you noticed that on hot, dry days, a rawhide rope or a *parfleche* is harder than when it rains?"

"Of course, but . . ."

"The air has been very dry, no?"

Beaver nodded.

"So," the trader continued, "we can't tie a knot as snugly as when the air is damp."

"Could we *wet* our packing strings? No . . ."

The trader had already started to laugh when Beaver realized the situation. Rawhide, when wet, will dry as hard as flint in hot, dry air. Then they could not *untie* the packs.

"Maybe we could put some grease on the ties," the trader pondered. "Let me think on this."

They did try, with possibly a little success, but then it rained, stopping the entire caravan for a day to dry out everything. Their rawhide ties shrank appreciably and dried stiff and hard to handle.

"This is very strange," the puzzled trader mused. "We have never had such problems in this region before. It cannot be the difference in climate. Dry air, as I had suspected, does not explain it."

The next day their misfortune continued. One of the pack horses, a bay mare, limped slightly as they saddled. Trades His Moccasins asked Beaver to lead the animal back and forth on level ground, with no obstructions.

"She still limps," he observed. "Maybe a thorn . . ."

He picked up the left forefoot and examined the frog. Then he cleaned the foot carefully, scraping the sole with a flint he kept for that purpose.

"I can find no thorn. A stone bruise, maybe. I don't know."

The trader created a padded shoe of soft-tanned buffalo leather, stuffed with a handful of hair shaved from the woolly part of an old buffalo robe and mixed with tallow. He gathered the upper edges of the skin and tied the contraption around the pastern with a thong.

"There! Now, lead her around a little. Yes, some better."

They repacked, giving a heavier load to one of the other horses. Most of the other travelers had already straggled out of the now abandoned camp, heading in a long column toward the north.

"We'll catch up this evening," assured the trader. "No matter, anyway. We'll leave them in a day or two, when they head farther west."

⟨⟩

The trader's small party arrived at the temporary camp site just as Sun Boy painted himself with brilliant colors and sauntered over Earth's rim. It was hard to find a spot to camp not already occupied by cactus, thistles, or other travelers.

They finally managed to find forage for the tired animals, and a place for the obligatory campfire. Cactus Flower tossed the ceremonial pinch of tobacco into the fire to appease the spirits, and the tired travelers settled in for the night, chewing some pemmican from one of the packs. It was too late to consider cooking. None of the three adults at the trader's fire mentioned one fact that all had noticed. The bay mare's limp had not improved at all. Maybe, even, it was slightly worse.

⟨·⟩18

"Have we done something to offend the spirits?" asked Beaver. "Maybe it is something I have done. You have not had trouble here before, when I was not with you."

"No, no, that is not it," Cactus Flower insisted. "I am made to think it is something else."

"I, too," agreed her husband. "There is something that we have overlooked here. The spirits may be offended, but *what* spirits, and why?"

They had parted company with the other travelers when it became apparent that the mare's limp was no better. They traveled another day with no pack load on the crippled animal, but even so, the limp became worse.

"Maybe a snake bite," pondered Trades His Moccasins. "Yet, I cannot see fang marks. A twisting injury, maybe."

He threw his hands up in dismay.

"We must move on, and this horse slows us. We have to leave her behind."

"*Leave* her?" asked Beaver.

"Yes. She has been a good mare. She is still young, too. Maybe she will recover, but now she holds us back. It is better for the mare and for us if we leave her. Look, there is good grass here, and water. Probably other horses, wild ones. She will get along, rest, and heal her injury, whatever it is . . . I cannot tell."

"Will you come back this way?" asked Beaver. "Maybe you can find her again, after she heals, on your way back."

"That is true," agreed the trader. "But there are other horses. We can find a replacement. Probably, among the people where we trade next."

"Who will that be?"

"I don't know. Probably one of the Lakota bands. It does not matter. But everyone has horses to trade."

They left the mare in a meadow that seemed ideal, with a crystal clear stream murmuring over a white gravel riffle. The grass in the bend of the stream was heavy and lush.

"Enjoy it, little lady," joked Trades His Moccasins. "Not many horses have it so good. May you heal well!"

It was evident that despite his bold talk, the trader hated to lose the animal. Not necessarily for her value, but more of a feeling that somehow he had failed in his responsibility to care for the horse.

As they bedded down that night to prepare for an early departure, there seemed a heavy feeling over the little camp. There was no point in discussion. All of the travelers felt it. No other course of action would have been of any help.

It was puzzling, though. All of them seemed depressed, out of all proportion to the problem. The loss of a horse, easily replaced, should not be so serious. They would travel a bit more slowly, with the remaining pack animals carrying extra burdens. They had no fixed schedule anyway, and really had little knowledge of where and when they might encounter people with whom to trade.

Their concern and frustration, their sheer sadness, seemed to make no sense at all. They tried to joke about it, but the jokes fell flat.

"We are missing something," Trades His Moccasins said thoughtfully.

"You mean, we have left something behind?" asked Beaver.

"No, no." The trader smiled wistfully. There were still some problems with language. "Not that way. I mean, there is something that is wrong that we have not noticed."

"But what, Uncle?"

"*Aiee*, you call me Uncle? I am not much older than you!"

Beaver was somewhat embarrassed by the reprimand.

"But you *are* older," he stammered.

"That is true," agreed Trades His Moccasins, "but I had not thought of it that way. I am a young man."

Cactus Flower, nursing her baby across the fire from the men, was shaking with laughter.

"I cannot believe it," she sputtered. "Two young men, who cannot accept the honor of being called 'Uncle', lest they be thought old and feeble!"

"It is not that," mumbled Beaver indignantly. "It is a matter of *respect*. I respect my friend Trades His Moccasins, no?"

"Of course," Flower agreed, still giggling. "But, the startled look on my husband's face!"

"What started this?" demanded the trader irritably.

"You said we have left something behind."

"Oh! That was it! No, I said . . . Or meant to say . . . There is something that we have not *thought* about. Maybe there is a *reason* why our horse goes lame, our packs slip."

"Something we have done?" asked Beaver.

"Maybe. Or maybe, something not done, something we should have."

"But what could it be, my husband?" asked Flower. "We have offered tobacco over our night fires to honor the spirits. Sage and sweetgrass, too. Is there some incense dearer to these northern spirits; something missing?"

"Not that I know about," the trader mused. "We have had no such trouble before."

"If we break a taboo, a custom, because we don't know about it . . ." Beaver began, but was interrupted by the trader.

"I think not, Beaver. One tribe is not held to the ways of another. We observe each other's ways sometimes out of politeness, but it would not anger their spirits . . . Well, look . . . Kiowas do not eat bears, but their friends the Comanches do. Yet, they hunt together. If a Kiowa is offered bear meat, he responds simply 'No, I am Kiowa,' and no one has broken a law. The Comanche still eats the bear meat, sitting next to one who does not."

Beaver nodded. "Our people do not eat bears, either," he observed.

"I know. That's why I chose that example. But I don't know . . ."

"It must be something other than a local custom, then?" suggested Cactus Flower.

"It would seem so," agreed her husband. "Something we don't know about. Then, *when* did it happen?"

"After we parted from the band we traveled with?"

"No, that was *why* we parted. It had already happened. The mare went lame . . ." the trader mused.

"Something about the mare?" asked Beaver.

"Maybe. We have to leave her anyway. Maybe that will stop the misfortune."

There was nothing to do but wait and see. They bedded in for the night, hoping for a good day to travel. No one shared further thoughts, but it was possible that all three had noticed other problems: the unexplained slipping of the packs, the difficulty with the ties . . .

Beaver lay awake a long time, thinking along these lines. There was just enough worry in the thoughts that scampered through his head to prevent his falling asleep. Several times he was almost there, only to waken and not know why. There were many strange things about this whole summer. Puzzling things, some of which he could not even begin to inquire about. Like the matter of the Little People, for instance. It had been some time since he had thought about that.

He drifted off to sleep, and dreamed he was watching a ceremony around a fire. A number of Little People were dancing, it seemed, gyrating wildly to the music of the crackling logs and the shimmering dance of the flames.

It was one of those times when one knows it is a dream, yet does not wake. To waken would stop the dream, but Beaver felt that he needed to experience it. He must *know* more, though he did not quite understand why as he hovered between the two worlds.

Then, he did waken, drawing up and out of the dream setting and back into his blankets by the campfire. The dream, so real and near, seemed far away now, and he was puzzled as to why it had seemed important only a moment ago. He must talk to Snakewater again. But no, she was many days' travel away to the south, with the People for the Sun Dance. He tried to think about where they might be now. He had not kept count. That was probably a mistake . . . Just now, he had no idea whether the Sun Dance was over, or yet to come.

It might be going on right now. Maybe that was the reason for his strange dream of the dancing Little People. Or, maybe not. He was still having trouble sorting dream from reality. He thought he could almost see a small human-like figure now, silhouetted against the northern horizon. No, he decided, that must have been a left-over fragment of that dream, or vision, or whatever it was.

Or had any of it happened at all? Was it all part of the process of existing?

Maybe, a familiar thought struck him, *maybe our daily world is the dream, and the visions we see when we are resting are the reality.* It was too much to ponder just then, and he rolled over and slept.

<> **19**

They woke next morning in the rain. There had been no signs when they retired that such a change in the weather was imminent. Looking back later, they might have suspected something. There had been an ominous feeling over the little camp, but the three young people had not given it much thought. It was easy to attribute their feelings to the loss of the mare, and the problems it had created.

They struggled for a little while to keep the fire alive. It would be needed to dry their baggage after the rain stopped. A makeshift lean-to devised from one of the canvas pack covers would do.

This was quite successful as the strange little shower rumbled across the prairie . . . From the wrong direction, Beaver noted. Summer storms come from the west or southwest, but this one, from the northeast. Odd . . . There was much more thunder and lightning than expected in a morning storm, too. They huddled beneath another of the pack covers and watched a spear of real-fire strike a giant old cottonwood a few hundred paces upstream. The boom of the thunder an instant later was deafening, and they stared in frightened wonder as half of the shattered tree fell ponderously away. It crashed to the ground, where it lay smoking and steaming in the rain. The scent of the acrid smoke mingled with the unfamiliar smell that follows the bolt of real-fire, the weapon of Storm Maker.

Nervously, Cactus Flower tossed a pinch of tobacco into their own struggling fire, and fanned its smoke upward to counteract the influence of the storm's spirits. She put the baby to breast, and covered its head against the next flash and the boom of Storm Maker's drum.

The shower passed on quickly, but they would lose a day's travel while they began to spread the packs and their contents to dry. It was only a short while before they discovered a corner of the canvas pack cover had been burned in the process of trying to shelter the campfire. It could still be used, but with difficulty. A makeshift patch job at best.

The clouds moved on, taking with them the flickering orange of lightning within their gray mass. The rumble of the distant thunder died to a mutter, and Sun Boy's torch blazed forth in all its glory. Birds began to sing again. The day was looking more promising. Then they discovered, almost accidentally, that one of the packs containing furs, for which they had traded, was wet. At some point, the lashing had slipped or loosened. The leak had allowed water to trickle into the tightly packed furs.

"We'll have to dry everything," observed Trades His Moccasins. "I never saw a pack of furs hold so much water!"

The skins were spread over patches of brush and small willows, to allow the sun's warmth and drying rays to remedy the problem. Untanned furs might easily mildew, or even begin to rot, if not kept dry.

"Look!" said Flower suddenly, pointing toward the sky.

A pair of buzzards circled, riding the rising currents of warm air. It was quite obvious that their point of concentration was the camp of the travelers.

"They see the furs," observed the trader. "This must look to them like a big kill. They are looking for carrion."

So it seemed. The puzzled birds studied the situation for some time and then, circling for a bit more altitude, soared off toward the west.

Next, a trio of crows flew past, circled back for another look, and then landed in a cottonwood a bow shot away, cawing indignantly. They seemed to sense that something was wrong with this unusual situation.

Oddly, Beaver began to feel a similar emotion. Many times in his life, he and his family had experienced such an event. When a lodge cover leaked, or when travelers were caught in an unexpected storm, they and their possessions might be soaked. An inconvenience, but a part of life. No great concern . . .

His thoughts were interrupted by angry words between Cactus Flower and her husband.

". . . then do it yourself!" she shot at him.

Beaver was shocked. In the entire time he had been in their company, he had never heard such words between them. The baby, sensing that something was wrong, began to cry.

The young man longed to be of help, but what could he do? Best to keep his mouth shut and his thoughts to himself . . . He walked away from the camp and from the scene of the argument to avoid intrusion on such a private matter.

He was very uncomfortable with it. There had been times when he had felt that he, as an outsider, had been invading the privacy of Flower and Trader as a couple. They were quite affectionate. Their soft giggles as they snuggled in the robes at night were very suggestive and intriguing to the inexperienced Beaver. He admired their relationship and their happiness together, and only hoped to find such a partnership himself some day.

All of these feelings made it doubly hard for him to watch a quarrel between these two for whom he had such admiration. Something was very wrong. The unusual storm, the odd behavior of the buzzards and the crows, both carrion creatures . . . The display of anger between two such devoted people . . . The mysteriously soaked pack, the burned pack covers . . . And, of course, the loss of the mare. It appeared that the little party was being subjected to something evil. A bit of bad luck from time to time could be expected, but all of this at once seemed almost impossible.

Could it be the spirit of *this place*? He thought not. The troubles had started two or three days' travel away. If it had been associated with a place, they would have left it behind. Instead, the bad luck had seemed to travel *with* them.

Even the horses seemed restless and jumpy, nervously skittish at any unexpected sight or sound. They, too, seemed to sense that something was wrong. Of course, horses and dogs sometimes see, hear, or smell things not perceived by mere humans. This seemed to be something more. Rather than a single event or object or entity, this was a dark, threatening presence that hung over the party like a gray cloud. Maybe tomorrow's travel, taking them out of this area, would change the dark mood that had fallen over them all.

<>

There was little conversation for the rest of the day, as they all worked to salvage, dry, and repack everything. Nobody seemed willing to break the overwhelming silence that had fallen over them.

Except for the baby, of course. The tiny girl, usually a happy child, seemed to have an anxious expression on her infant face. It was a look of dread, as if the baby held knowledge of danger unavailable to adults. Beaver found this a worrisome thing.

As purple shadows began to blossom in the gullies and distant canyons, they repacked, to the best of their ability, most of the trade goods and furs. In the morning, their sleeping robes and a few personal items could be quickly packed and loaded for an early departure.

<>

It was not to be. The horses were still jumpy next morning. As the last pair of packs was placed across the back of the bay gelding, the animal began to buck. Not the little nervous crow-hop that sometimes occurs when the cinch is tightened, but a high-flying, head-down, bawling, squealing bucking fit.

At about the third jump, one of the paired packs seemed to burst, scattering small items of trade goods across the ground. This in turn allowed the weight of the other bundle to swing it in and under the horse's belly. The normally calm gelding seemed to panic, bucking and squealing as he tried to dislodge the clinging, bumping burden.

In the space of a few heartbeats the incident was over. Most of the trader's goods, even most of the party's possessions, were scattered from the camp toward the top of the hill, over the space of a long bow shot.

"*Aiee!*" said the trader softly.

In the shocked silence of the morning, the baby began to cry.

<>

They started by recovering what they could. Small items were strewn along the faint game trail which had been the path of retreat for the panicky horse. Here and there lay a small bundle or packet, or the scattered contents of a container which once held trade beads. They would never be able to salvage even half of such a spill. A person might spend a day or more picking up the tiny "seed beads."

To a person not in tune with the mind-set of the trader, the disaster was total. Trades His Moccasins however, had grown up with trading. A trader sometimes makes a good trade, sometimes a poor one. Win some, lose some. A poor trade is only temporary, and the next one may be much better.

Beaver did not yet have the experience to completely understand the situation in this way. He only saw objects of value, scattered on the path or hidden in the thick grass alongside. He was trying frantically to pick up the spill when the trader called to him.

"Don't try to pick up everything. We have to camp here another day now anyway. Beaver, go catch the pack horse. He's stopped, over there."

He pointed. The bay had kicked loose from the damaged pack, and was quietly grazing. Pieces of ropes and straps dangled from the pack saddle, which hung at a crazy angle on the horse's left hip.

The thought crossed Beaver's mind that such an object might easily cause a skittish horse to continue to buck, but it had not. Once rid of the pack, the twisted saddle seemed not to concern the animal at all. This curious fact seemed of no consequence, and was quickly forgotten in the need for some action. He started up the path toward the horse.

As he walked, he watched closely where he stepped. The scatter of items from the pack was almost uniform, and he could hardly take a few strides without some risk of stepping on the valuable objects. It would be a long and tedious day. A whimsical thought crossed his mind, the old saying that "the spirits have a sense of humor." But this seemed more serious than whimsical. Their luck had been overwhelmingly bad for several days, and worsening as the days passed.

Beaver caught the pack horse with no trouble at all. This, too, seemed a little bit unusual for an animal that had seemed so crazy only a short while ago. But one does not question the *good* things.

He was nearly back to where the others were picking up the spill and beginning to establish a new camp site. Cactus Flower suddenly cried out, straightened, and jumped back from something on the ground . . . *A snake?* He wondered, as he hurried toward the spot to help if he could.

She stood, staring at a small object in the grass. It appeared to be a buckskin pouch. It seemed familiar, somehow, though it had no striking difference from a hundred others he had seen. Such a pouch might be used as a warrior's medicine pouch.

"What is it?" asked Trades His Moccasins. "Just part of the . . ."

He stopped short.

"*Aiee!*" said Beaver softly, as he now recognized the beaded design.

The three people stood staring at the pouch that had held the beautifully crafted eagle's head pipe carved from the red stone.

"Is the pipe still in it?" asked Trades His Moccasins.

"I don't know. I didn't touch it," said Flower softly.

Cautiously, the trader knelt to pick up the pouch. The polished eagle's head slid smoothly into his palm, and he quickly but gently slid it back with a deep sigh, almost as if it was hot.

"I thought that you refused that," said Beaver.

"I did," said the trader sadly.

"But . . ."

"The woman . . . She must have slipped it into our pack," Cactus Flower mused. "She thought to thank you for your kindness. I'm sure she tried to do us good."

"Maybe," said her husband. "Or, she saw a chance to get rid of the cursed thing."

"She did not seem to be a person who would harm others," said Flower. "Maybe she did not realize . . ."

"Maybe," he agreed. "Anyway, her problem is ours, now. We know why our luck is all bad."

"What do we do now?" asked Beaver.

"Leave the thing behind," said Trades His Moccasins, "with its curse."

He carried the pouch to a nearby outcropping of stone on the shoulder of the hill, and respectfully positioned it on the ledge.

"Now, let us pick up the damage."

⟨⟩

The entire day was spent collecting, cleaning, repairing, reorganizing, and repacking. By evening, they had restored a semblance of order, and it was good to look forward to a night's rest. Now, maybe their lives would be able to return to normal.

These were Beaver's thoughts as he rolled into his sleeping robe. Yet there was an uneasy feeling that he was overlooking something. Finally, he drifted off to sleep, still troubled.

◀·▸20

It must have been along toward morning that the dream occurred . . . Again, if it *was* a dream. Beaver was never certain about that. A vision is a vision, whether it occurs during the course of the day, or when one is resting. Maybe it comes more easily then, with the mind relaxed and receptive to that which it does not understand.

The fire had burned down to a handful of red-orange coals. Beaver could not remember later whether the moon was visible. There would hardly have been enough light from the stars to see what he saw. Yet the whole event seemed so logical and ordinary, despite what his reason attempted to tell him later.

A little person sat, cross-legged, beside the nearly dormant embers. In his dream, this seemed not unusual. Beaver glanced beyond the apparition, toward the sleeping couple across the fire. He could hear soft, restful snores, indicating sound sleep. He looked back at the visitor, and even under these strange circumstances, noted to himself that this apparition seemed quite familiar. Had they met before?

As if in answer to his unspoken question, he seemed to understand that yes, this was the being that he had thought he saw against the rising moon, and on another occasion or two. Those incidents had been nebulous and indistinct, but somehow he was made to think that yes, this was the same entity.

"'Siyo," said the little person.

This was puzzling . . . A word not in his own tongue, yet one he understood. It was a greeting, one he had heard before, used by Snakewater, the old medicine woman who lived with the People. *She* used that as a greeting. And Snakewater was Cherokee. The greeting, "'siyo" was Cherokee, then, and the Little Person before him, must be also.

He was more curious than alarmed, and it seemed logical to him, in this dream-like state, that he should be here, conversing with a Little Person.

"*Ah-koh*," he answered in the tongue of the People.

Even as he did so, he tried to remember all he had learned about the Little People of the Cherokees. Snakewater had made it clear that one who sees a Little Person must never admit it, or he dies. So, there could be no description. *Now*, Beaver wondered, would *this hold true for Cherokees only, or for anyone encountering a Cherokee Little Person?*

The Little Person by the fire seemed to know his thoughts, and chuckled.

"That," she said," is for you to decide."

She? It was the first time Beaver had ever thought about gender among Little People. But if they are *people*, then there must be men and women and babies. He had never wondered about it until now. This entity was clearly female from her shape. Not a particularly attractive female . . . A bit chubby, maybe.

"You're no prize catch yourself," she said sarcastically, as if she had read his thoughts.

Hers was not a face that could be described as beautiful, or pretty, but there was about it a certain dignity and confidence. The face of a capable woman, one of wisdom. He noted, without serious study, strong cheekbones and jaw line. An appearance not unlike that of Snakewater, actually. Had not the medicine woman hinted that if one actually saw a Little Person, it might resemble a small Cherokee? Beaver's impression was that this was a young adult, though who could tell how the Little People might count time? *Are their years measured the same as ours?*

He tried to remember any of the other things he had been told about the Little People, especially those of the Cherokees. Even as he tried, he had trouble convincing himself that this was anything but a dream. It seemed to have no connection to the real world.

But what was it that he had been told about the purpose and the function of the Little People? Snakewater had said they are in charge of unsupervised children and of lost objects. This seemed to have no bearing on the present situation.

As he shaped that thought, there was a mischievous giggle from the visitor.

"You are wondering whether you are a lost child or a lost object."

It was a statement, not a question, and it was irritating, the idea that she was reading his very thoughts.

"Of course not," he muttered.

His irritation was further fueled by the thought that this was really only a dream, and of no importance anyway. He would try to change the subject.

"What is your name?" he asked. "How are you called?"

"Ah! You want to talk about something else. Very funny!"

She broke into her odd chuckling again.

"Are you only a dream?" Beaver blurted in confusion.

There was a pause in the giggling, and the apparition spoke again, more seriously.

"That is mostly your choice. As to your other question, my name . . . What does it matter, if I am only a dream?"

She giggled again, a not unpleasant sound, he now realized.

The dim outlines of the Little Person began to fade. For some reason he found this alarming.

"Wait! Don't go yet."

"Ah! You have decided, then, that I *am* real?"

Her tone was teasing, taunting.

"Maybe so."

"Ah! Then *maybe* I can help you."

"Help me?"

"You have a problem or two?"

Beaver thought of how confused his life had become in the past few moons. Question upon question, all the trouble of the last few days, over the red stone pipe.

"Maybe so," he admitted.

Then the thought struck him: *The Cherokee Little People are said to be the custodians of lost objects!*

Could this be a connection? The pipe, along with what seemed to be a curse on its possessors?

"*Oh-keh*," said the other. "Now you begin to use your mind a little."

Again, Beaver had the strong impression that she had been reading his thoughts.

"What about the pipe?" he blurted.

She smiled, a coquettish, teasing expression.

"What would seem right to you?"

This was becoming quite irritating. He was virtually offered help, and when he agreed to accept it, he was told to figure it out for himself.

What was she trying to tell him? They had found the pipe, with its suspected curse, and had taken steps to rid themselves of it. What more was there to say or do?

The shape was beginning to fade again.

"Wait!"

"You can think about it . . ." she giggled.

"Come back here, Giggles!" he demanded.

The apparition became more distinguishable for a moment, and the unique laughter rippled again.

"*Wa-doh*," she said. "You are learning!"

"Don't leave! I don't . . ."

But the dream was over. He was now awake, and the possibility that the experience had been anything but a fantasy seemed remote. He tossed a couple of sticks on the fire, and walked a little distance to empty his bladder outside the camp circle. But as he turned back to his sleeping robes, he would have sworn that he heard the now familiar giggle.

There was a gray-yellow glow in the east which said that dawn was near. He would try to sleep, but it seemed unlikely that he could.

Trades His Moccasins crawled out of his bed and answered to the call of his bladder, returning to resume his rest. He was soon snoring, but Beaver lay wide-eyed and awake. He doubted for a moment that he could *ever* sleep again, but finally he drifted off . . .

Beaver wakened with the sun in his eyes, as it rose above the distant hills. It took a few moments for him to relive his vision and all that it implied. It answered some of the questions that had been bothering him for nearly a moon, but raised others.

Instinctively, he knew that he could not tell the others of his dream. He was certain that it had been real, but had some doubts about its meaning. Even more doubts as to what he must do about it.

<>

They finished packing, and left their camp site as quickly as they could. Beaver turned for one last look at the beaded bag with its bad luck contents, lying on the rock ledge in the yellow rays of the rising sun. They would be well rid of it, and now, surely, their luck would change.

They had not traveled half the morning when that theory was shattered. One of the pack horses began to balk, refusing to move across a certain spot on the trail. Horses and dogs, of course, see things not perceived by mere humans. The animal could not be pushed, pulled, or dragged beyond that spot.

Finally Trades His Moccasins tried to lead the animal *around* the invisible obstacle. The horse reared and fell, and in the struggle to rise, rolled on and broke one of its packs. The other pack horse became excited, and in its panic trampled over the spilled trade goods.

By the time the damage had been remedied, it was too late to travel a full day's distance. They managed to find a camp site with water and a little grass, but a cloud of gloom hung over the travelers.

"That cursed pipe has done this!" said the trader over their evening fire. "I thought we would escape its spell by leaving it."

Beaver's thoughts were racing. He, too, had thought so. But now . . .

Suddenly a thought struck him.

"Uncle," he said respectfully, "maybe it is not enough to rid ourselves of the pipe that carries tragedy. Maybe we are to return it."

"Who would you return it to?" asked the trader. "They are dead, except for the woman. She has thrown her curse on us."

"I doubt that she meant to do that," said Flower.

"She wanted to give us the only thing of value that she had, to thank you."

"Whether she intended or not," said Trades His Moccasins," she has transferred the curse to us. I thought to leave it behind."

He sighed deeply and squatted by the fire.

"But, Uncle, if we took it back, not to where it was given to you, but to where it came from . . ."

"What do you mean?"

"The quarry! Back where it started."

"Carry it? Bring its trouble with us? That makes no sense, Beaver!"

"But we *have* its trouble even without the pipe itself."

"That is true," said Flower softly. "It has followed us."

"I am made to think," said Beaver, "that this is what we must do. I will go back and bring it here. Then, to where it came from, if we can find it."

There was a long silence, and then the trader spoke, almost sadly.

"I have no better thoughts, Beaver. Go back. We will wait here."

<·>21

Beaver was plagued by many doubts on the way back to their previous camp.

Trades His Moccasins had suggested that perhaps *he* should be the one to return and retrieve the pipe. It was the trader to whom the bad-luck talisman had been given.

But Beaver had been given the vision.

"You should stay here with your family," he insisted. "I'll be back tomorrow."

No one felt really good about this plan. However, the same was true about their entire situation. The recovery of the pipe was felt to be essential. Beaver, a young man on his first journey away from the People, had been thrust into more responsibility than he expected. Actually, this duty should have been that of Trades His Moccasins. But it was overshadowed by the trader's greater responsibility to his family. He could not leave his wife and child in the care of the inexperienced Beaver overnight. That would not be acceptable in the custom of either of their nations.

The only alternative that they had discussed at all was that the entire party could go back. But a single rider, unencumbered with pack animals, could travel much faster. Finally, it was decided that this was the best of several options. It was to the credit of Trades His Moccasins that he could accept this gracefully.

"I only hope that this does not place the bad luck on your back," the trader said.

Beaver shrugged.

"I am made to think that it has already touched the backs of us all, Uncle. And the dream was mine."

He had not gone into detail in recounting his experience. Such things are private among the People. He only explained that he had been given a dream in which he was made to think that the pipe that carried the curse must be returned. And dreams must be taken seriously, in any situation.

<>

Beaver felt good as he loped easily along the back trail. For today, at least, he had direction and purpose. His blue roan was traveling well through the beauty of the prairie. He loped until the mare began to show signs of tiring. Then he would pull her in to a walk, letting her blow until she recovered her wind and seemed ready again for a faster gait. After the last few days of trouble, this was a wonderfully satisfying experience. He could not refrain from noting to himself that his interpretation of the dream sequence must have been right.

Even as that thought flitted through his head, it was followed by another. It was something like an accusation.

Are you sure that you would have thought of it yourself?

The feeling was so strong that he pulled the mare to a stop for a look around. He half expected to see the mischievous face of the Little Person in his dream, but he saw nothing.

"Are you out there?" he asked aloud. He felt a little foolish, and was glad he was alone.

It was time to rest a little anyway, so he dismounted and drank from a cool spring that wandered out from under a rocky outcrop. He allowed the mare to drink, also, but because she was hot and thirsty, limited her intake. He certainly did not want to invite problems with a colicky horse. There were already enough troubles.

They rested only a little while, but during that time his feelings and thoughts were good. A time or two he felt that there was another presence there. Not a threatening thing, but a friendly, helpful spirit. He became convinced that it had to do with the Little Person of his dream.

Once he turned quickly to look behind him. He had sensed something there. He could even imagine that he saw a shadow of motion, which disappeared as he turned.

"Are you out there, Giggles?" he asked mischievously.

Anyone passing by would have seen him talking to empty air. In reality, he was. There was nothing to be seen. Yet his action was only half joking. He *had* felt a presence, and had he not *seen* the Little Person fade and reappear? In his dream, of course . . . This reminded him once again of the puzzle in separating the dream-world from that of everyday reality.

Maybe one should not even try to separate them. White Buffalo had once said that they are the same anyway. A flat stone from near a stream may have two sides. One side is damp, the other dry. But it is the same stone. Might not existence be similar? That which is seen, held, and felt; and the unseen side, though invisible, is yet equally powerful. Possibly even more so.

He rose to go, and smiled to himself. It was a comfortable thing to consider such thoughts. He would try to do so again, when opportunity offered. He swung to the horse's back, and spoke over his shoulder.

"Come on, Giggles."

Was the faint ripple, like that of laughter, only the sound of the water in the spring under the rock?

As he rode, there was more time to think. He was just beginning to comprehend the vastness of the unseen world out there. Maybe, when opportunity offered, it would be prudent to take his vision quest. There had never been a time when it would have been practical. He had always been busy with day-to-day tasks and relationships. Parents, relatives, friends, learning the needed skills of one of the People.

Now, he was curious. Eager, almost. What had happened to change his attitude? The thought came to him quickly . . . Nothing had changed. But he was now ready. He had not been, before.

There was joy in the realization, but frustration, too. He had no idea when an opportunity would be permitted him. He was committed to stay with the trader's family for now, in addition to his quest for the meaning of the red pipestone.

Childhood had been so simple compared to the responsibilities that now faced him.

<>

He arrived at their previous camp site well before dark. He dismounted, glanced around the familiar place, and walked over to the outcropping shelf of rock where the buckskin pouch had been. The flat stone shelf was bare.

Panic gripped him, quickly followed by a wave of relief. If someone else had picked up the pipe, the bad luck might be transferred to *him*. A pang of guilt followed quickly, that he would so easily wish bad luck on another, a stranger.

All of these conflicting emotions whirled, collided and disappeared as he saw the pouch where it had fallen, in the grass below the rock. He picked it up with a sigh of relief, and tucked in inside his buckskin shirt.

"Ah!" said a whisper of a voice at his ear. "You are not quite so stupid as I thought."

Beaver whirled and his eyes found only empty air. Had he imagined this, or had he actually said it to himself? No, the voice had seemed familiar . . .

"Is this going to be a game?" he asked, still looking around.

There was only silence, though he imagined that he heard the mischievous giggle again.

<>

As he considered preparing for the night, a thought occurred to him. He could save nearly a day's travel for the trader's party by starting back now. If need be, he could stop anywhere for rest and to let the horse graze. He had only to follow his own back trail, the faint game trail they had been following north. He decided to try it, and as he swung onto the horse, he touched a hand to the pipe which had become so important in his life.

<>

As he rode, he began to wonder about the nature of the Little Person who also seemed to have entered his life. He had never actually seen her except in his dream. He was not certain that such an encounter would be valid. Yet, there *had* been those times when he had seen *something* against the rising moon, or the blazing colors of a sunset.

There were the times that he had *heard* the chuckling laughter. At least, he thought so.

Now, he was puzzled as to the nature of the Little People. If they actually existed. He was prepared to concede that, but . . . Apparently this one continued to follow him. Not the most comfortable thought, although he felt no threat over it. He thought of the feeling that "Giggles" had the ability to appear and to become invisible at will. How was that accomplished? Or, had that only happened during the dream?

But, the voice, at the rock where the pipe had been left . . . How would Little People *travel*? Could this one appear and disappear not only at any time, but materialize at any *place*?

A silent thought came at him, surprising him. It was like a familiar voice, but without words. A *concept* that bypassed voice communication to arrive in his mind.

Behind you, stupid!

Beaver turned quickly to look and saw nothing. He swept an arm behind him, over the horse's rump, but *felt* nothing, either. But there was the hint of a giggle. Maybe it was only the soft clatter of the roan's hooves in the water and gravel of the stream they were crossing. Even so, such things were beginning to seem like ordinary events. Unless, of course, he *was* going mad. But such thoughts seemed more humorous than alarming.

<>

He did not feel tired, and decided to continue to travel for at least a little while after darkness descended. The game trail was plain. The horse could follow it. Besides, they were headed almost due north, and the Real-star, the lodge of the Seven Hunters, would remain straight ahead. Maybe he could even doze a little as the horse followed the trail.

◁ ◦ ▷ 22

Occasionally, most of us need some time alone, to commune with ourselves, our own private thoughts. Since Beaver had been with the trader and his family, there had been virtually no time to be alone, to think, wonder about the future, to daydream of goals and ambitions.

Sometimes after the others were asleep, he would walk a little way out of their camp to enjoy the privacy of the prairie night. But that was not entirely an escape. There was the knowledge that Trades His Moccasins and Cactus Flower were within earshot. The baby, too; a marvelously tolerant child with a pleasant demeanor. Beaver enjoyed watching her. He had no younger siblings, and was fascinated by each new discovery or development on the part of this little one.

He had not really understood how much he needed an occasional escape until now, this night alone on the prairie. For the first time in many days, things seemed to make some sense . . . Well, a little bit . . . There were some big questions, and some new things that deserved serious thought.

At the top of a gently rolling hill he pulled the mare to a stop and dismounted. He sat on a boulder, still warm from the sun, and allowed his mount to graze, while he pondered all the complicated events that had come into his life this season. With some, he was quite comfortable, with others puzzled, with still others, frustrated at his inability to figure out meaning and purpose. He supposed it would always be so, but he was hungry for understanding.

A realization now dawned upon him. There was no going back. His childhood was behind him. He had looked forward to this, but occasionally a thought fluttered through his mind regarding how much easier it had been in the lodge of his parents, with no major responsibilities. He had had the wisdom and comfort of his mother, the strong protection of his father, the instruction of his uncle. He was missing all of these more than he had imagined.

On the other hand, he was finding a delight in new experiences, and an increasing understanding, which gave him *new* security. He felt that, for whatever reason, he had been given a gift of understanding about the bad luck of the red stone pipe. He did not see this as an achievement. More like a responsibility. When he returned to the People, this gift would not be something to boast of to Horse and his other friends . . . How childish some of their escapades now seemed to him!

Other parts of his experience this summer were more puzzling. That of the Little Person, whom he now thought of as "Giggles" . . . Had that actually happened at all, except as a dream? He couldn't answer. Yet it did seem that his understanding of the pipe's curse had been aided by the somewhat sarcastic remarks of the questionable person. If, of course, such a nebulous entity can even be considered a "person."

He touched the packet inside his shirt, through the buckskin, to reassure himself that the pouch and its contents were still there, still intact.

Odd, he thought, that somehow he was the one in the traveling trader's party who had been given the insight about the pipe and its curse. What a responsibility! It must have started several moons ago, he now realized, when his attention had been drawn to another example of the red stone's importance. A logical extension of this line of thought brought him to another realization: There must be more to come. There would have to be, he told himself. He had no real idea yet as to how, where, and when they would be able to restore the pipe to its intended function, whatever that might be, and remove the curse. To be an emissary of this task could bring him into danger, yet he felt a duty to carry out whatever was required. For now, he would turn the responsibility over to Trades His Moccasins.

The rest, the time alone, and the opportunity to think while the horse grazed were quite beneficial. He watched the Seven Hunters wheel around the Real-star, while he sorted out his thoughts. Finally, he decided that it was time to move on.

It was not long after daylight when Beaver trotted into the camp of Trades His Moccasins. He was greeted warmly, but cautiously.

"You found it?" the trader asked.

"Yes!"

Beaver touched the bulge of the pipe through his buckskin shirt, and swung down from the horse's back.

"It is good!" said Trades His Moccasins. "Did you have troubles?"

"No, none. I stopped to rest and think a while. Is it well with you?"

"Yes. We must be doing what is meant to be."

Beaver reached into his shirt to retrieve the pipe in its case, but the trader spoke quickly.

"Wait! It goes well now. We do not know whether . . ."

He paused, searching for words.

Beaver puzzled for a moment, and realized the concern on the part of the other. There had been no indication of anything amiss since he started back to retrieve the pipe. Now, if it changed hands, would it upset the delicate balance between the worlds, that of spirit and of substance? Apparently Trades His Moccasins held some doubt.

"It goes well now," the trader spoke with hesitancy, almost with embarrassment. "Would you . . . *Aiee*, if it begins to go wrong, I will carry the pipe!"

Beaver had looked forward to ridding himself of the responsibility associated with this powerful talisman, but he could see the point.

"If it begins to be bad for you, I will carry the pipe at any time," the trader said apologetically.

"It is good," agreed Beaver.

He did not actually feel as confident as he tried to sound. This was a very questionable situation. How were they to know what course of action to take? This was a situation completely foreign to everyone in the party, and with no previous experience on the part of any of them with such a curse. They would have to proceed slowly and with much thoughtful consideration. If it seemed that they were heading into a wrong course of action, they must be prepared to change, quickly and decisively.

For now, Beaver was comfortable with the feel of the soft buckskin pipe case against the skin of his belly. He would be glad when their ever-changing circumstances would rid him of the inconvenience, but for now . . . There was a certain amount of pride that he, a young man who had not yet even earned a reputation or taken his vision quest, would be trusted with such a powerful responsibility.

It did not take long to break camp and head on northward. It was good to note that their progress was completely different now. There seemed to be no trouble with loose pack ties, no lame horses. The entire spirit of the expedition had changed. There was a purpose and a goal, and so far, everything seemed to be going well.

"You have been to the quarry, that of the red pipestone?" asked Beaver as they rode.

"Yes, once," answered the trader. "I was with my parents. It was several summers past."

"Could you tell me of it?"

"There is little to tell. The stone is in a narrow layer, sometimes only a hand's span, with other stone beneath and above. Much like the way the blue-gray flint layer is found in the tallgrass hills of your people."

"I have heard it said," Beaver stated, "that such stone comes only from this one place."

"That is not quite it," said the trader. "There are some other places. None are said to be quite as good as this . . . The color, the hardness . . . Many tribes and nations come to the Pipestone Quarry, to dig the stone."

"Is it true," asked Beaver, "that even enemies do not fight at this place?"

"That is true, so I have heard," said Trades His Moccasins. "It is understood that it is more important than old hates. There is a truce there."

"How could it be agreed to by *all*?" asked Beaver. "There could be some from far away, who might not know."

"Ah, yes, but this is the country of Lakotas. They are numerous and powerful. Stronger than any party of outsiders. And if Lakotas respect the truce, who is to want to fight?"

This seemed a logical conclusion.

They camped in comfort that evening, with still no problems with the animals, the packs, the country over which they traveled, or even the weather. There was a great sense of relief as they settled in for the night.

The fading sunset, the gentle breeze from the south, the song of whippoorwills in the trees along the stream . . . All combined, with the distant cry of a family of coyotes in the distance, to produce the most comfortable evening they had experienced for days.

"It must be," observed Cactus Flower as the fire dwindled to a bed of glowing coals, "that we are doing something right."

And it was good.

<◇>**23**

It was the third day later when they encountered the other party. They had cautiously begun to relax after the run of extreme bad luck. It began to seem possible that the curse of the red pipe was past, but they remained uneasy. Even to mention it might bring back the misfortune that had struck them so hard.

Beaver continued to carry the pipe inside his shirt, now suspended on a thong around his neck to keep it from sliding around. He was becoming accustomed to the feel of the buckskin pouch against his belly, bumping gently to the motion of the horse. It was easy to imagine that such motion was initiated not by the swaying of the animal's gait, but by the pipe itself . . . A living thing, writhing or undulating, like the coils of a snake, rubbing against his own skin as it changed position. He tried to suppress such thoughts, with only partial success. There had been so many instances of trouble that *seemed* connected to the influence of the pipe, it was difficult to forget.

But, they had traveled well. The same lashings on the packs, which had been so troubling before, now remained secure. There was no problem with lameness in any of the animals, but their hooves were examined carefully at each stop, anyway.

The trail they followed seemed much easier now, the sun more comfortable, water and grass available when needed. The country appeared no different than that which they had crossed a few days before. How had it seemed so hostile, and now so welcoming? Its spirit reached out, comforting like the arms of a mother as she cradles her child. It was easy to relax, dreamily rocking with the repetitive motion. It was a good day.

Such dreamy preoccupation stopped suddenly as Trades His Moccasins pulled his horse to a stop with a soft exclamation.

"Aiee!"

They had just topped one of the low rolling swells that repeated themselves across the prairie as far as they eye could see.

"What is it?" asked Beaver.

"I don't know . . . Maybe wild horses."

He turned to speak to the others.

"Keep the pack animals behind the hill. We need to know more."

Trades His Moccasins reined back to put his own mount behind the summit of the ridge, and dismounted. The horse quickly took advantage of the opportunity, to make up grazing time lost to travel.

The trader motioned to Beaver to dismount and follow him. Bending low, they approached the crest again and cautiously peered across the wide valley.

"Your eyes may be better than mine," said Trades His Moccasins. "What do you see?"

Flattered by the confidence placed on him, Beaver lay on his belly and moved into a more comfortable position, sliding the pipe in his shirt to one side. Several dark figures stood out against the smooth green of the prairie.

"How far, do you think?" asked the trader.

"Ah . . . Less than half a day's travel, maybe."

In this area of far horizons, travelers by horse may often be able to see, for most of the day, the place where they will camp tonight. In the white man's terms, perhaps twenty miles would be a good day's travel with pack animals.

Distance is deceiving in several ways. The first quality to be distorted is color. It is possible to see a horse and identify *what* it is at a much greater distance than what *color* it is. A dozen large animals may appear as an irregular dark blotch, seen for several miles. Close behind, comes number. A slowly moving group of grazing animals might be estimated as fifteen, or twenty, or thirty. All will be perceived as dark in color at a distance beyond a certain range.

Now, Trades His Moccasins propped on his elbows, curled both hands, partially closing the fists as if he were grasping some object. With one fist in front of each eye, he peered through the tunnels formed by the palms, looking toward the distant animals.

"What are you doing?" asked Beaver, curiously.

"Try it," suggested the trader. "It keeps out light from the sides. From everywhere except what we want to see."

Beaver was somewhat confused, but he was discovering many things about this man. Trades His Moccasins had a wide range of experience. His contact with other tribes and nations as the son of a trader had taught him much. Not only language, custom, and tradition, but simple tricks like this.

The young man followed the suggestion of the trader. A bit of adjustment and experimentation . . . It was a pleasant surprise, as his eyes focused and the distant objects became clearer. He wondered how it had happened that he had never learned this before. Of course, he had never been on a war party or horse-stealing raid. The People were on good terms with most of their neighbors, allies with the Kiowas and Cheyennes. Beaver would probably have participated in a hunt this season, if it had not been for his quest.

"Ah!" he said. "It is good!"

"What do you see?" asked Trades His Moccasins.

"Horses. Some ridden, some with the pole-drag travois, maybe."

"How many?"

"About ten? No, more . . . Maybe another family . . . Yes, I am made to think maybe fifteen or twenty. Maybe, more."

"Good. You learn quickly, Beaver. Now, will trade be good?"

It was like Trades His Moccasins to think along these lines. Most travelers on the prairie would be thinking whether there would be danger. But, having been in a trading family all his life, Trader considered himself immune to such danger. A trader was worth more alive than dead. Besides, a reputation for having mistreated or killed an honest trader would not be good.

"It depends on when they last saw a trader," said Beaver.

"Of course!" laughed the other man. "You just thought like a trader, Beaver." He was pleased.

The other party seemed to be approaching the line of travel of the trader's party. The newcomers were traveling in a northwesterly direction. Their course would probably arrive at a conjunction with that of the trader near the end of the day. In fact, a small grove could be seen that probably marked the junction of the two trails.

"Let us travel on," Trades His Moccasins decided. "A party with travois has women and children. They will not be looking for trouble."

It could soon be seen that the party of strangers were led by and followed by scouts, as would be appropriate. A flanking rider could be distinguished beyond the column. A well-organized party, it appeared, appropriately traveling with outriders. Not much more could be told.

Trades His Moccasins decided to continue on their present course, plainly in the open, to assure the strangers that they had no evil intentions. Remounting, they topped the rise and started down the other side.

It was a short while before one of the scouts across the valley noticed the trader's party. There was a flurry of activity as the larger party drew together and stopped, studying the newcomers. Neither group could determine much about the other at this distance, and it would be late in the day before their paths converged. Both would spend most of the afternoon watching each other and trying to determine more about them.

There were times during the afternoon when, in the shimmering heat of the summer sun, distant objects became somewhat blurred, almost indistinguishable as they watched. Then the heat waves would ripple and shift on the breeze, and the scene would clear, only to blur again.

<>

By late afternoon they had a much better estimate of the other travelers. A small band, no more than three or four families, traveling with their possessions. Five, possibly six men, counting warriors and older youths. An appropriate number of women, a few small children. At the distances that separated the two parties for the rest of the day, they could distinguish little else.

The others, too, would be watching them. Beaver tried to speculate on the observations of the other party. The trader's little band would obviously not appear as a threat. It would be apparent that although there were only three adults, they drove several pack animals. Probably the strangers had already identified them as a trader's party.

<>

The sun was low when they approached the small grove, which Trades His Moccasins had correctly identified as a camp site, probably used for centuries. There would be a stream or spring for water, some shelter from the rocky bluff behind, and good grass for the animals.

The other party had reached the site first, and now, as the trader's party approached, three men rode out to meet them. The tall man in the middle was the oldest, and apparently their leader. All were armed, but as they drew their horses to a stop, the tall man raised his right hand, palm forward, in the signal for a peaceful greeting.

Trades His Moccasins motioned for Beaver to ride alongside him to greet the other party. He returned the hand sign, and added another.

How are you called?

There was a moment of confusion; the strangers were apparently acquainted with, but not expert in the use of hand signs.

We come from the east, the leader signed.

He accompanied the signs with spoken words, which the trader did not completely understand.

"They must have come from a long way," said Trades His Moccasins. "But, no matter. We will find a way to talk."

<·>**24**

Trades His Moccasins, true to his profession, worked hard at finding a way to communicate with the other travelers. The actual trading was not a problem. That could be done with gestures and by pointing to the objects under consideration. Even those unfamiliar with hand-sign talk could understand.

An experienced trader, however, would realize the importance of the trust that can more quickly be established by two-way dialogue. He would try to discover a common ground in which two persons may converse.

There would be several tongues, and around the fire that evening, he tried most of them. Kiowa, Cheyenne, Pawnee, Comanche, his own Arapaho, and that of the Elk-dog People. Mostly, the results were disappointing. The rudimentary hand signs used by the strangers were inadequate, but better than most of their other attempts.

"How is it," asked Beaver, "that they do not use hand signs? Everyone uses signs."

Trades His Moccasins pondered for a few moments.

"I have heard," he mused thoughtfully, "that east of the Big River, hand signs are not used very much."

"Why? How can they talk?"

"I don't know. Let us think on this. I have heard that they use a sort of traders' talk . . . A mixture."

He turned and signed to the leader of the other party.

Do you know the trade talk?

The other man became excited, nodding and smiling, talking rapidly.

"Ah, but we *don't*," said the trader, mostly to himself. He signed the same comment to the other party, and the countenances fell.

"There must be a way," Trades His Moccasins said, almost to himself.

Suddenly he brightened.

"From east, across the Mississippi," he said thoughtfully. "Who do we know . . ?"

There was a twinkle in his eye as he turned to Beaver.

"Maybe *Cherokee*?"

The reaction of the other party was almost instant. Their leader smiled broadly and nodded his head.

"Tsallaghee!"

The man continued to talk rapidly in the tongue that Beaver recognized as that of old Snakewater, though he was not fluent in its use. The trader, of course, with his vast experience through trade, had been in contact with migrating Cherokees in the southern plains, and as far west as the mountains.

"You are Cherokee?" asked Trades His Moccasins in amazement.

"No, no," the other answered, still in the language of the Cherokee, "but we know them. We trade with them."

"Wah-do!" said the trader, smiling. "It is good!"

Almost instantly, they could communicate, now that a language had been identified which was at least somewhat familiar to both parties. It would be a slow and sometimes halting dialogue, but it was at least possible.

<>

The trader's party learned that night that the other group had fled from increasing pressure in the east. More and more whites moving in, moving westward. The white man's chiefs and soldiers were pushing to move the inhabitants on to the west, across the Mississippi. Along with this rose conflicts between those on the move and those through whose country they passed.

This particular band had fallen on hard times in their home territory. They had been both growers and hunters, but white growers were crowding in, occupying land where these people had farmed for many lifetimes. At the same time, hunting became more and more difficult, with the whites taking many deer as well as small game. With the firearms of the whites, used by both white and Native hunters, meat was becoming scarce, and people more numerous. They had packed what they could and set out to the west.

To do so, however, they passed through territory that had long been disputed. Their neighbors had also been in *their* fields and farms for many lifetimes. In some seasons there had been an easy tolerance. Mostly, when crops grew well and hunting was good. In a year when conditions had not been favorable, there had been less tolerance for each other.

"It makes a difference when the children are hungry," explained their leader.

This was a truism that could not be denied.

The leader was called Hungry Hawk. He was not quite as proficient in Cherokee as his wife, who did much of the talking.

"How is it that he is called Hungry Hawk?" asked the trader.

The wife smiled. It was plain that she was proud of her spouse.

"Because that is his name," she explained.

Trades His Moccasins let the matter drop. Some things are not meant to be explained. At one time, there must have been events worthy of note which had contributed to such a name. Over a period of time, the original event had been forgotten. The phrase that comprises the name takes on more association with the person than with an almost forgotten event in the past.

The trader smiled to himself as he thought of the significance of his own name, and its origins. In his case, it had become an advantage to tell of his name's origin. It usually brought a laugh and a feeling of sympathy for a gullible child. Such a feeling might easily impress a potential customer favorably, and provide a trading advantage.

<>

Hungry Hawk and his party had been attacked several times during their journey thus far, he related. It seemed that their old enemies had decided to move west, also. For growers, the timing of any move was important. It must be at a point in the growing season when the travelers could carry the seeds or roots or cuttings which they would need for next season's planting. Their traditional enemies, too, were limited by the same problems. They must move after the harvest, but before winter. They must also find a place to grow next year's corn. That was difficult, at best.

"But, the corn is growing now," observed Trades His Moccasins, "yet you are traveling."

"Ah, yes," said Hungry Hawk. "We had begun to plant, and were attacked. We were forced to move on. Many were killed."

"And you have no seed to plant?"

"Only a little. It is too late now to plant for this season."

Trades His Moccasins nodded.

"Your troubles are many," he said sympathetically.

Only now was he beginning to realize just how bad the situation was for these people. There could be little trading, because the resources of the pitiful band were practically exhausted. He had noticed much wear and tear on their equipment and their horses, but he had had no idea how really desperate their situation was. From previous contact with growers, he realized that each year's crop was essential to survival. Among the hunter tribes of the plains, a good autumn hunt was greatly hoped for, to provide winter supplies, and to trade with the growers of the area for corn and pumpkins to vary their diet.

In this case, the travelers had nothing to trade, and might have to eat their seed corn to survive the winter. Then, they would have nothing at all to plant. It began to appear that their only chance for survival was a successful fall hunt. This would be very difficult in unknown country and in competition with local hunter tribes who might consider them intruders. Besides, it appeared that they could probably mount only six or eight hunters.

"How is it that you are so few in numbers?" asked the trader. "Your towns are this small in your country?"

The saddest of expressions flitted across the face of Hungry Hawk.

"Ah," he said sadly, "not this small. We were once prosperous. We lost many to the white man's sicknesses, more in fighting. You see that each of our men has two or three women. Their husbands have been killed. They join a sister's family."

The trader nodded.

"It is so among our people, too. What other way is there? But you have only these men left?"

"That is true. Very few. I am made to think that even now we are followed by enemies from our old homeland."

"*Still?* You have been gone for two years."

"Yes, but some of our old neighbors have moved west, too, for the same reasons we have. They are the ones who will not let us alone. They would want to kill us all. Maybe to steal our children and younger women to sell."

Everyone in the trader's party now fell silent. They had not realized how desperate the plight of these travelers had actually become. Conversation lagged, and there was only the crackle of the fire, and a few calls of the night creatures in the narrow wooded strip along the stream.

"Do you have a plan, to go to any special place?" asked Trades His Moccasins.

"We had hoped," said Hawk, "to find the place where the red stone for making pipes may be dug. This might give us something to trade."

Well, thought Beaver, at least they had a semblance of a plan. He did not know yet whether it might interfere with his own.

"Are your enemies still following you?" asked the trader.

"Maybe. We are not sure," said Hawk sadly. "We must prepare to defend ourselves anyway."

It was true. If they were not followed, there was no way to know. It was possible, maybe even probable, that they were *not* pursued. Still, they must prepare for the worst.

<> **25**

"*Aiee*," said Cactus Flower when they were alone, "is it not dangerous to be with these people? There are those who want to harm *them*, and . . ."

"That is true," interrupted her husband, "but what can we do? We are going in the same direction. Do we want to tell them to stay away from us?"

Beaver, inexperienced as he was, had been with the trader long enough to recognize the depth of this problem. A trader must do his best to relate to everyone. If he gives the impression *no, I do not want to be with you*, the people involved will tell others. A trader must trade. He must not earn a reputation of favoritism or of avoidance for any tribe or band. Where does one draw the line?

And, if Trades His Moccasins did decide to part ways with this unfortunate band of travelers, how could it be accomplished? Would they simply stay behind for a day? The only alternative would be *not* to camp for the night, but to continue on, into the night, which would be ridiculous in unfamiliar territory.

The thought came to Beaver that it would be possible to *pretend* some problem. A lame horse, perhaps, or a retying of a pack. No, he decided, that would be an obvious deception. Even worse, possibly, than to say, in effect, "We don't want to be with you."

So they moved on together, becoming better acquainted as they traveled. They exchanged the traditional stories of each of their nations. In so doing, they gained more understanding, and became closer. Within a few days it seemed strange that they had ever considered trying to find an excuse to part from these people. Maybe, even, a little embarrassing. They didn't talk further about it.

The country through which they traveled was changing. It was apparent that the climate differed. The dim trail that they followed brought them to a sizable river.

"The *Miss-oo-rie*, I am made to think," said the trader.

"You have been here before?" asked Hungry Hawk.

"Not this way. Farther west."

"Do we cross the river?"

"Maybe. This has been a good trail. If there is a place to cross, the road should lead to it, no?"

The trail meandered a little. It approached the river at a point where the riverbed was broad and apparently shallow. The ripple of the stream's current was plain where it broadened over an expanse of white gravel. They could see, from where they stood, the point on the far bank where the trail began again. A gravel bar formed a long arc upstream. It was obvious that this was a crossing that had been used for a long time by many generations.

"I'll try it," suggested Hawk.

"Let me join you!" said Beaver, reining behind him.

The two had little difficulty in crossing. At one point Beaver's horse, water up to her flanks, found no solid footing and began to swim. Almost immediately, however, she found her footing again and proceeded on. It was a great help to be able to see the trail on the far side, where it emerged from the stream.

The two riders, back on solid ground, waved to the others. Trades His Moccasins had already tied ropes to the pack animals, and now entered the stream, riding and leading the first horse. The second was tied behind. Cactus Flower brought up the rear, riding and carrying her child, and the other party began to cross.

It was more complicated to cross with dragging lodge poles and baggage. These travelers, though their dwellings had not originally been constructed with skins or canvas and poles, had adapted to some of the ways of the plains. A horse can move bigger and more cumbersome loads by the use of the drag-poles. In turn, the poles become a part of the portable dwelling when a destination is reached. This little band had seen the practical advantage in some of the customs of the prairie dwellers, and was putting them to good use. It became a different matter, however, in crossing a stream of this size.

Some of the men made several trips across and back, dividing the baggage into loads that must be carried and those which could survive being dragged through the water.

By the time the crossing was completed, the sun was low in the west. One pack and a couple of lodge poles had been claimed by the river. Except for that, the crossing had been successful.

While others made camp, a couple of the young men rode back along the river and managed to salvage the sodden pack and one of the poles. They could find no trace of the other pole, they reported. It must have been drawn into the main current, and might be far downstream by this time.

⟨⟩

It was decided to camp here for a day, to spread and dry water-soaked blankets and the assorted possessions that each family carried.

Trades His Moccasins and Cactus Flower, more experienced with travel, had suffered little damage. Their skill in packing and unpacking constantly was valuable, Beaver realized.

It also occurred to him that now would be an ideal time to leave the other party. The others had chosen not to travel, and the trader could easily give the impression that he must move on, that it was critical to his occupation.

Beaver considered mentioning the possibility of moving on, but decided against it. They were becoming better acquainted with their traveling companions. It was much easier now to accept the theory of strength in numbers. To stay together might be wise in this situation. He suspected that Trades His Moccasins might be thinking along the same lines, but neither mentioned it.

They spent another night at the ford, and moved on.

< >

One of the young women in the party caught the attention of young Beaver. She had a small baby, no more than a few moons old. She was quite attractive with a natural beauty and a quiet, shy smile. She appeared to have no man, but traveled with an older couple. There was a look of sadness about her, and Beaver assumed that the girl had lost her husband in the conflicts the party had suffered. Cautious inquiry revealed that his theory was correct. Her man had been killed before her baby was born. Beaver's heart was heavy for her. Without fully realizing what he was doing, he began to smile in greeting, and to show her little kindnesses. He felt an urge to help and protect her, which he did not fully understand.

She was about his age, and he learned, little by little, that she was the eldest daughter in the lodge of her parents. She had no sister whose husband could take her as a second or third wife, so she had moved back to her parents' lodge. Obviously, she would be looking for a husband. If she had been at all aggressive, Beaver would have run like a rabbit. On the contrary, he found that her very shyness reached out, causing him to want to help her.

His concern for the girl was duly noted by Trades His Moccasins and Cactus Flower, who teased him about it.

"This is good, Beaver! You could have a wife and a child, just for the asking, without the inconvenience of bedding the woman," observed the trader.

Beaver was embarrassed, and a bit of anger flared.

"I do not think of Pale Moon in that way," he snapped.

He lied, of course.

"She has suffered much loss," he went on. "She needs the help of someone."

"Yes, poor thing," said Flower. "Her parents cannot attend to her needs."

"But they have other children," he began. "*Aiee*, you are teasing me! Look, I have not . . . I don't . . . I only try to help her a little."

"Of course, Beaver," said the trader seriously. "If the girl invited you to her bed, you would naturally, refuse."

Beaver, embarrassed and angry, turned and walked away.

Good weather continued, and they traveled well.

"How much more travel until the pipestone place?" asked Hungry Hawk one morning.

"I am not sure," said Trades His Moccasins. "I have been there only once, several summers ago. Maybe four or five days."

<>

It was the next day that they encountered the Lakotas, a hunting party of perhaps a dozen. There was considerable anxiety on the part of the traveling band. The reputation of the Lakotas as fighters was known far and wide.

"I will talk with them," said Trades His Moccasins in Cherokee. "I have traded with them before, and I will tell them of your wishes, and the troubles you have had."

Three capable-looking warriors rode out to meet them. Trades His Moccasins, flanked by Beaver and Hungry Hawk, rode forward, and the two groups reined in a few steps apart. The trader displayed his right palm in the peace sign, and the Lakota leader returned it, adding quickly the question gesture and the sign for travel.

Where are you going?

I am a trader. This is my helper.

Who is this? signed the Lakota, gesturing toward Hawk.

They are people we met on the trail.

Then the trader changed his tactics.

"Let us speak in your tongue. You are Lakota?"

The other smiled.

"Of course."

"I was here with my father, a few seasons ago. He was a trader."

"Ah! Maybe I remember that," mused the other man. "Arapaho, no?"

"Yes, partly, anyway."

"But who are these?"

The Lakota indicated Hungry Hawk.

"They come from the east. They were pushed out by the whites, and were attacked by some of their neighbors. They lost several men."

"So it appears," said the Lakota, looking over the newcomers. "What do they want?"

Might as well tell it all, the trader decided.

"They have been growers," he explained. "They were attacked and lost most of their seed corn. No crop this year, of course. They may even be pursued by some of their old enemies, those who killed their men."

"But what do they want?"

"Mostly, a place to stop, I am made to think."

"There is no place here. Too many coming in already!"

The face of the Lakota was grim.

"My chief," said the trader in a placating way, "they have asked no special favors. They inquire about the pipestone place. They had heard that it is a safe haven. Even enemies do not fight there, no?"

"That is true. But then what?"

"They had hoped to dig a little of the stone, to make some things to trade, until they can grow a crop, next year."

"They will hunt a little?"

"I suppose so."

"But you said they lost their seed corn?"

"Most of it. They have some. And maybe pumpkins. Do you not trade with growers for these things?"

"Sometimes. Where would they try to settle?"

"They do not know this country. Their first goal was to find the pipestone, I am made to think."

"But you come to trade?"

"That is true."

The Lakota considered for a little while, and then spoke.

"Let us think on this. Our camp is beyond the hill, there. Come, camp with us, let us trade."

"What about the others?" asked the trader.

The Lakota shrugged.

"Let them come along. Our council will listen to them."

"It is good. Who is your chief?"

"Bull's Horn. You know him?"

"I think not. Maybe when I was here as a boy."

The other man nodded. "Well, come along. You can tell these things at the council. Bull's Horn will listen."

◁ ▷ 26

There was much question as to whether the newcomers would be accepted by the Lakotas. The hunting party may have overstepped their authority by bringing such a large group of travelers to their camp.

Beaver did not understand enough Lakota to know all that was said, but the general theme was apparent. The Lakota hunters insisted that they only sought to bring the trader, which was good. The travelers from the east simply came along. This was not so good, apparently. There was a short but stormy discussion among a few of the Lakota leaders. It ended with the departure of a couple of the older chiefs, who stalked away stiffly toward their own lodges.

"They will talk of it at a council fire tonight," Trades His Moccasins explained to the other travelers, in Cherokee. "How do you call yourselves? I will need to speak for you."

There was a short discussion over this language problem. Nearly every nation's name for themselves will translate simply as "The People." In this case, translating by way of a tongue not native to any of those present might be slow and cumbersome, but necessary. And the only one present who could do the necessary explanation would be the trader, whose vocation and experience made it possible.

<>

As shadows started to lengthen, people began to bring wood for the council fire. Normally, in the trader's travels, this would be a time of amusement, the telling of stories, of becoming acquainted. The storytellers would exchange accounts, each telling the age-old creation stories, "How *our* people came to be."

This was a more serious meeting. Strangers, encroaching on the hunting grounds of the Lakota, might be at risk any time. Without the help of a translator, which was pure coincidence anyway, there might easily have been violence. There could be, yet.

The Lakota camp, Beaver noted, consisted of about thirty lodges, mostly canvas, and mostly, large. Most of the cooking was done outside the lodges in good weather, using buffalo chips to augment wood in areas where wood was scarce. Here, it appeared that wood was in good supply along the streams.

The fire grew, from small orange tongues licking and flickering up through the small twigs and sticks, to ignite some of the larger branches. People were drifting in, curious about the newcomers, and finding places to sit. Dusk deepened, and the fire began to eat through some of the brushy fuel, allowing the sticks on top to fall. This produced a shower of sparks, rising high into the darkening sky like a swarm of fireflies, only to quickly disappear.

The leader of the encampment arrived with dignity, a bright blanket over his shoulder. Not that a blanket was needed for warmth, but to demonstrate his authority and his affluence. He was flanked by two able-looking sub-chiefs, and all three seated themselves in an area which seemed designated for this purpose.

A young man, apparently a pipe bearer, filled and handed the instrument to the chief. He then brought a blazing stick from the fire, and the leader ignited the tobacco, blowing a puff to each of the four winds, to the earth, and finally to the sky. He then handed the pipe to the man on his left.

The ceremony proceeded around the circle of warriors on the front row. When it reached the chief again, he knocked the dottle into his palm, tossed it into the fire, and handed the pipe to the pipe bearer.

"It is good," he announced solemnly. "I am Bull's Horn, who speaks for this band. Now, who speaks for the visitors?"

"I will, my chief," said Trades His Moccasins, in Lakota. "As you know, I am a trader."

The chief nodded, and the trader continued.

"These are people whom we met on the trail. They come from the east, across the Big River."

"How is it that you speak their tongue, trader?"

"I do not, my chief. We could not talk at first. They do not use hand signs where they come from."

Bull's Horn nodded, a bit irritably. "Yes, get on with it."

"Of course. We discovered that both the people of Hungry Hawk, here, and myself, understand the tongue of the Cherokee."

The chief nodded.

"I have heard of them."

"Do you know their tongue?"

"No! Go on!"

"Yes. This is how I speak with them."

The chief seemed impatient, so Trades His Moccasins hurried on.

"So, my chief, their story is one of trouble. They were pushed from their homes by the whites. Some of their neighbors, old enemies, would not let them stay in *their* area, and they moved on."

The chief nodded, and spoke again. "So what do they want?"

"They have been growers, and hunt a little."

He was certain that the men of the hunting party had already told all of this. Bull's Horn was merely formalizing the facts for the listeners.

"So, they want to plant?"

"They cannot until next season, my chief. It is too late. They had asked us about the pipestone quarry."

"Why?" the chief grunted bluntly.

"They had given thought to using enough stone to give them something to trade, for now, until they can plant."

"That is a long time."

"Yes. But they need to do something. I am made to think that these people work hard."

Bull's Horn grunted, showing a bit of indignation.

"Growers!" he said, as if it were a dirty word.

Then a new idea seemed to strike him.

"What happened to their men?" he asked, gesturing to the area where most of the growers were seated.

"Their neighbors are old enemies. After they planted corn and pumpkins, they came and drove them off, killing some of the men."

Another non-committal grunt. "Why should we help them?"

The trader appeared to think for a moment, deciding on his course of argument.

"Maybe you shouldn't," he shrugged carelessly. "It makes no difference to me. I was made to think that Lakotas sometimes trade meat or skins to those who grow vegetables. You could show them where you want them to be."

Now, Bull's Horn paused for a long time.

"Maybe so," he said at last. "But what about the pipestone?"

"Only something to trade until next season, I am told," said the trader. "They have heard that even enemies cannot fight in that valley."

"It has been declared so by our people," said Bull's Horn. "It is a sacred place, not to be violated by killing. So be it."

"You will let them stay?"

Trades His Moccasins wanted no misunderstandings.

"For one season, anyway. We will tell the other Lakota bands. Then we will talk of it again, as we trade for their vegetables."

"May I tell them these things?"

"Yes, go ahead."

Rapidly, the trader explained to Hungry Hawk.

"Bull's Horn says that you may stay one season. Then, talk again. They will tell the other Lakotas."

"And the pipestone?" asked Hawk. "We may dig it?"

The trader paused to verify.

"They may dig pipestone?"

"Yes," agreed Bull's Horn. "For now."

"Winter there?"

Now Bull's Horn pondered for what seemed an eternity. Maybe they had gone too far.

Finally, he nodded.

"One season!"

They could ask for no better.

<>

Trading went well. They spent three days with the Lakotas, during which they received specific directions to the quarry, about two days' travel, they were told.

Trades His Moccasins had said nothing about the red pipe which had become so important to the lives of the trader, his wife, and young Beaver. That was a personal thing, one to be dealt with, but not dwelled upon.

They would travel with the outlanders, however. This was made clear to the Lakotas, who in turn would spread the word that the party from the east was to be tolerated.

"If anyone asks," advised the chief as they parted, "tell them that Bull's Horn says they are to be respected."

Beaver had a strong impression that this endorsement by Bull's Horn would carry a considerable amount of weight in this north country.

<>

Beaver found himself continuing to be drawn toward the widowed girl with the baby. He would have denied anything but sympathy for her plight, but his sentiments were clear to Cactus Flower. She gently teased him about it.

"The girl needs a husband," she hinted.

"I do not think of her in that way," mumbled the embarrassed young man.

"Maybe you should, Beaver. She likes you."

"No, no, Flower. She only appreciates that I am polite to her."

"Does she know the Cherokee tongue?"

"I don't know."

"But *you* do. Maybe you could ask her."

"It doesn't matter . . ."

He was more and more embarrassed.

"Maybe it should," she teased.

"Stop it, Flower!"

"What is it?" asked Trades His Moccasins, who was just approaching. "You two are arguing?"

He appeared puzzled.

"No, no," said his wife with a sly giggle. "Beaver has feelings for Pale Moon, the girl with the baby."

"I have not," insisted Beaver, blushing.

"Ah, that one," observed the trader. "You could do a lot worse, Beaver."

"I am not looking for a wife," the young man insisted.

"Of course not," said Cactus Flower. "No young man thinks of such things, does he, my husband?"

"Maybe sometimes."

"I will go see about the horses," said Beaver.

<∙>**27**

It was that night that Beaver had a different dream. It was not an erotic dream. Those, he understood. This was a dream that, though mildly stimulating, was more a feeling of comfort and security. Of reassurance, maybe. The identity of the woman in the dream was sketchy and poorly defined. As he thought about it later, his impression was that the dream woman had not been a stranger, but someone he knew. The problem was that in the dream state, he could not identify her.

In the dream, his face nuzzled in the hollow of the woman's neck; he could not see her clearly. He hesitated to draw back far enough to be able to look at her face. Such an action might spoil the moment and the embrace. He had no desire to do that, because what he was dreaming was perfection in itself. He had never experienced such feelings before, or this sensation that it was so appropriate.

Through all of this confusion, he still seemed to have the recognition that it was, after all, a dream. This feeling did not diminish the experience. In fact, it may have enhanced it. He realized that he had felt this way before about a dream . . . A reluctance to waken and leave the experience. He was enjoying it too much. He couldn't remember when, or what it was about.

Someone was laughing at him, a musical chuckle. Was this part of the dream, or part of reality?

He opened his eyes. It was still dark. Their fire had burned down to white ashes and a few glowing coals seen dimly in the starlight. A gray-yellow streak in the east told him that dawn was not far off. Also, that he *had* dreamed the woman in his arms. She was not real. At least, there was no one here now. He could hear the soft snores of the trader, bundled against the chill of the prairie night. Trades His Moccasins shared his bed with his wife, and Beaver wondered if their embrace was as comforting as that he had experienced in his dream. He still had no clue as to the woman's identity. But, the laughter in his dream . . . Had that been real or part of the dream? It had sounded like the voice of a woman, but not the one in the dream embrace. A familiar chuckle. The Little Person, maybe? He was confused by so many puzzling experiences.

He lay there, pondering, thinking of the unidentified person who had laughed softly in his dream, or in the real world. Maybe *both*, a laugh overlapping both worlds. It was a sobering thought, and why would it have occurred to him just now, when he was *between* two worlds?

From the corner of his eye, against the lightening eastern sky, Beaver thought he detected a hint of motion. Cautiously, he turned his head, and for the space of a heartbeat or two, caught a glimpse of what appeared to be a human form. The sensation was much like the previous glimpses that had puzzled him. It could have been a person at a distance, or a very small person at closer range. The light laughter suggested a woman or a child. Again, he longed for a chance to talk of this with the holy man, or better, with Snakewater, who knew much about the Little People. He was ready to concede this now. The events he had already experienced made him ready to accept the Little People. *Why me?* he thought. I didn't ask for *this*, Giggles!"

As he considered the concept, another thought occurred to him. Always in the past, when someone mentioned Little People, it had seemed to Beaver that they were talking of little *men*.

Over all of this thoughtful perusing of the subject hovered an idea that had begun with the childish (or feminine) laughter as he wakened: If there are little *men*, as he had always envisioned the Little People, where do they come from? Not the place, but the *origin*. Among humans, a man is borne by a mother, a *woman*. It must be the same with the Little People, no? As any human must have a father and a mother, would it not be the same with Little People? Little men, little women, little children, even. *Family* groups?

He was at a loss as to why he found himself thinking along those lines. Family. In the excitement of his vision quest and the adventures of traveling with the trader, he had not considered that he might miss his family. The excitement was "out there . . ." The coming of age, the thrill of becoming his own person, had masked his feelings for a little while. The world outside that of the People had seemed so inviting.

Now, it seemed much larger and more complicated, filled with mysteries and unknown threats, and there was no place to retreat. The safe haven of his mother's arms, which he had thought to abandon as he became a man, now seemed desirable. Except, of course, that one cannot become a child again.

Maybe, he thought, he was being affected by the plight of the outlanders with whom they were traveling. Among the People, there had been hard times that he could remember. From time to time there was a death. An accident, an illness, a sick child, who crossed over earlier than most. Occasionally a man was killed in a skirmish with another tribe, but it was uncommon. The People had been at peace with most of their neighbors for many seasons now.

If a death occurred, the People carried out the ritual mourning period, singing the traditional songs. They placed the deceased on the scaffold with food and water for the journey, and after the three days during which the spirit crosses over, they returned to the ways of the living.

Beaver recalled one winter when food was scarce. Many of the adults became very thin because they had given what food they had to the children.

Cold Maker had done his worst that season. It was impossible to hunt or trap. One respected old warrior, Runs Ahead, had gone out to fight the storm, singing the Death Song.

"The grass and the sky go on forever,
but today is a good day to die."

Had Runs Ahead lost his mind? But, this action had drawn not only approval, but admiration from the adults of the People.

It was much later that Beaver realized the significance of the act. The Death Song was that with which the warriors rode into battle, a boast to threaten the enemy. Runs Ahead had been the boldest of warriors. His name, in fact, had been earned by his habit of leading the charge into the fight.

On the day of his last Death Song, the People were starving. Runs Ahead had walked into the teeth of the blizzard, knowing that in this last battle, he would die. But in so doing, he would defeat Cold Maker. The absence of Runs Ahead would provide more food for the children who would be the future of the People.

The old warrior's challenge had been successful. It was only a few days later that Sun Boy lighted his new torch to begin the time of Awakening.

< >

Even so, Beaver had not been exposed to death in a way that had affected him like this, his contact with the party from the east. He was now traveling with, talking to, sharing food with, people little older than himself, who had seen the young men of their families killed before their eyes. This was a new experience for him.

It is probable that for every person there is a moment when he realizes his own mortality. Until then, it may seem that such things as death happen only to others. We see ourselves as observers, not as participants.

This moment came to Beaver as he lay in his blankets that morning, waiting for the dawn. He considered rising quietly to feed a few sticks to the fire, but abandoned that idea, unwilling to risk waking the others. Instead, he lay there and pondered.

They should reach the pipestone quarry in another day's travel, or so they had been told. He was eager to experience the place he had heard so much of, and which seemed so important to his life. He moved his right hand to touch the bundle inside his shirt. Each time he did so, there was a sensation of its importance. In another day, maybe he would be able to carry out the ritual he was certain would answer many of the mysteries that he found troubling.

He was not sure just how it would happen, the restoring of the red stone pipe to its place. That in itself was part of the mystery. Would there be a high point of rock where he could place it, or should he rebury it? He tried to convince himself that when the time came, it would be revealed to him. In this, he was not entirely successful. He wondered if he would ever know the right thing to do.

But now it was growing light, and the camp was beginning to stir. Smoke from newly kindled fires brought a familiar fragrance to the morning air.

Trades His Moccasins stood up and stretched sleepily. Beaver laid a couple of dry sticks across the coals he had been watching, and blew gently to bring back the glow. The trader nodded a morning greeting, and Cactus Flower sat up to put her baby to breast.

Beaver looked across the camp to try to catch a glimpse of the young widow, Pale Moon, as she rose. But if he had been asked, he would have denied that it was intentional.

28

They arrived at the valley of the red stone the following day. It had been decided better to enter the area with most of a day before them. There were marked disadvantages in arriving just before dark. There would be no opportunity to look around for a good camp site, to feel the spirit of the place, and begin to relate to it.

It had been a restless night, with excitement building as they thought of tomorrow. They would take some time to look around, to find water, and an area in which to camp for a period of time.

Beaver had given little thought to how long, and Trades His Moccasins had given no hint. The trader, by his occupation, had a tendency *not* to make long-range plans. When camping with others, if the trading was good, it was easy to prolong their stay for another day. If not, it was as easy to move on. Beaver had fallen easily into this pattern. Nothing had been said about how long they might remain here, or in association with the fugitives from the east. Plans could change easily.

The main object to the trader's visit here was to rid himself of the curse placed on him unintentionally by the widow. At least, they had assumed it unintentional. There was no clear plan as to how the situation would now be handled. There was not enough information to go on. Somehow, somewhere, the pipe would be restored to its place of origin, and hopefully the trader would be free of its influence.

Beaver's part in the visit to the quarry was less defined. His role was unclear, even to himself. He had become obsessed with the secret of the red pipestone . . . Ah, so long ago, it seemed, now. His dreams, his waking thoughts and experiences, his odd position now as custodian of the object of the trader's curse. Beaver had not asked for this, or sought it; it had simply happened. He had given little thought to what might come next, or to how long he might need to spend here. The family of the trader, of which he had become a part, would be moving on, as there was little trade to expect here.

He felt, somehow, that his own quest would take longer. They had not discussed it, but it was a natural assumption. His was a quest, a thing to be experienced, not planned. Ah, well, time would tell.

‹ ›

As he looked at the valley, he was struck with the thought that it would be hard to describe. There was a large, open flat, big enough for the entire Southern Band of the People to have camped. The vegetation was short at this season, but of the familiar tallgrass prairie. It would grow tall with the approach of autumn.

In the distance he could see the reddish wall of a low bluff which partially encircled the flat. His heart leaped for a moment at the sight of the red color. Then he realized that this was only red clay and shale, eroded by wind and weather. The stone of the pipes would not be so exposed, but must be dug from between the layers of other material.

There was a small stream, meandering past the area where the party stood, winding its way into a rough and rocky ravine on the left. In places, the canyon appeared to be heavily timbered. Oddly shaped outcrops of stone jutted from the floor of the canyon, and footpaths or game trails wound their way among gigantic boulders.

The stone was reddish, but its texture was not that of the soap-smooth pipestone. It was more like the stone in the country of the

People, except red instead of white. Beaver wondered at this, but quickly remembered that in every mention of the special pipestone, there had been reference to "digging" it from the quarry.

This was a long-anticipated moment, but he was puzzled at his own reaction. He was not certain what he had expected. Some sort of uplift, a spiritual awakening, maybe? A sudden understanding or communication with the spirits of the place, or even a connection with the whole spirit world.

Instead, there was nothing. He found this disappointing, if not downright alarming. A beautiful place, it was true. But he had expected excitement, a thrill, a spiritual experience. He had anticipated so long, and now, nothing. Just another pretty place.

He looked around at the others in the party, wondering if they were feeling the same. He saw nothing that would give him any information. There was only the usual preparation to select camp sites, convenient to water and to grass for the horses. Maybe, he thought, he could find some answers by walking the game trail down the canyon. He turned to help unload the packs and set up camp.

⟨⟩

By mid-afternoon they were settled in. The symbolic fires had been kindled, to announce their presence to the spirits of the place. Some of the families began to erect their shelters, or to cook their first meal in this camp.

Beaver voiced his intention to walk the trail in the canyon.

"It is good," agreed Trades His Moccasins. "Maybe you can tell how we are to return the pipe."

"I will try," agreed Beaver. "I don't know . . ."

He wondered if the trader or his wife had any feeling of the confusion he was experiencing. They seemed to show none, beyond natural curiosity about a new place. He gathered an armful of dry sticks for Cactus Flower's cooking fire, and placed it conveniently near.

"Thank you, Beaver," she smiled. "You will be a good husband for someone."

Her eyes sparkled with mischief.

Beaver blushed, embarrassed, and turned away. He wished she wouldn't tease him like that.

He turned toward a point where the path dropped over the ledge of stone and began to slope down, circling and hugging the face of the cliff, around and among the jumble of oddly shaped boulders. Here, he began to feel a stir of excitement. One huge mass of rock resembled a human face seen from the side. Another reminded him of a huge bird of prey. The color was red. He stroked the red stone wall beside him . . . No, this was not the pipestone, but of a sandy texture. He was puzzled. He moved on, still trying to get some feeling for the place.

He came around a shoulder of the wall's face, threading between the cliff and a massive pilaster which rose from the canyon floor like a giant tree trunk. It was a nearly round cylinder, on end, flat across the top at the same level as the cliff's top itself. The flat top appeared to be two or three paces across, no larger or smaller than the pillar's trunk. The cliff at this point was about three times the height of a man.

An odd idea occurred to him. With a running start, it would be possible to run along the edge of the cliff and jump to the top of the pedestal.

He heard a chuckle and turned to see a young man about his own age. The stranger smiled and spoke, in a tongue not familiar to Beaver. He believed it to be Lakota.

Quickly, Beaver gave the peace sign, right palm forward, and the other nodded.

You are Lakota? Beaver asked in signs.

Yes. You?

No. Elk-dog People. South.

Ah! I have heard of them, the other signed. *Yours are the ones up there?*

He pointed in the general direction of the newcomers' camp.

No. I am with a trader. Arapaho, "Trader People". We met these others on the trail.

The other nodded again.

We heard someone was coming. You talked to Bull's Horn?

Beaver had been puzzled that the young man had not seemed surprised to see him, and had expressed only curiosity, not suspicion. Even given that the area was a sacred site where even enemies must not fight, this was an unexpected attitude. A young Lakota would hardly be so friendly, in most instances.

Then he realized the uncommon familiarity of this young man, his almost friendly greeting, was likely due to Bull Horn's decree.

Yes, that is true. We met on the trail, signed Beaver.

Bull's Horn is my uncle, the young man explained.

Beaver was unsure, from the sign, whether the term "Uncle" was used in the same way as the People used it. A blood relative, or just a term of respect for a male adult older than one's self? He guessed it didn't matter much.

I am Beaver, he signed. *How are you called?*

I am Spider. You were looking at the Lover's Leap when I saw you.

Lover's Leap?

Yes. The stone, there. He pointed. *If a man wants to impress a girl he will show that he can jump to that rock without falling off.*

Sometimes they fall? asked Beaver.

Oh, yes. But maybe the girl will honor his bravery, or take pity on him.

What happens if he lands safely?

Beaver had been at this point of wonder when the other approached.

What do you mean? asked Spider.

How does he get back? There is no room for a running start.

An amused expression flitted across the face of the young Lakota.

The jump is a test of bravery, not wisdom, he signed.

Spider's expression was sober, but his eyes twinkled with humor.

Beaver liked this young man from the start. It was good to meet a person of his own age with such a sense of humor. Spider carried a bow, and a quiver of arrows was slung over his back.

You camp near here? asked Beaver.

A day away. I came to see the trader when Bull's Horn's party told of it.

We just arrived. No trade yet.

Of course. I, too, just came.

You have a woman? asked Beaver.

Spider smiled.

No. I have not been foolish enough to try the leap!

Both laughed, but Beaver was a bit uncertain. Did the young man mean the Lovers' Leap, or the leap into matrimony?

Or, maybe both.

29

Beaver spent the rest of the day exploring the valley, its hidden places and those which were more spectacular. He was puzzled. This was completely different from what he had expected. He had to admit that he had not known exactly what to anticipate. A spiritual event, like that of a vision quest, maybe. At least, some experience that would mark it as an important event of his lifetime.

So far, he had found nothing of the sort. In fact, he *felt* nothing at all. It seemed to him that somehow the place was empty of spirit, and he found that difficult to understand. He had tossed a pinch of tobacco from his own pouch into Cactus Flower's cooking fire to draw the spirits into contact, yet it had seemed to have little effect.

He wandered down the canyon, among the giant rocks which had, through the millennia, split away or fallen from the wall of the main body of stone. In places, growth of trees and shrubs hugged against the canyon's wall, hiding the rocky shapes.

It was entirely by accident that Beaver stumbled onto an important feature of the place. Stumbled, quite literally . . . The shadow of a large bird as it flew overhead caused him to glance aside from where he was walking. The toe of his moccasin caught for just an instant on a protruding shard of reddish stone in the nearly overgrown game trail, and he pitched forward. Completely off balance, he fell heavily. Instinct caused him to throw his hands forward to break his fall against the wall of stone. But the fall was not broken, and he struck the ground heavily on his stomach, the breath knocked from his lungs. The eagle screamed as it veered away over the cliff and disappeared. *His guide?* Beaver's vision plunged into darkness for the space of a few heartbeats as he struggled to catch his breath.

As coherent thought returned, he realized that he had fallen into a clump of climbing, viny growth that clung to and nearly obscured the cliff's face. His senses had told him that he was falling against a solid wall of stone, but that was not the case. His head, having pushed through the curtain of vines, was thrust partly into an opening in the stone. Dim light filtered down from some crevice overhead. There was a musty animal smell. As his eyes adjusted, he realized that he was looking through a narrow opening into a low cave. Possibly, this had in other seasons been the den of raccoons, coyotes, or even a wintering bear. It was not large enough for him to stand erect, and no more than a few paces in breadth or width.

Embarrassed by his own bumbling, he backed out of the opening and looked quickly around to assure himself that no one had seen his clumsiness. The tangled vines fell back into place, and everything was as before. Except, of course, for the discomfort of a scraped elbow, a bruised knee, and a bump where his head had struck the side of the opening as he fell.

He paused a moment to feel the bulge of the carefully wrapped packet in his shirt. It seemed intact. He would be glad when he was able to rid himself of the responsibility of the cursed pipe.

His main injury was to his pride. He would say nothing to anyone about his fall. A quick glance up and down the trail reassured him that no one had witnessed his clumsiness. That, at least, was good.

Beaver gathered an armful of sticks as he made his way back toward the campfire of the trader's family. He felt the need to justify his activity, and certainly did not want to answer questions about his exploration.

⟨ ⟩

There was one other curious incident that evening which was as puzzling as most of the day's other happenings. As he made his way back to rejoin Trades His Moccasins' family at their camp, he passed the mouth of a small gully, branching off from the main canyon. He heard an odd, metallic sound and glanced in that direction.

A few paces along the streambed was a man in buckskins. He was standing in the rocky channel of the waterway, dry at this season. The man held an iron bar, and was striking at the stone shelf that formed one bank of the watercourse. At that point the bank was twice the height of the man. It was mostly of whitish layers of shale-like soft stone. At the point where the man was striking and prying, however, Beaver could see a layer of stone of a different color. Red. It was possibly as thick as the width of a man's palm, and ran horizontally in both directions for a space of a several paces.

Near the stranger's feet was a small pile of the red stones. With a thrill of excitement, Beaver realized that this was what he had come all this way to see. The man was unceremoniously prying out of the rock, slabs of the mysterious stone which seemed to carry such importance to so many.

Perhaps sensing Beaver's stare, the man straightened, looked full into Beaver's eyes, and nodded a solemn greeting. Then he returned to his work.

Beaver moved on, more puzzled, perhaps, than ever.

⟨ ⟩

Back at the campfire, he tossed down his load of fuel.

"It is good," said Cactus Flower. Then she looked toward him and gasped.

"What happened to your head?"

Self-consciously, Beaver reached toward the bump above his right eye. He struck a tender spot, winced, and stared at his fingers, smeared with blood.

"You are hurt!"

"No, I just bumped my head a little," he protested.

Still, he was startled to find that the bump on his head was bleeding. There was a certain numbness about it, as expected with a head wound, but the sticky wetness was completely unexpected. The bleeding must have stopped now, he realized. Otherwise, it would still be trickling down his face.

"Here, let me clean it," Cactus Flower said.

She dampened a small cloth and gently dabbed at the injury.

"It's not very big," she noted, half to herself. "How did you do this?"

"I . . . I slipped and fell," Beaver stammered.

"On your *head*?"

"What's happening?" asked Trades His Moccasins, returning from a look around.

"It is nothing," insisted Beaver. "I stumbled on the path, and fell against the rock. I did not even know it was bloody until Flower told me."

"Just like a man," Cactus Flower scolded. "You could bleed to death without knowing it if there was no woman to look after you. You need a woman, Beaver."

"I am not bleeding to death!" Beaver protested. "See, it has stopped now."

"Yes, that is true," admitted the young woman. "You might have survived, even without help."

Trades His Moccasins was laughing.

"I don't understand how you bumped *there*, over the eye."

"It was not difficult," Beaver said irritably. "I tripped, fell against the rock. That is what happened."

"Of course," said the trader, still with an amused smile on his face.

Beaver was irritated. He had intended to tell the whole story of his odd experience, but now . . . Somehow, the mixture of Flower's concern and her husband's amusement embarrassed him, and put him on the defensive. For reasons he could not have explained, he was determined to say nothing more about it.

"Will you set up for trade tomorrow?" Beaver asked, to change the subject.

"Of course. I haven't decided how much to display. I am made to think that people are here for other reasons. Maybe we can tell more at evening fires. I'll put out some goods and see."

It was not mentioned that most of the people camped at the quarry were the refugees from the east. They were here, of course, *because* they had nothing.

<>

"Have you thought of how it would be best to return the pipe, here?" asked Beaver a little later. He touched the bundle in his shirt.

"I have been thinking on that," mused the trader. "It has done well for you to carry it, but now . . . I even wonder if your, uh, 'accident' could have some meaning."

Beaver bristled, but the trader went on quickly.

"No, no. I am serious, Beaver. It seems to me that when the time comes to *return* the pipe, it is my problem."

"But how? Where?" asked Beaver.

"I don't know. Could your fall mean that you should be rid of the pipe?"

"Maybe. Do you want to take it now?"

The trader was quiet for a little while.

"I will if you feel I should, Beaver. I am not eager, of course, but I want no harm to you."

Beaver was reluctant to say any more about the little cavern into which he had blundered. He could not have told why, except that there had seemed to be powerful forces at work. Now, he had begun to feel this more strongly. There must have been a reason. He was equally convinced, however, that this reason had no connection whatever to the powerful curse on the bundled pipe that he carried in his shirt. These were two separate matters, but he was deeply involved in both.

"I am made to think," he said slowly, "that you will know when and where to return the pipe. Is it not so?"

The trader nodded.

"It would seem so. Let us talk of this again when either of us feels that it is time."

"It is good."

"Let us smoke," suggested Trades His Moccasins.

This was a solemn event. The two had talked seriously, man to man, on a new level. Both realized it, and it seemed of enough importance to mark the event with a ceremonial smoke.

They carried out the entire ritual, blowing a puff to the four directions, to earth and to sky. The pipe was the trader's, as the older of the two, but the tobacco a pinch from the pouch of each, mixed and packed together.

"Mmm. That's pleasant," said Trades His Moccasins, after the rituals were completed. "Juniper?"

"Just a little. Some sumac, a touch of catnip."

The trader nodded approvingly.

"I saw a man digging the pipestone," Beaver recounted a little later as they headed back toward the camp.

"Oh?"

"Yes, he had a stick made of iron, and he was striking the ledge, prying out pieces of stone."

"Were you made to think you should try it?"

"No, no. I had no feeling of that sort."

Or of any other sort, Beaver thought to himself. This, maybe, was the strangest mystery of all.

Except for one, the one he had not mentioned to anyone. It involved the mysterious human-like Little Person who seemed to turn up sometimes in the margin of his vision, and her low, chuckling laughter.

He had been somewhat stunned when he fell and bumped his head, and he had seen nothing. Maybe he had, in his dazed condition, only imagined that he heard the laughter, too. He had said nothing to anyone about that.

But in his heart, he knew he had heard it.

◁ ·ᐅ**30**

Beaver was deeply troubled. He had been confused after the accident, and irritated by his clumsiness. The trader and his wife teased him in a friendly, concerned fashion, which did not bother him very much.

His concern, however, was linked to his own reaction to the pipe-stone quarry in general. He had not known what to expect, but of all the feelings he might have had, none was anything at all like what he was experiencing. More accurately, perhaps, feelings that he was *not* experiencing. There was no contact at all with the spirits of the place, and this was completely new for him.

He had heard it said that white men have no recognition for the spirits of objects other than humans, and maybe some animals. He found that hard to believe. Among the People, all things have a spirit. Every tree, every rock, every *place*. How could the white man deny this, when even as he says it, he talks of a gloomy thicket, a happy clearing, or a threatening stretch of the trail? Beaver had never understood that, but it had never worried him. That was the white man's problem, and of no concern to Beaver. His concern now was that he, himself, felt no spirit here.

Was it possible, he wondered, that so much of the red stone had been removed over a long period of time that there was no remaining spirit? He pondered this for a little while. He had felt the spirit of the carefully wrapped pipe that he still carried inside his buckskin shirt. Maybe, he thought, the fact that for many years pieces of this stone had been removed, little by little, and carried away, had weakened the underlying spirit of the place itself. Power, misused, can be dangerous to one who possesses it, he knew. Had the powerful medicine of this place somehow been carried away in bits and pieces until there was nothing left?

Or, on the contrary, was it Beaver himself who was missing some critical factor here? It was almost frightening to consider that he might be missing something that was very important because of his ignorance or carelessness. Maybe, even, his clumsiness, he thought as he ruefully touched the still-swollen knot on his right temple. Maybe he had jolted something out of its proper position in the world's well-ordered design. Or in his own confused head . . .

"Beaver!"

His thoughts were interrupted by the approach of Trades His Moccasins.

"Ah! Here you are!" said the trader, seating himself on a rocky outcrop near the boulder where Beaver had been perched. "It is good. Let us talk."

There flashed through the young man's head the thought that maybe he had done something that the trader would not approve. That was only a passing thought, however. The look on the face of Trades His Moccasins said that the concern was not for Beaver, but for something nearer himself.

"Beaver," he began carefully, "you still carry the eagle-pipe, no?"

"Yes . . . I wondered . . ."

The trader nodded, even as he went on.

"I know, Beaver. It is not right that I have let you carry the pipe, when it was mine to do."

"I am made to think it was right, Uncle," Beaver protested. "We have had no problems . . ."

"Yes, yes, that is true," said the trader as he hurried on. "I have not felt comfortable about it, but it has somehow done what we need. Its spirit was pleased. But now, what?"

Beaver was silent, lost in thought, and Trades His Moccasins continued.

"We must move on. I had thought to stay here a little while, maybe do some trading with those who come to dig the pipestone. But that is not good."

"Not good?"

The trader gestured toward the camp of the easterners.

"Not good! Good *people*, hard workers . . . They will do well, but not now. Just now, they will be trying to dig some of the pipestone. We cannot carry much of the rough stone. It is too heavy. And we can't wait until they carve and work it, though I understand that they can do this well. But, a trader must trade, so we must move on."

Beaver nodded. For a moment a stray thought fluttered its way through his mind . . . *What will happen to Pale Moon and her child?* He thrust it aside.

"What shall I do with the pipe?" he asked.

"Ah, I was wondering about that," said the trader. "Have you any thoughts?"

"I had not thought about it. I am made to think that such a choice is yours, Uncle, how to restore its medicine. It was given to you."

Trades His Moccasins nodded sadly.

"That is true, of course, though I really had no choice. *Aiee*, it has done so well to have *you* carry it!"

Both chuckled at the obvious inconsistencies of this odd situation, and then settled back to more serious thought.

"I am made to think," ventured Beaver, "that it would be good to leave it in a prominent place."

"I, too," Trades His Moccasins agreed. "To hide it in some secret place might be offensive. It must be plain that we honor it."

But where?

"Let us walk the trail," suggested the trader. "Maybe we will see the spot where we may place it."

There seemed no better idea, and the two rose and started along a path which meandered through the whole area.

<>

"Here, maybe?" Beaver suggested.

"No, too public a place."

"Hang it in a tree?"

"Maybe. It would be seen as a sacrifice, though."

"Most would honor that."

"But not all. We don't know what travelers might come here. Ones whose ways we have never heard of."

Nearly half the day was gone now. They had walked the entire circle of level prairie bordered by the bluff on one side and the canyon on the other, without finding a place that seemed appropriate. How could they honor the spirit that appeared to be that of the pipe without exposing it to possible theft or dishonor?

"Maybe the finder should take the risk," Beaver suggested.

"No," said the trader thoughtfully. "We tried that once. Our bad luck continued, remember. No, we must be sure it is right this time."

<>

They were on the second circuit of the gully's rim when an idea struck Beaver. They were just passing the freestanding rock formation that had been described as the Lovers' Leap.

"There!" he exclaimed.

"What? Where?"

"There!"

Beaver pointed to the flat round area on the top of the column.

Trades his Moccasins studied the scene for a moment.

"No, no, Beaver. I doubt that either of us . . . Ah, wait! You do not mean to jump, but to *toss*! Of course. And no one is likely to disturb it. A young man who makes the jump, if anyone can . . . *Aiee*, if his medicine is that strong, he should be in no danger!"

Very quickly, it was decided. This was the place. Beaver removed the bundle from his shirt and handed it to Trades His Moccasins.

"Should it be unwrapped and placed on its pipestem?" Beaver asked.

The trader pondered for a few moments.

"I am made to think not. It might risk damage. No, I think it should remain wrapped. The bundle will protect and honor it. Do you want to toss it?"

He extended the bundle toward Beaver.

"No, no!" Beaver said hurriedly. "It was given to you. It must be you who restores it. Is it not so?"

The trader shrugged, an expression of resignation on his face.

"I know," he admitted with a wry smile. "But it was worth a try. Its spirit was quiet when the pipe traveled with you, was it not?"

"That is true, but . . ."

Trades His Moccasins waved a hand to assure him that the discussion was at an end. He moved toward the edge and paused, seeming to estimate the distance of the toss and the likelihood of too long a throw. Or, if the bundle happened to bounce. The flat surface on which the pipe must land was no more than two or three paces across . . .

Beaver held his breath, trying not to let his anxiety show. A bit too much force would bounce or slide the packet on over the edge. Too weak a toss might as easily cause it to fall short.

Only then did it occur to him that there was very little actual risk. If worst came to worst, the bundle would fall to the ground near the base of the stone column. The pipe was padded to protect it from accident anyway, and it should suffer no harm. The height of the fall was no more than three times that of a man. It would require only that one of them descend by the rocky path to retrieve the bundle for another try.

Despite his attempt at self-assurance, Beaver held his breath as the trader leaned over the edge as far as he safely could. His right arm swung at full extension, back and forth, once, twice, a third time

. . . He released the bundle, and Beaver watched as it seemed to float across the space between.

Too short . . . No, too long . . . Aiee! Just right!

The bundle containing the pipe struck the flat top of the stone column, bounced and rolled another hand's span or two. It came to rest almost exactly in the center of the intended target.

"*Aiee*! It is good!" Beaver almost shouted.

He turned to look at the trader, whose face was pale and beaded with sweat. The expression on that face, however, was one of great relief. Plainly, this was an important turning point.

The two returned to their camp, where Cactus Flower waited with the baby. She rose to greet them.

"It went well?" she inquired, though she already knew from their faces.

"Very much so," Beaver assured her.

Quickly, he described the scene, and the skill with which Trades His Moccasins had tossed the eagle pipe onto the stone pedestal at the Lovers' Leap.

Cactus Flower's happy face fell, and her expression became one of concern.

"The Lovers' Leap? What if some young lover *does* manage to jump over to the landing place?"

"I don't think it can be done," said her husband. "I am made to think that is just a story. But if anyone does, it becomes *his* problem. I have taken care of mine!"

Beaver said nothing, and tried not to notice the uneasy feeling that had begun to creep over him. It was a feeling that somewhere along the line, something had been overlooked. Something of great importance.

◁·▷31

"We'll move on tomorrow," Trades His Moccasins announced to his companions that evening at the fire. "There is no trade to be done here."

Although he knew the circumstances and the reasons, Beaver was not ready to move on so quickly. He had been drawn to this place, by other forces and for other reasons. It had been a powerful call. Now he was here, and though the purpose of the trader's visit had been accomplished, his own had not. He was no nearer to an understanding than when he started. The satisfaction of having been able to return the powerful eagle pipe to its place of origin was overshadowed by his own problem.

Maybe it was even worse now. He had not been prepared to feel absolutely nothing of the spirit when he reached this place. The journey and quest which was to have answered his questions had not only failed to do so, but had raised more.

In addition to all of this, there was another confusing factor that he could never have expected. He was concerned for the well-being of the young widow in the party of outlanders from the east. Cactus Flower had seen it in his eyes, and had correctly interpreted his feelings. He had denied it, of course, out of embarrassment, but

Flower knew. She was a woman. He did not understand how women know such things, but has any mere man ever understood women, in all the world?

During the past days, Beaver had come to have more and more attraction toward the unfortunate young mother. He had been unwilling to admit it to himself.

Pale Moon . . . He had actually talked to her very little. He had been unsure whether such contact was even to be permitted among her people. A widow. Was there a time period after the loss of a husband that would restrict her talking with a single man? How long before she would be considered eligible for courtship? Even such thoughts alarmed him. Was he ready for such thoughts as he now pondered?

In addition, there was the language problem. But sometimes the voices of natural attraction seem to leap over such barriers. The two seemed to communicate without words, and Pale Moon's people did not seem to object. So, with the apparent consent or at least tolerance, of her family and her people, they had shared very shy advances. If it had been put into such words, both of the young people would have denied any communication at all, and truthfully so. Beaver did not even want to think about the fact that they would soon be parting.

Now, that time was upon him. He should have realized that Trades His Moccasins would have to move on. He had, in his innocence, pushed the reality aside, refusing to look at some of the major decisions that came looming at him now.

He lay sleepless in his blanket, facing such decisions with a suddenness that seemed overwhelming. *Aiee*, to be a child again, and have others make the decisions!

He must decide by morning whether he would move on with Trades His Moccasins and Cactus Flower or remain here with the struggling people of Pale Moon. That in itself must be decided *now*. If he stayed, it would imply a relationship that he was not sure actually existed. It had been only a few days . . .

Maybe his biggest stumbling block, however, was that none of it seemed to have any connection whatsoever to the quest on which he had been so powerfully called. He was here, at the quarry itself, and he felt nothing. Nothing at all.

So, what was he to do? He lay awake for what seemed an eternity, watching the Seven Hunters circle the northern sky, wishing, almost pleading, for some sort of direction. If there was to be a change in his quest, why couldn't he see and feel it? His quest had guided him here, and in spite of it all, he had been given no answers. Could it be, then, that he must remain here until he found some sort of guidance? To move on with the trader would, in effect, be to abandon the cause which had beckoned him.

Then a new thought struck him. Maybe the quest for meaning in the red pipestone *had* been fulfilled with the restoration of the old warrior's pipe to its place of origin. Yes, that must be it. His task, and that of Trades His Moccasins, had been fulfilled when the bundle with the eagle pipe landed on the top of the rock. Of course!

There was only one problem with this theory. He lay there, running the sequence of events over and over in his mind. Each time, he had to come back to the same unsatisfactory conclusion: There was no *feeling* of fulfillment. For the solution to the trader's problem, yes. The eagle pipe had been returned, much to the relief of Trades His Moccasins and Cactus Flower.

But that had not been Beaver's problem, except accidentally. His connection had been quite unrelated. He had happened to be of help, but it was not enough for him to have experienced the powerful guidance that he had encountered. It must be, then, that for Beaver, there was something unfinished. There must be more to come.

He had a strong feeling, too, that whatever was to come must be linked to this *place*. Whatever would happen was somehow linked to the pipestone quarry. The conclusion was inescapable: He could not leave, and he must tell Trades His Moccasins in the morning.

With this settled in his mind, he drifted off to sleep. It was not an easy sleep, but one with dreams. There were odd questions and bizarre situations. For a short space of time he felt trapped between the reality of the world and the shadowy, unknown Other Side. He saw faces which reflected the entire range of human emotion: joy, happiness, love, and pleasure, but also those with fear, puzzlement, question, anger and tragedy. One, the face of a dignified old man, seemed to want to communicate with him. Beaver felt strongly that there was something the man wanted to tell or to ask him, but was somehow unable to do so.

There was a time in which he had a more conventional dream, similar to one he had experienced before. It was a welcome respite from the anxiety and unknown fears of his other visions. His safe haven was, as before, in the arms of a woman. As before, he could not identify her, except that she represented safety, and the sense that now, all was well. He felt the confidence of childhood again, as if in the arms of this woman, he was protected from the rest of the world. It was not a maternal protection, however, but one of partnership and understanding. The sort of understanding that he had seen in the lodges of couples who seemed to enjoy each other as friends as well as lovers. And yes, again, as in his previous dream, there was the physical warmth and mildly stimulating satisfaction, just short of outright eroticism. He buried his face in the warmth of her neck and shoulder, and it was good. Good, to be held and comforted, to feel the soft, yielding body against his, and to know that he was also providing warmth and comfort to her.

He woke, somewhat reluctantly, because he had been happily enjoying such a reassuring dream. The sky in the east was just turning from dark blue-black with countless pinpoints of light to a gray-yellow. The stars were fading with the approach of dawn. It would be a decisive day in his life, but now he knew what his decision must be. His quest here was unfinished after all. He must live out the rest. He could not forsake the young woman whose need was so great, who had suffered so much loss, and whose spirit seemed to reach out to him. He would stay here, where his quest had led him, and let the rest of it happen. He was pleased to have been able to help in the restoration of the red pipe to its proper home. That, he decided, was an incident in which he had been privileged to take part. He had been in the right place, the right time.

⟨⟩

It was growing light now, and the twinkling stars began to pale and disappear. Trades His Moccasins stirred, rolled over and rose, gently replacing the corner of his robe over his sleeping wife's shoulder. It warmed Beaver's heart to see such affection.

The trader made his way toward the area which, by common consent, the men of the party had selected for the purpose, and emptied his bladder. He turned as Beaver approached. He was still adjusting his breechcloth and redressing himself.

"Good! You are up for the day. Shall we get an early start?"

Beaver hesitated. This would not be easy.

"I . . . Uncle, I would speak with you of something."

"Of what, Beaver?"

"Of moving on. You know that I felt a call. A quest."

"Of course. Ah, Beaver, you have been a great help to me. How would I have been able to return the eagle pipe without you? I am made to think that you have a powerful guide!"

"It was nothing," protested the embarrassed Beaver. "My help, that is. Anyone would have done the same."

"Not just anyone," the trader insisted. "But, what did you want to speak of?"

"I cannot go on, Uncle."

"What? Why not?"

Beaver hesitated, then took a deep breath.

"There is something wrong."

"What is it?"

"I do not know, Uncle. I was made to think that it was something about the red pipestone."

"So you have said."

"But, it is hard to explain. It does not feel finished."

"We returned the pipe that carried the curse," said Trades His Moccasins.

"That is true. And your heart is good, because of it, no?"

"Yours is *not*?"

"It is good for that, of course, Uncle. But would I have been called to a quest for that alone?"

The trader was quiet for a little while, and when he spoke, it was softly.

"You have had another vision?"

"Not exactly. I dreamed dreams, yes. But, I am made to think there is more."

"What will you do?"

"Stay here. Wait, I suppose."

The face of Trades His Moccasins showed frustration, a trace of anger, and disbelief. Still, one does not question the visions of another.

"Are you sure, Beaver?"

"I must be. I was led here."

"But, maybe to help me return the eagle pipe?"

"That is part of it. But I was not really needed for that. You could have done that yourself."

"Ah!" said the trader with a sudden burst of insight. "I know! The woman of the outlanders. The widow. Pale Moon, is it? Yes, the way you look at her . . ."

Beaver blushed, embarrassed.

"That is not . . ." he began, but the trader waved him down.

"It is good, Beaver, if that is it. She needs someone, and she should make a fine wife."

"Uncle, what you say is true, but I am made to think there is more. I was drawn here on a powerful quest, and it does not seem finished. I must stay and try to find the part that is missing."

"Of course," said the trader. "I would not question anyone's vision."

But there was an amused twinkle in his eye as they returned to their camp.

<　>**32**

Once decided, and once the trader and his wife had been informed of the decision, Beaver had expected the change to be easily accepted. He felt a sense of relief himself. At least, he tried to believe it was so.

The two men returned to the fire, and Trades His Moccasins spared Beaver the problem of how to inform Cactus Flower.

"Beaver is leaving us."

"*What*?" the woman sputtered. "But, he . . ."

"His quest," explained the trader, "has led him here."

"Then it is finished, no? He can move on with us."

Then, a suspicion seemed to dawn, and a mischievous look crept over her face.

"Ah, yes, Beaver. The outlander girl! It is good."

Beaver blushed again, and was quick to protest.

"No, no, that is not it, Flower."

"Of course not," she giggled. "You have hardly noticed her. Well, never mind. We will struggle along as best we can."

"Don't tease him," said the trader gently. "This is not an easy decision for him."

"I will help you pack," offered Beaver.

There was little packing to do, since the trade packs had not been spread open since they arrived.

Cactus Flower displayed mixed emotions during the preparations to break camp. She joked and teased him as usual, but from time to time it could be noted that her attitude was one of sadness. Beaver was reminded that her dejection was much like the reaction his mother had exhibited on the day of his departure from the People . . . Sadness, mixed with hope for success.

He, too, was experiencing mixed feelings. For the past moon or more, the trader couple had been like family to him, the only family he had. Trades His Moccasins was only a few seasons older than Beaver himself, and in some ways supplied the role of a brother. The trader had admitted to feeling rather foolish when Beaver addressed him as "uncle." It appeared that he, too, felt the brotherly tone of their relationship.

Where Cactus Flower was involved, however, the connection was a bit different. Here was a person even nearer his own age, but with a far different status. Flower was a parent. Yes, it was obviously true of Trades His Moccasins also, but it was not nearly so apparent. The young woman had borne a child, changing her status completely not only in Beaver's adolescent mind, but in everyday observation. A young man of his age and status must be quite aware of Flower's care of her infant. Her day was filled with motherly tasks, not the least of which was that of putting the child to breast at frequent intervals, day and night. He had seen such activity all his life, of course, among the People. It was nothing new.

What was new in this case, however, was that Cactus Flower's parenthood, with its accompanying duties and activities, placed her in a different role from most of the girls of Beaver's age. Flower was not like the girls with whom he had grown up. When they had met, her role was already that of a mother. In turn, her attitude toward young Beaver was largely maternal. At least, in his mind.

Her gentle admonitions, her teasing, her advice and cautions, were not really much different than her remarks to her husband. Is this not a woman's role? Is it not appropriate to the maternal instincts of many women to mother the males in their sphere of influence? What man, falling asleep in a dwelling occupied by a woman, has not sometimes wakened to find himself covered by a blanket?

Such was young Beaver's perception of the trader's wife, and he recognized her concern for him in the present situation. The young couple had come to think of him as family, and without realizing it, Beaver, too, had accepted such a relationship. A time or two as they prepared to depart, he thought he saw a trace of a tear in the eye of Cactus Flower. He said nothing about it, but choked back the lump in his own throat as their departure neared.

There was no valid reason why it should have taken twice as long to prepare for departure as it usually did, but it was so. The sun was already high when the trader and family were ready to break camp.

"Will you stay here, or move nearer the outlanders?" asked Trades His Moccasins.

"I don't know," answered Beaver. "Maybe be alone a little while. See if I find a vision."

"It is good," agreed the trader.

"Take good care of the widow," chided Flower.

"But . . ." Beaver started to argue, but saw no point.

"Of course," he said, laughing.

But there was that lump in his throat again.

"Seriously, take care of yourself," said Trades His Moccasins. "We will be thinking of you. May our trails cross again soon."

Beaver only nodded, reluctant to try to speak.

"The baby and I will miss you," said Cactus Flower. "Be careful, Beaver."

He nodded again, as she lightly touched his elbow with a motherly pat. The baby, in the cradle on her back, smiled at him as Flower turned away, and his heart was heavy.

⟨ ⟩

Beaver decided not to move just yet. The section of the shallow canyon below where they had camped was heavily wooded. It should provide some small game to extend his meager supplies of dried meat and pemmican. He had seen squirrels. Not the best of animals to hunt with a bow. A miss might easily lose an arrow in such a wooded area. With a smile, he recalled the skills of old Snakewater, the medicine woman. She hunted squirrels with darts from her blowgun, a favorite hunting weapon from her Cherokee background. A lost dart was more easily replaced than a precious arrow, but the People had always favored open prairie, and relied very little on small game. Consequently, no one he knew except Snakewater even owned a blowgun.

Odd, he thought, as he readied his bow and quiver of arrows, that he would be thinking of Snakewater just now. Well, maybe he could find a squirrel or two without risking too many arrows.

He had no qualms about leaving his camp site unattended. The fact that he had left a fire burning would signify to any passerby that the camp was occupied. He had few possessions anyway, but it was considered common courtesy among the various tribes and nations *not* to molest another's unguarded possessions. Except, of course, in time of war, with a known enemy. In this case, there was the extra protection of the noncombatant status of the area itself. And, there being no white men around as far as he knew, his camp should be secure during his absence.

He made his way down the path he had followed before, moving slowly and pausing to observe any sound or movement. He fitted an arrow to his bowstring to be as ready as possible.

The timber was full of sounds, mostly the territorial calls of songbirds. Beaver was not entirely familiar with these species, some being unknown in the range occupied by the People. None of these, however, would be those sought by humans for food, except in emergencies.

He moved down the path, listening for the barked warning signal of the squirrel. It could easily be mistaken for a bird call, he had learned. He expected to catch a glimpse of a squirrel or two running across the treetops in their unbelievably acrobatic style, but he saw nothing. He stepped very slowly. A sudden move on the part of a hunter of any species might alarm his quarry.

The first squirrel that he saw startled him considerably. He had expected a running animal, and almost missed seeing it because it was not moving. The creature was lying flattened on the upper surface of a limb that grew horizontally from the bole of a giant sycamore. He first saw the reddish-brown shape as a bump or knot on the chalk-white surface of the limb. It was a moment later that his eyes focused on a small spot, dark and shiny, on the knot. In the space of a heartbeat his perception of the knot changed and he was staring into the eye of a large squirrel, frozen in immobility. Now that he recognized it, he did not see how he could have overlooked it before. The eye stared at him, unmoving, and he could almost feel the pressure of the animal's gaze. Moving even more slowly, he turned to raise the bow. It took the space of several heartbeats to do so without startling the animal into motion.

He had almost drawn the arrow to its head when a thought occurred to him. The squirrel, flattened on the upper surface of the limb, presented a very narrow target. Less than half a hand's span, in fact. A trifle high, even if he hit the animal, his arrow would fly beyond, across the rocky streambed and into the bushes. A trifle low, the flint point of his arrow would strike the limb of the sycamore and certainly be destroyed. Either way, or even with a perfect shot, the food available from a single squirrel was not enough on which to risk a good arrow.

He lowered the bow and smiled as he spoke to his quarry.

"Not today, brother. May it go well with you."

It was some distance and some time before he saw any game that was even a possible meal. A woodchuck, surprised as it grazed on a patch of lush green grass by the stream, waddled hurriedly toward a jumble of rocks. Then it paused, altered its course, and clambered up the slanting trunk of a fallen tree. It stopped and turned to look, above the ground about half the height of a man. It was odd behavior for the ground-dwelling creature. Even so, it was an easy shot, and well worth the risk of an arrow.

The woodchuck fell with a thud, transfixed by the missile, and Beaver ran forward. For some reason, he felt the need to perform for the dying creature the same apology used by the People for the first buffalo kill of the hunt.

"We are sorry to kill you, my brother, but on your flesh our lives depend, as yours do upon the grasses."

The woodchuck was fat and healthy and would provide enough meat for several meals. Even cooked, there was some danger of spoilage in the hot summer days.

It took him only a little while to decide that he must share with someone, and in an even shorter time he realized it should be with the family of Pale Moon.

<· >**33**

Beaver walked into the camp of the outsiders looking for the family of the young woman. He carried his woodchuck, which attracted quite a bit of attention.

There were several makeshift lean-to type dwellings of nondescript construction. These people, he realized, had not yet discovered the entire advantage of the conical tent supported by poles, used by the nomads of the plains. These had been growers, and had probably lived in permanent structures of logs and poles, maybe partly dug into the ground and with earth bermed around the outside. He had seen Pawnee earth lodges, big enough in which to winter an extended family of twenty or thirty people, with a few of their best horses included. Maybe some similar dwelling had been used by these people in their former location. Beaver pushed aside his feeling that these strangers were inferior just because they did not understand how to build a practical dwelling. But he was certain that he could not tolerate the close, confined and smothering feel of a lodge with no fresh air and ventilation. *Well*, he thought, *that is THEIR problem.*

But just now, his problem was to find the lodge of the parents of Pale Moon. He was not even certain of their names. He suddenly felt stupid, wandering among a camp of people with whom he could not even carry on a conversation, and carrying a dead woodchuck. Maybe he should have gone with the trader . . . But no, he was made to think that this was to be.

There were four; no, five of the brush shelters, with a few skins and blankets tossed across the tops to provide some degree of shelter. The thought flitted through his mind that to winter here would require a great deal of preparation. Maybe down in the timber there might be shelter, but it was already late summer. In his own culture, the People would be trying to guess when Cold Maker would sweep down from his ice cave in the northern mountains to drive Sun Boy southward with his torch.

On top of this problem was that of their primary purpose here. These people hoped to quarry enough pipestone to trade to someone, *anyone*, for supplies. They would be able to harvest some nuts, acorns, and berries, and possibly dry some meat before Cold Maker settled in for the winter. But it would certainly take hard work to accomplish all this while also trying to quarry pipestone. He hoped to help by hunting, at least for the family of Pale Moon.

Beaver paused to look around. There were not many people in sight. Others might be digging stone, he supposed. He now realized that he had overlooked his lack of language skills. He had relied on the trader to communicate. Beaver, like most of the people of the prairie, was fluent with hand signs, but these easterners were not.

How had he been so stupid, he asked himself. Without the trader couple, how could he talk with the people of Pale Moon?

He stood there feeling foolish for what seemed an eternity, unsure what he should do next. Then it occurred to him that Trades His Moccasins often tried to find a tongue that both could speak. But the trader spoke many tongues . . . How could he, Beaver . . . *Wait*! Had not the trader discovered that some of these people could speak Cherokee? Beaver was limited, but had often heard Snakewater speak in her tongue, and the youngsters had sometimes in play attempted to learn it. Maybe he could try to remember enough to get ideas across.

Just then an older woman stuck her head out from behind the hanging skin at the open side of one of the brush shelters. She smiled in recognition, and offered a wave of the hand. Beaver recognized the woman whom he assumed was Pale Moon's mother. He moved in that direction, extending his woodchuck in a giving gesture.

The woman nodded, but the look on her face reflected suspicion.

"Pale Moon," he mumbled, using the only words he knew in this woman's tongue.

Then he switched to a combination of hand signs, Cherokee, and the talk of his own, the People, a jumbled mix which seemed more ridiculous to him by the moment.

"Food!" in hand signs. Then "Pale Moon" again. "I want to help. Give. Eat."

He accompanied his words with the hand signs, among which *food*, *give*, and *eat* can almost be interpreted by anyone, especially, if the giver has food in his extended hand. In some cultures a dead woodchuck might not be considered an appropriate gift for a young suitor to offer. In this case it was understood, welcomed, and accepted enthusiastically.

The mother of Pale Moon used the method commonly utilized when speaking to someone not familiar with the same language. In simplest form, speak slowly and very loudly in one's own tongue.

"IT . . . IS . . . GOOD!"

Beaver nodded enthusiastically.

The woman took the bloody animal, hefted its weight and smiled broadly, nodding her head in turn. She felt the plumpness of the flesh beneath the fur, nodded and smiled some more.

Beaver was pleased.

"COME BACK WHEN THE SUN GOES DOWN," said the old woman, using the same linguistic skills as before.

Beaver would never have understood a word, except for her gestures at the sun, the sky, the horizon, and the earth at their feet.

And, after all, hand signs are, in effect, only a refinement of such gestures. The young man turned away, his heart soaring as he nodded in agreement.

⟨⟩

When he returned at sunset, it was apparent that the whole encampment had heard the entire story, and probably a great deal more. There were smiles, waves, and friendly greetings in their own tongue. At least, he thought so. It was completely foreign to him, but after all, what other language would they be speaking?

Their acceptance seemed so complete and so effortless. *Maybe this is moving too fast*, flashed a warning in the back of his mind. He wondered for a moment whether he might have accidentally blundered into an unknown ritual of these foreigners. What if the presentation of a woodchuck is, to these people, part of a prolonged marital ceremony? Would he now be expected to assume the role of a husband? To sleep with her and to take on the responsibility of the child? A chill of something like an icy finger crept up his back, between the shoulder blades and toward the base of his skull. He shook his head to clear it.

Of course not, stupid . . . A ridiculous idea. They are only showing gratitude and hospitality, he told himself.

Surely, it was only appreciation for his having brought food when food was scarce. His efforts to convince himself became gradually more successful as the evening progressed.

It undoubtedly helped that when Pale Moon emerged from the brush shelter she was wearing a garment that he had never seen before. It was a dress of finest white buckskin, ornamented skillfully with beads and quills. *A wedding dress?* Panic gripped him again, with a sense of helplessness, but this time it passed more quickly.

After all, he told himself, if the situation became threatening enough, he could simply ride his blue roan mare out of here and away. But so far, the prospect of staying seemed much more attractive.

<>

It was obvious that the girl's people were anxious for this potential romance to proceed well. He could understand such a situation. In any setting since creation, there are likely to be more women than men in a group larger than the immediate family. It has always been so. The men are more exposed to the dangers of the hunt, or to war, for whatever cause, good or bad. Men have been killed or incapacitated by the hazards of the males' daily occupations through the ages. They leave behind widows, mothers, and daughters, many of whom have no means of support.

The solution has, in all settings and cultures, been similar. Men with power have acquired multiple females, especially those of grace and beauty.

In a more modest setting, a widow might be taken into the home of her sister, or that of her husband's brother.

In the current situation, the traveling band from the east had been so decimated by their traditional enemies that family groups were unable to absorb the survivors. The availability of an apparently capable young man with connections to a trader was a powerful factor.

<>

The evening went well, except for the inability to communicate. There was a lot of laughter and chatter that Beaver did not understand, some of which he suspected, related to him. But the beauty and dignity of the young mother, Pale Moon, was such that he largely forgot everything else.

It was somewhat later in the evening that Beaver began to have a few doubts. Things were moving too fast. There was altogether too much friendly familiarity on the part of the older women . . . More teasing. Someone would voice a few words in a happy, jocular manner in an obvious reference to the provider of the meat, and the others would laugh. It was probably merely the joy of *having* something to eat, meager through it might be. But to Beaver it began to look somewhat contrived. It was almost as if he had lost control of the ongoing events in his life.

Then, as it grew later, the flickering firelight illuminated a scene of serene faces. Despite their troubles and the questionable status of their very survival, here were people who would do their best with whatever challenge presented. They had come a long way against overwhelming odds. They were willing to work hard and had proved that. Beaver began to feel honored that he was accepted by such a group.

It helped considerably perhaps, that across the flickering fire sat one of the most beautiful young women he had ever seen. Her graceful manner and her classic form and figure could not help but draw his attention. She smiled, hinting at potential rewards, drawing his feelings toward her like the attraction of a cool spring to a thirsty traveler.

He did not fully know where all of this was going, but in that moment he was willing to follow wherever the circumstances might lead.

< > 34

Beaver made his way back to his own camp by the light of a three-quarter moon. He was already thinking about tomorrow, and moving his camp a bit closer to that of Pale Moon's people. A solitary camp might be the only way to experience such a thing as a ceremonial vision quest, but it certainly had lonely qualities about it. Especially, when there was no spiritual incentive.

He was not thinking in terms of spiritual enlightenment, however. His mood was one of excitement and anticipation, but on a more visceral level. He still did not know how to proceed with a courtship. What would be proper, and what frowned upon, or actually forbidden in the customs of the outsiders? Still, the girl's family, as well as the others in the encampment, seemed to look with favor upon him.

Especially, the older women. It had been quite embarrassing, the way women older than his own mother smiled and flirted outrageously with him. He knew that this was largely a matter of teasing a young man searching for romance. He had seen such actions among the grandmothers of his own people. This, however, was the first time he had personally experienced such attention, and he found it uncomfortable, to say the least. Of course, as he *showed* discomfort, it awakened in the old matriarchs the adolescent sense of humor of their own younger years. The flirting had become more blatant, more suggestive, and more embarrassing.

He had no way of knowing what earthy comments might be tossed back and forth among the women, but he could guess. He could see the old eyes roving over his body with exaggerated appreciation, the raised eyebrows, the nods and giggles, the long pause by one old crone, to stare at his loincloth, while the others laughed uproariously.

⟨⟩

He tossed a couple of sticks on the coals of his campfire to keep it going, and rolled into his blankets. Staring up into the starry sky, he was sure that sleep would come slowly. After the tension and excitement of having spent time among Pale Moon's people, it was hard to come back down to reality. He tried to plan his next moves. One would be a physical move, closer to the camp of the others.

A more important one, however, involved how he could manage to procure enough game to impress the extended family of the pretty widow. He must be able to acquire more than a woodchuck or two. That kill had been largely luck, anyway. To be really effective, he must be able to offer a major kill. An antelope or an elk, perhaps. Maybe even a buffalo. That would provide enough meat to dry some for the coming winter, as well as fresh meat for their current needs. He knew that one or two of the men in the party were also hunting. He could join them . . .

No, he decided. It would make a bigger and better impression to be able to do it himself. He could visualize himself, leading his roan mare into the camp with a fat buck deer slung across her back. That would quickly place him in high esteem, and surely enhance his attempts at courtship. He finally drifted toward sleep, trying to decide in which direction to ride in the morning. He would defer moving his camp until after his hunt. That might look better to those whom he wanted to impress.

As if in reaction to such a thought, he seemed to hear a muffled chuckle or giggle. It seemed familiar. He had experienced this before, but each time, it had been as he neared sleep or as he woke. Part of a dream, maybe? He had not been able to decide. Each time, it had also been associated with a fleeting glimpse of shadowy motion, or of the human-like figure of the Little Person, silhouetted against the sunset or rising moon. He had, each time, been unsure as to which was reality.

He rose to an elbow, looking around for any hint of motion. Maybe there! Was that the child-like shadow that he had *almost* come to recognize?

"Where are you?" he demanded. "What do you want, Giggles?"

There was a brief period of silence, and he spoke again:

"What? Buffalo? To the west of here?"

Silence, enough for an answer.

Then: "It is good! I will do so."

Beaver was quickly asleep.

⟨⟩

He wakened the next morning, well rested but confused. What had he dreamed? It must have been just after falling asleep. A conversation with a Little Person?

As he rekindled his fire, his thoughts were racing. Could the dream or vision have been *before* sleep, something that had seemed so *real*?

He must get started on the hunt that might be so important to his courtship plans. He glanced around in all directions, taking in the woodlands along the stream, the red bluff that partially encircled the area, and the distant prairie. Which direction?

West, came the instant answer, somehow inside his head. Had he not been told that somewhere? Ah, maybe part of that puzzling, half-awake dream, if that was what it had been. This whole thing was more and more confusing.

Beaver saddled the mare and mounted, carrying his bow and a quiver of arrows. He nudged the mare into an easy trot, heading westward. As for exactly why he chose that direction, he could not have told. It seemed the proper way.

<>

He saw the animals at a distance, dark specks on the green of the prairie. Maybe ten or fifteen, he judged. Probably buffalo, though at a great distance, colors became more difficult to distinguish. These could be elk, or antelope, though none of those would appear this dark, he thought. Possibly bears, but unlikely in such numbers. The way they moved as they grazed, their massive build and their gait, all suggested buffalo. The distance was too great to distinguish whether they were all the usual shade of brown. In the northern herds, buffalo of a dun or yellowish color were not uncommon. Occasionally a mousy gray-blue individual would be noticed. That skin would be highly valued.

Beaver was not concerned with that as he rode carefully toward the little herd. All would taste the same. On this hunt, the primary purpose was for meat.

He chose a casual route. The vision of buffalo is poor at long distances. The animals might see the rider in motion before they identified him as a man on a horse, a possible danger.

In addition, he needed to approach from downwind. His quarry might easily catch the scent of man and horse before they could *see* a danger. He might not have more than one shot, if the buffalo started to run. If he could manage another, so much the better. He had made only one kill in the course of the group hunting parties he had joined back among his own People. This would be different, with no need to adjust his approach to anyone else's position or actions. His bow was ready.

Some of his friends had adopted the use of the lance instead. In most cases, it was a matter of personal preference, bow or lance. However, the change in weapons requires a different horse. The horse instinctively *chases*. Some approach the running quarry from the right, some from the left, by the horse's preference. To shoot a bow from horseback, the approach must be from the right, or it is impossible to draw the bow. The lance requires an approach from the left, because the rider will carry the lance beneath his *right* arm.

For a hunter of Beaver's status, usually the choice came to depend on which horse might be available. An older, more experienced hunter with some prestige or more wealth might take the other course. He might seek to acquire a horse which runs right or left to match his own expertise.

In Beaver's situation, he had little experience with the lance. There was no problem, because his blue roan ran to the right anyway, permitting use of the bow.

He took a wandering approach, watching the animals carefully. The breeze was in his face, very light and a little southeast in direction. He would have to circle southward a bit to prevent a tricky gust from betraying him. Each time a suspicious animal raised its head, he changed direction slightly, to prevent the threat of direct approach. In this way, he drew nearer. He did not want the quarry to begin to run. Not yet. When they did, the horse would be faced with the task of pursuit.

⟨⟩

He had spotted the wary old cow who appeared to be the matriarch of the little herd. She was the one to watch, because the other animals, even the mature bulls, would follow her lead. The cow raised her head frequently to look around, sniffing the air for any scent of danger. Beaver altered his approach several times to give the impression that his was a wandering path. The cow's poor long-range vision would perceive a random pattern which should present no danger. The light breeze continued to cooperate with his purpose.

A young bull, closest to the advancing horseman, lifted his head to stare. Now, success would rest largely on how much closer the hunter could come before the entire band started to run. A little further . . .

There was a sudden snort from the old lead cow, as she wheeled away toward open prairie. The whispering wayward breeze, shifting constantly as it stirred the tall grasses, may have wafted her way. Whatever the means by which she became aware of the danger, she was now alarmed, and sprang into a full gallop.

Beaver dug his heels into the roan's flanks and charged toward the nearest animal, the yearling bull. The bull wheeled to flee, and the roan mare, ears flattened to her head, sprinted in pursuit. She did not need to be guided. The running buffalo had hardly come to full speed when horse and rider drew alongside. Beaver's arrow flew true, entering just behind the ribs and ranging forward and down, into the vital heart-lung area. The animal took a few more frantic leaps and collapsed as horse and rider swept past.

The horse would have pursued the herd, but Beaver drew her in and circled back to where the dying animal lay, kicking weakly as the eyes glazed over.

He dismounted and waited until the kicking ceased. Then he straightened the head, placing it in a more lifelike position, and performed the ritual apology.

"I am sorry to kill you, my brother, but on your flesh our lives depend, as the grass supports yours."

The roan mare grazed quietly a short distance away.

<・>**35**

Beaver's next problem was plain to see, although he really hadn't fully realized it until now. Here he was, a considerable distance from his camp, or from that of Pale Moon's people. He had successfully carried out his hunt and had acquired meat. He was proud of his success, and of the way his horse had performed. His own use of the bow had pleased him. The thought flitted through his head that it was unfortunate that he had no one to witness his skill. He had performed the ritual apology and . . .

Aiee! The most important thing now was something he had not even given thought to. Here he was. His triumph lay before him, and the carcass of the yearling bull, nearly as large as his horse, must be butchered immediately, before it began to spoil.

He had helped with butchering sometimes. Everyone among the People did, when necessary. In the case of a highly successful hunt, every person beyond infancy would work through the night if necessary, to salvage every possible scrap of meat, skin, horn, and bone that could be utilized. The women were in charge, directing the tasks of the men with the heavier work, and those of the children, as they were able.

Here, there were no women to direct the process, or even tell him how to proceed. It was odd, he thought in passing, that he had never noticed this important function of the grandmothers.

There were several problems here. He knew that it was important to disembowel the kill to retard spoilage, especially in this heat of late summer. The intestines could be used for the storing of pemmican, as the white man uses those of cattle for the making of sausages. But they must be cooled and cleaned quickly on a day this warm. It might be better to waste the intestines, gutting out the kill to let it cool while he went for help in the butchering. The women back at the camp would know. Yes, he would do that first procedure and then hurry for help. He drew his knife.

Just at that moment a shadow swept across the prairie before him and he glanced up. A pair of buzzards circled overhead, riding the warm rising current, but now beginning to drop slowly with each circuit. The eyesight of Buzzard must be the world's keenest, he thought.

This brought another problem. If he removed the inside organs, even if he decided to discard them, this would give Buzzard and his mate access to the inside and to the desirable flesh of the kill. Buzzard's habits are unclean. On the heels of that thought, another: It was afternoon, and by dusk there would be coyotes, gathering for their rightful share of the kill. It has been so since Creation. Any leavings after Man takes his share of a kill belong to Coyote and to Buzzard.

Quickly, Beaver decided: He must have help. It was better to leave his kill intact, to avoid as much contamination as possible from Buzzard and Coyote.

He turned and stepped toward his roan mare, grazing quietly now that the excitement was over. Only then did he look beyond, to the crest of a low rise. There, calmly watching, was a party of well-armed warriors. His heartbeat jumped excitedly for a moment. Then it came to him. This was a good thing. They were probably members of Bull's Horn's band. He raised his right palm to signal his peaceful intention, but the newcomers did not return the greeting as they came forward. A cold dread crept over him, prickling the hairs on the back of his neck.

Six warriors. They rode slowly, deliberately, without a care, as if to show their contempt. He was a lone hunter, virtually helpless against the haughty, well-armed party if they chose to show force. At almost the same moment he realized that these were not Bull's Horn's people. Not at all. Their garments and weapons were not at all like those of the Lakotas. Who, then?

One of the men carried a large wooden war club. It was carved in a single piece, resembling a round hardwood ball with a grace-fully turned handle. There was ornate carving around the heavy ball and a vining leaf pattern up the handle. Even at the time, he thought it odd, the familiarity of that design. He had seen such carving somewhat recently.

Then it came to him, all at once. Pale Moon's father, the digni-fied old man from far away, had a pipe whose stem had similar vining leaf patterns. There was a moment of joy, quickly quenched by his next realization. It came like a plunge into cold water on a hot day. These warriors must come from a culture far away, some-what similar to Moon's people. His brief hope was dashed by the obvious explanation. These must be warriors of the "enemy" that Pale Moon's people described as pursuing their party of travelers. The former neighbors, who had killed many of the men, including Moon's husband.

Anger rose in him, but his main reaction was a wave of fear. These men had shown by their actions their disregard for the rights of others. Even for lives.

Beaver tried to remain calm as he continued to hold his right hand aloft in the sign of peace. The dark shadow of Buzzard's next circuit swept past across the open space between them as the riders approached. Their leader was tall and thin. Young, no more than thirty winters, Beaver thought. Probably ruthless. There were chuckles among his followers, still younger. Warriors still trying to prove themselves. A bad situation. He must try to communicate, and quickly. The others from the east had little experience with hand signs, but with these he was not certain. He must try something. Carefully, he lowered his raised hand and began to sign.

How are you called?

There was no sign of recognition or response. Not good. He tried again.

I have meat, he pointed to the freshly killed bull. *Let us camp and eat.*

This was a more obvious series of signs, and he thought he saw a tendency to relax a little. A very small amount. What next?

He pointed again to the fresh kill, and made the horizontal sign for hunger across his belly. There was a questioning look of partial understanding on the face of the young leader.

Beaver beckoned an invitation to dismount and camp. He was trying to think ahead, wondering what to do next. If he could induce the newcomers to give their attention to the fresh kill, he could possibly gain some time in which to try to devise a plan.

Moving slowly, talking in his own tongue, he pointed to some dead sticks in the scanty brush of a small gully.

Fire? he signed.

After what seemed a long moment, the leader nodded assent, and spoke to the others.

Almost instantly, they began to dismount, to talk among themselves, and to examine the buffalo kill. They pointed to the bull's right flank, where the feathered end of the arrow still jutted out. Beaver was proud of that shot himself.

He wondered if these men were accustomed to hunting buffalo on horseback. He had in his mind the idea that much of the eastern region was similar to the woodland area of the Eastern Band of the People, where they often wintered. He had never been there, but had heard their descriptions. It was virtually impossible to hunt on horseback among the trees. It was a puzzle to him, why people would want to live in such a place, with no chance to look at a distant horizon. But, to each his own.

Moving slowly, Beaver drew his knife and approached the buffalo carcass. He slit the belly and reached inside to pull the warm and still squirming intestines into the open. They could be discarded under these circumstances. In fact, the kill itself was now not as important as the attitude of these newcomers. They had already proven to be quite dangerous to the refugee party from the east.

Beaver had in mind building a fire and sharing food to establish better contact with these strangers. It is harder to consider one an enemy if you have eaten together. With this in mind, he chose a spot to pile some of the dry twigs for kindling a fire. As he did so, he motioned toward the kill, suggesting that they might proceed with the butchering. Two of the men did so.

As he drew out his flint and steel to start the fire, however, the leader of the newcomers intervened. With unmistakable gestures, the warrior indicated, even without hand sign experience, a very urgent fact.

No fire!

Beaver nodded agreement. What else could he do?

With several knives busy, it did not take long to convert a substantial amount of meat to portable dimensions, bundled in pieces of the animal's skin. Each rider prepared to carry as much as he was easily able.

Of course, thought Beaver. *They have their families traveling with them.*

They began to mount, and Beaver waited. There would be enough meat left for him to bundle together and return to Hungry Hawk's refugee camp at the pipestone quarry. He could still make a good impression on the family of Pale Moon. He considered, even, using the roan mare as a pack horse. He could tie all the meat possible to the animal's back and walk on foot himself. He could carry more meat that way. Not the most comfortable way to travel, of course, but more advantageous. Yes, that would do.

He was beginning to bundle some of the better cuts of meat into a portion of the hide as the others began to mount. It would be more comfortable, he thought, when they had departed. He turned back to his task.

There was an impatient gesture from the leader which could mean but one thing.

Come on!

Beaver was surprised, but there was no misinterpreting the gesture. He tried to improvise some signs. Even without sign talk experience, some gestures are almost universal.

He shook his head.

No. I go this way!

There was an angry, impatient expression on the face of the leader as he very firmly expressed the facts of the situation.

No. You come with us!

It was not an invitation, but a command. For the first time, Beaver began to realize something he had overlooked until now.

These people considered him their prisoner. Quite possibly, their surly leader thought that he was being generous to let a lone stranger live. They could have killed him already, but had not done so, because he offered food.

A chill crept up Beaver's spine as he hurriedly finished his ties and vaulted onto the roan's back behind the bundles.

<· ·>36

They arrived at the camp well before dark, and a curious group
of women and children gathered to stare at the stranger. They were
closer to the camp of the newcomers than he had thought.

Beaver was not certain of his status here. He did not seem to
be considered a captive, but he was watched closely. He was glad
that no one tried to take his weapons. He had not decided what
he would do in such a case. It would have to depend on the
apparent circumstances, he supposed. All in all it was a very uncomfortable situation. There was a tentative air, as if these people did
not know his status either. He was not treated as a captive, but
neither as a guest. He estimated that if he had not just made a
buffalo kill and offered to share, he might now be in real trouble.

With these thoughts in mind, he took his bundle of meat and
placed it with some of the others as a friendly gesture. His experience with Trades His Moccasins had taught him about communication when vocal language is not possible. Much can be done
with attitude, facial expression, and body language. He must not
show fear, or too much arrogance; interest, but not prying
curiosity.

Gradually, the tension relaxed as the women began to cook some of the meat from the kill. The stiff, reserved attitude of the men began to ease somewhat, and there were more attempts at communication, with mostly poor results.

The leader of the warrior-hunter party remained arrogant and aloof. A couple of older men, who had not been with the hunting party, made an effort to communicate, apparently trying several languages, but without success. None of the attempts produced even a word that Beaver could understand.

Then, suddenly, one of the old men spoke to the other, almost excitedly. The other looked surprised, then nodded, and both began to talk at once. They turned back to Beaver, still talking, and beckoned to him to follow them. Seeing no reason to do otherwise, he did so.

Resting in the shade of a brush lean-to was an old woman. Her skin was an expanse of tiny wrinkles, as if it had been exposed to the heat of many summers and the chill of the intervening winters. Her face was placid, and her eyes sharp and knowing. She appeared bright and alert, and it was apparent that among these, as among his own people, the elders were honored.

Beaver waited while the two old men talked to the woman. He did not understand a word, but one thing was plain. They were asking for something or some action on her part, and she was refusing with a shake of her head.

They continued to plead, and finally she shrugged in surrender. Instantly, the two men were smiling and nodding, both talking at once again. The old woman silenced them with a gesture and turned to look at Beaver. Her eyes swept him up and down, and he somehow felt that she was looking into his very soul.

Finally, she nodded slowly, and spoke to him. The words were familiar, though poorly spoken, and for a moment he did not recognize the tongue she was using. It was not his own, but somewhat familiar . . . *Ah!* He realized, now. A neighbor of the People, the Head Splitters, used this talk. The two tribes, once enemies, had long ago become allies in a defense against a mutual enemy. They now camped together, sometimes hunted together, and attended each other's Sun Dance and other festivals. This old woman must have had contact, at one time, with the Head Splitters.

Beaver, while not proficient in the tongue of this allied tribe, could use it a little.

"You . . . The Head Splitters, Grandmother?" he asked.

The old woman turned and spat, narrowly missing his moccasin.

"You . . . One of *them*?" she asked haltingly, as she remembered the unfamiliar sounds.

"No, no," he assured. "I . . . a trader."

He thought it just as well not to mention the close ties of the People to a tribe she obviously detested.

"You know their tongue, Grandmother?" he asked.

There was a string of bitter invective, some of which he did not understand. As far as he could tell, it was mostly in the language of the Head Splitters, and included reference to a variety of unpleasant topics, mostly involving excrement. He gathered that she had been with the Head Splitters as a captive, probably long ago. Possibly she had been sold to them, perhaps as a slave wife.

"You were a captive?" he continued.

The woman nodded.

"They bought me, to wife!"

"You had children with them?"

"No!" Her temper flared. "I cut the throat of the man who held me, and ran away, back to my people!"

She used several unmistakable gestures during this tirade. "Cut the throat" was obvious.

Beaver shuddered, feeling a mixture of emotions. Here was a woman, probably a beauty in her day, who had been kidnapped and sold into slavery. Possibly sold and resold, subjected to abuse, cruel and sadistic treatment. Such things were not uncommon. But she had managed to escape and find her way back to her own people. Such a woman would be admired and cherished among Beaver's tribe.

"It is good, Grandmother," he said respectfully.

"Who are you? What do you want?" she demanded.

"I am called Beaver," he answered, using the hand sign for "beaver" also, because he was not certain about the word in the tongue of the Head Splitters.

The woman nodded impatiently.

"I came here as a trader," he went on, "looking for the place of the red pipestone. Your people came here from far away?"

"Yes. From East."

"I am from the South."

She nodded, something like a sneer flitting across her face.

"Yes. Head Splitters!"

She gave him a dark look.

"Not Head Splitters, Grandmother. I am Elk-dog People."

"Just as bad!" she snapped.

This was not going well, and he decided to change the subject.

"I was trading with a party from the East," he began cautiously. "They are growers . . ."

A bitter and derisive sneer crossed her face.

"Yes. Enemies. We kill them."

It was plain that she understood, and did not approve of his contact with the people of Hungry Hawk's party.

The two men who had made the introduction were standing, watching the conversation unfold. Their facial expressions indicated that they were amused at the progress. One of them spoke to the old woman, and she turned to Beaver with a question.

"Why you camp alone?"

Then, before he could phrase an answer, there was another pointed exchange between her and the old men. She turned to him again.

"They say, where you camp?"

"Place of red stone," he pointed.

Instantly, he knew that it was a mistake. These were surely the enemy of Hungry Hawk, and of the woman Beaver loved. Now they would be able to find the other party, and more killing was likely. Maybe, even, he had now caused even more danger to Pale Moon and her people. The old woman was relaying his answer to the two elders, and they were talking with intensity to each other and to the old woman.

She turned.

"Where your trade goods? You no trader!"

He must stick as closely as possible to the truth . . .

"Not here. My . . ." he struggled with the unfamiliar words of the Peoples' neighbor . . . Partner? Brother? Yes, that would do in this case. "My brother and his woman . . . That way!" he pointed.

There was a long silence, and the two men looked at each other, exchanged a few words, and turned to the woman again. She listened, then spoke to Beaver.

"They say you lie. We saw trader, woman, baby. Trader not say about you. You lie!"

"No, no. I was with them, before. We . . . Uh . . . Split." He supplemented with hand gesture. "Back together, maybe so, later."

He was running thin on ways to express himself to these people.

There was another brief discussion between the old men, they spoke to the woman again, and she turned back to Beaver.

"You not trader. Hunter! For who?"

"Other people. At red stone place . . ."

He might as well stay as close to the truth as possible. He continued. "Place of safety. Sacred place. Nobody fight, there."

The woman translated, there was another discussion, and she spoke to him again.

"Who says, no fight?"

"Lakota," Beaver answered quickly. "*Their* sacred place. No fight, no kill."

This was passed on, and received with indignant grunts, some more conversation, and the old woman turned back.

"They say, *we* say about no fight, not Lakotas."

These people did not understand the might and strength of the Lakotas, Beaver decided. He knew of no way to convince them.

"Very strong, many warriors, Lakota," he told her. "Big. Many sleeps, Lakota all around."

He felt that he was not really able to express the power and size of the mighty Lakota nation. These people simply did not understand. They also seemed to fail to see the concept of a "safe" place, where by decree or agreement there would be no killing. His attempt to explain seemed to fall on deaf ears.

Evening was coming on, and he had no blankets or robe. He must determine his status, and whether he would be permitted to leave.

He noted, as he ate the meat that had been handed to him by one of the women, that the two old men were talking seriously with the young warrior who had been the leader of the hunting party. The thought crossed his mind that they might be discussing what to do with him. There had been no action on the part of anyone which had seemed threatening, but he had been watched closely.

An idea came to him, and he strolled over to the woman who spoke a little of the Head Splitter tongue.

"Grandmother," he said respectfully, "I must go. My camp, my blankets. Night comes. You tell them?"

She studied him a moment, then yelled in a remarkable strong voice, something to a group of warriors at one of the fires. An elder, one of those involved in the earlier conversation, rose and approached. The woman apparently told him what Beaver had said, and they conversed a little. Then she turned back to Beaver again.

"They say no," she said. "Give you a blanket. Here!"

She handed him a threadbare trade blanket, then gave him a big toothless grin.

"You sleep with me?"

It was with great relief that he realized she was teasing, but he blushed deeply at the general laughter over the old woman's joke.

He hoped that the blanket was relatively clean, and free from vermin. In any case, he doubted that he could sleep.

<>**37**

Beaver chose a spot near one of the fires, and spread his borrowed blanket. He was still somewhat concerned over the possibility of lice or other parasites in the fabric. Still, there was no other alternative that he could see. It made no sense to attempt to leave as darkness fell, since he was in unfamiliar territory. In addition, his status as a stranger in the camp of an unfamiliar tribe made him cautious. There was no point in asking for trouble.

He expected to have difficulty sleeping, but it had been an arduous and exciting day. He woke once to find, to his surprise, that considerable time had passed. The stars of the Seven Hunters had rotated through a wide segment of the night sky. It was puzzling, because he had thought that he had only dozed for a moment. He shifted to a more comfortable position and stared at the sky for a little while. An owl glided noiselessly overhead, blotting out a patch of stars in its course as it passed. A distant coyote yodeled his song. Finally, Beaver fell asleep again.

He dreamed the now familiar feeling that he was wrapped in the warm embrace of a woman. Yet, as before, he could not identify her. It could be, however, none but the beautiful young widow, Pale Moon. Thoughts of her flitted through his mind continually, like a bright butterfly attending the blossoms of the orange prairie milk-weed. It must be something intended to be. The possibility excited his entire being, causing his heart to beat faster and his breathing deeper, and the excitement wakened him.

Again, Beaver felt the odd puzzle he had experienced before. He must try to distinguish between the dream world and that of reality. Which was the dream, and which real? The unidentified woman in his bed had seemed so real, so warm and desirable, yet had proved to be only a dream. Now, the same dream had wakened him again, and he lay there in frustration, trying to make sense of what was happening to him.

He could hear the soft snores of some of the other sleepers in the immediate area. It was just enough of a distraction to keep him awake for a little while. He listened to the night sounds, and wondered what the dawn of the coming day might bring. To this point, he did not know the intentions of these people, or even which direction their travel might take them. Would they expect, or even demand, that he accompany their party, or would they assume that it was time to part ways? If he could determine somehow which direction was their intent, he could choose another. If, in fact, they would allow him to do so. Of that, he was still not certain.

It would seem, however, that if he were considered a captive, there would not have been certain kindnesses, such as the blanket that now warmed him against the night's chill. Or, in fact, the attempt to communicate through the old woman which had not met with much success.

Still, these people and their leaders seemed more curious than aggressive toward him. It was a fortunate thing, he realized now, that he had made a buffalo kill. If he had not been able to offer them meat, the contact with these warriors could have been far different.

He sighed, and rolled to his side to change positions. Even with a blanket, the ground is a hard bed.

From the corner of his eye, Beaver glimpsed a light, and turned to look. There, on the eastern horizon, the edge of a crescent moon pushed its way silently above the horizon. He had always found it fascinating to watch the rising moon, especially when it was full, or shortly after. He recalled that some of his most impressive experiences were related to such an event. This moon was well past full. In fact, a mere sliver of bright reflection. Still, it was impressive, spiking up above earth's rim like a tongue of orange flame.

Even as he pondered on this scene, his attention was distracted by a sound. The sound of female laughter. It was not like the hearty laugh of a boisterous male, but more like a soft murmur of water over stones. He now recognized its familiarity, with a bit of puzzlement as well as irritation. It was the sound he had heard before when he had seen the small human-like figure against the horizon.

Yes, there, against the thin slice of moon-glow, like the slice of a pumpkin at harvest, he could see motion. It was much as before. The small figure, becoming familiar now, was welcome to him, the most reality he had experienced since he encountered this militant group of warriors.

There was also a new and different feeling this time, entirely different from previous experience. Previously the human-like chuckle seemed to tease and taunt. It had been an irritation to him.

Now, in this setting, where he was in a potentially dangerous situation, it came as a comfort. He did not understand it, but he now remembered the wise words of one of the elders. Words to the effect that some things are not meant to be understood, only experienced.

These words came back to him now. He had originally been puzzled, startled, a little frightened, maybe, by the small figure he had seen or thought he saw. He had thrown into the scene a doubt, a denial. He had not been able to accept what now appeared to be an attempt to help.

With this reassuring thought, his attitude toward the apparition was changing rapidly. From a question and denial, he was quickly altering his position. He was ready to accept, not deny or challenge, what he saw and experienced. *Yes, it is real. I do not have to understand.*

As this mood of satisfaction came over him, he began to feel a sense of communication with what he now regarded as the Little Person. There was no time or incentive to question now. Whatever was in progress was already happening, and it was good. The soft rippling chuckle still had a teasing tone, but it was now supporting, rather than annoying. He found that although words were not spoken, the ideas came clearly. They seemed to flow through or around the audible sounds, not the same, but related. The sounds were not a language, but a means to convey ideas. Yet, what is that, but language?

Do not try to understand came at him again.

"Let it be so," he murmured wearily.

Yes! came the thought back at him. *Now we can begin.*

"What am I to do?"

There was no answer.

He rose to an elbow and peered toward the moon. Its full crescent had now floated above the horizon, and he could not see any trace of the small figure.

Had the whole thing been a dream? It was possible. But, if so, how had he now come to feel that he was receiving help, in some strange way? He still did not understand, but he had acquired a sense of confidence that enabled him to return to sleep.

<>

When he woke again, the yellow-gray of the false dawn was beginning to pale in the east. People were stirring, some moving away from the camp to empty bladders or bowels as nature called.

Beaver rose, shook out his blanket and folded it to return it to its owner. Then he attended to his own bladder's call and went to seek out the old woman who was his only means of communication. As he did so, one of the two older men who had set up that line of communication joined him.

Beaver felt a great deal more confident than he had last evening. Somehow, the world was a better place.

It may have been only a dream, he told himself, but *does it matter*?

Don't try to understand. Accept. The thought drifted through his consciousness, and he smiled to himself. Somehow, he was learning, was realizing that there are many things intended to remain mysteries to mere mortals. He was feeling a revelation; he imagined it to be somewhat like that on a vision quest.

Yet, here I go again, trying to understand. But the thought was amusing now, not troubling. There might be troubles ahead, but he was gaining patience and confidence.

He handed the borrowed blanket to the elder, with smiles and gestures to indicate his thanks. It seemed that there was mutual understanding, and he saddled the roan to depart.

A short while ago he would have been concerned whether he would have been allowed to leave. Now this concern was largely behind him. He realized that having become more confident had made his presence more acceptable. Now, it was logical to these travelers that he go on with his own affairs.

There was a lingering dread. He was certain that these travelers must be the "enemy" referred to by Hungry Hawk's party. If so, they were in grave danger, and he must warn them.

An even more serious danger seemed to cast a cloud over the entire situation. Beaver had the strong impression that his erstwhile hosts were somehow lacking in leadership. The young warrior who had led the hunting party he had encountered seemed impulsive. Spotted Crow was his name, Beaver had learned through the old woman. There seemed to be no real leader with the maturity to exercise good judgment.

The elders who had helped him were probably concerned. They may have been leaders in the hunt or in war, but were now past their prime. The young men would follow a charismatic leader like Spotted Crow.

Beaver's concern was for the people of Pale Moon, who felt secure in the safe haven of the pipestone quarry. They had been told by the Lakota chieftain, Bull's Horn, that they would be safe there.

At this point, however, neither Bull's Horn or the leaders of Pale Moon's party knew that the newcomers under Spotted Crow had no intention of honoring the safe haven.

Beaver kicked his horse into a gentle lope. He did not know how much time he might have.

<> **38**

"Where have you been?" asked the old woman who spoke enough Cherokee to talk with him. "Your fire was dead, but your pack still here. We were worried."

Seeking out Hungry Hawk, leader of the refugee band, Beaver explained, through the woman, what had happened, and his estimate of the danger.

"But, this place, the Lakotas said it is a safe haven."

Beaver nodded. "True," he agreed. "But I am made to think your enemy will not honor it."

A look of grave concern came over the face of Hungry Hawk. Beaver was just beginning to realize the grave danger that now faced this party. They did not have enough fighting men to defend themselves against an attack by the band with whom he had spent the night. He could help, but he was only one, and with no fighting experience. They would still be badly outnumbered.

He looked at the young widow, his heart reaching out to her. He wanted to hold her, as he had held the woman in his dream. She smiled, and his heart melted. At that moment, he would have done anything for her.

Die for her? his inner thoughts demanded.

There must be a better way.

⟨⟩

He had no idea how much time there might be available. The other party was apparently moving about, looking at the country. They could arrive here at the quarry today, tomorrow, or not at all. But, he realized that there must be some sort of a plan. He could not wait until the attack occurred, or even until the enemy arrived. That would be too late.

In the back of his mind dwelt another concern, too. Trades His Moccasins had been under the influence of the eagle-head pipe, whose owner was deceased. They had assumed that restoring the pipe to its place of origin would remove the curse. It lay where it had been tossed, but was there any real reason to think that the curse was lifted?

That thought had nagged at him from time to time. He would ponder it later, but for now there were more pressing problems. A plan for defense, or escape from attack was desperately needed.

As if on demand, an idea struck him. What about the hidden cave into which he had fallen? Had this been a sign?

He started for the cave to look again. Could it be that the entire party could fit into that hidden space?

As he passed the Lovers' Leap, he noted the wrapped parcel with the pipe that had caused so much trouble. At least, *maybe*. There was something about that . . . Well, no time now. He could ponder that later.

The cave was as he remembered, wide but low-ceilinged. An adult could sit cross-legged and upright with little difficulty. But was there space for all? He counted quickly. Nearly twenty people, he estimated. He crawled around in the dim, green-tinted light, trying to visualize people sitting here. Yes, he thought. Crowded, but enough space for the purpose. He tried not to think of what would happen if they were discovered. A fire at the entrance, smoke sucked through the cavern and out the crack at the top . . . He did not want to think about it.

<>

He returned to his own camp, pausing a moment as he passed the Lovers' Leap. Again, he was attracted to the carefully wrapped pipe, lying in plain sight on the flat surface of the stone column. It was as if its very spirit reached out to him. He squatted on his heels for a moment, staring at the buckskin packet. Its mystery seemed so near, yet so far. It seemed to have no connection to his present problems. Yet, why was he constantly distracted by this object, when he should be thinking of some manner of defense or escape? He rose, and hurried back toward the camp.

<>

It was late afternoon now. Beaver had explained, as best he could with the difficulty in language, about the hiding place. He had taken Hungry Hawk and a couple of the leaders to show them the possibility of concealment in the cave. He dreaded the idea of close, cramped confinement in the cavern. He had grown up on the open prairie, in wide open spaces with the family dwelling a skin lodge. Later, a lodge of canvas. He had, a few times, entered a more permanent house, such as the growers used. Always, he had felt the close, uncomfortable sensation of being trapped in such a structure, with no means of escape.

All of this now came back to him as he demonstrated the possibility of hiding the entire party in this hidden cave.

The elders examined carefully, talked between them, pointing here and there, nodding sometimes. It was apparent that they saw the same advantages and drawbacks that Beaver recognized. On the other hand, these men had grown up in permanent dwellings of logs and earth.

Finally, they nodded approval. They returned to the camp, and as they gathered around the evening fire, the leaders explained the plan. At least, Beaver hoped so. He understood very little of the dialogue but had to assume that the leaders had the wisdom to explain the plan to the others. It was critical to the survival of them all. One slight mistake could lead to the deaths of everyone in the party.

<>

It was in the afternoon of the following day that the scouts who had been posted saw riders in the distance. It would be some time before they were near enough to identify, but it was necessary to act, now.

The plan had been carefully outlined. There was no possibility of concealing the fact that a number of people had camped here. It was also impossible to carry all of their possessions into the hiding place. Some things must be left behind to be plundered by the enemy. Maybe that activity would distract them from further search.

In his heart, Beaver knew that it would not distract the raiders for very long.

<>

The move to the cave was orderly. It must be so, very deliberate and well planned. The horses had been herded to a distant canyon where there was water and grass. They would not wander far. At least, it was hoped so. But the two young men who had moved them would remain in the area to keep watch, rather than rejoining the rest of the band. If the group survived, they would need the horses.

It was not known how long their concealment must last, so every waterskin and gourd flask had been filled. Food was scarce, but for a few days . . . No one knew, of course, how long the enemy might choose to stay.

The women, children, and elders were settled in the cavern, while the scouts continued to watch the approach of the expected enemy party. Beaver remained outside with two others until it was necessary for them to retreat, also.

There were about ten or twelve riders in the approaching party. Maybe, thought Beaver, it would have been possible to defend themselves. But no, he quickly realized. These riders were well-armed warriors, bent on destruction, and outnumbering Hungry Hawk's fighting men anyway.

As they drew nearer, the fugitives quietly retreated down the footpath to the canyon, drew the curtain of vegetation aside, and slipped into the cavern. The few children in the party were cautioned again by parents, and everyone settled in uneasily to wait for whatever was to come.

⟨⟩

It was not long. They heard the sound of hoofbeats, a surprised pause, and warriors calling back and forth over the discovery of an abandoned camp. It was apparent to the intruders, of course, that the occupants had left hurriedly, leaving many possessions behind. They could hear the riders calling to each other in surprise.

The next thing, of course, would be the search. What if they were discovered? Almost in a panic, Beaver felt trapped, with no way out.

No! he told himself. *Stay calm*!

He took a deep breath or two. This was going as expected. They must stay still. Any sound could cause the death of them all.

On the positive side, the day was drawing to an end. Through the foliage over the cave's entrance, Beaver could note the change in the quality of the light outside. The hot white of the afternoon sun was fading to a soft golden glow, as the day began to make way for night.

There was a sound of motion on the footpath outside, the soft shuffle of moccasinned feet on earth and stone. A lone warrior, Beaver guessed. Maybe two. A shadow fell across the mouth of the little cavern and moved on.

Just then, there was a quiet chortle from the infant in Pale Moon's arms. The footsteps outside ceased suddenly as the warrior stopped to listen. Beaver turned to see, in the dim light, the young mother covering the baby's mouth with her palm, preventing any outcry.

Apparently, the warrior outside, hearing no further sound, decided to investigate no further. He moved on up the trail.

It was darkening rapidly now, heavy shadows smothering the canyon like a thrown blanket. It was apparent that the enemy would be camping above, probably plundering the camp site and stealing anything worthwhile. Meanwhile, it was essential to remain quiet through the night, until the intruders departed.

It was a restless, terrifying night for everyone in the cramped quarters of the cave in the canyon. It seemed forever before the yellow light of dawn began to filter through the crack in the stone overhead, and through the curtain of vines that covered the entrance to the cave.

They could hear the activity of the war party above. Beaver had hesitated to think of it as a war party, but now had to concede. They had hidden for their lives from men who wanted to kill them.

It seemed to take forever for the party above to prepare to leave. It grew gradually lighter in the cave, but until the enemy departed, they must remain here, and remain still.

Beaver looked around the cave through the gradually retreating darkness. How had everyone fared? More to the point, how had the beautiful young Pale Moon fared? There had been a time or two during the night when he considered trying to find her in the dark. He had a feeling that the night might have been much less unpleasant in her arms.

Now, in the dim light of early dawn, he searched for her. Finally, he saw her, at the far corner of the cavern. She bent over the infant in her arms, crying. Two other women sat next to her, appearing to comfort her. But *why*?

The awful truth descended on him now, making the blackness that lingered in the corners of the cave seem evil and ugly. It was something that he had not even foreseen, and could hardly accept, even now.

Pale Moon had seen that her baby was crying out, and would reveal their hiding place. She had smothered it to save her people.

<⬩>39

Before the sun was high, the enemy party had departed.

Beaver was completely overwhelmed by the shocking discovery that the infant of Pale Moon was dead. It was an event that would have seemed impossible to him had he realized what was happening.

Then, too, a death should be mourned. Among his own people, there would be the singing of songs of mourning. The ritual would continue for three days, until the spirit was assumed to have crossed over, and then the People would return to the ways of the living.

But this was an entirely different situation. He did not know the ways of Pale Moon's people. Of one thing he was certain, though. The girl had saved her people. Thinking back to the evening, he recalled the shadowy figures on the trail outside the cave. There had been a moment when there was a muffled sound in the dimness of the cave, the small animal sound that an infant makes. He had noted it, as had everyone in the cave. That had been a critical moment, while everyone almost hesitated to breathe. It had passed, and the enemy warrior outside had moved on. There was little doubt that the man had heard something. But, since only silence had followed, he had probably assumed that it had been a small wild creature. A mouse, perhaps, or a chipmunk. The man was satisfied.

Now, Beaver struggled with a knowledge that he had not even realized at the time. He could visualize the terrible decision on the part of Pale Moon. Crouched in the darkening cavern while the enemy lingered outside, listening . . . What a dreadful choice! If the child had cried out again, they might all be dead by this time. Or more likely, before darkness fell last evening.

He found himself torn between two feelings. He admired the courage and strength that it had required to suffocate her baby, her own flesh and blood, the only part of her deceased husband that was left to her. Such strength of purpose, such courage. The young mother's decision and her deed in saving the others would be told and retold around the story fires for generations: "The one who saved her people." Probably her name would be changed to commemorate the event.

He realized now that he had already decided, even before the event in the cave, that he must have this woman. His heart had gone out to her, in the sorrow of her bereavement. That of her husband, not this new loss. He had accepted the fact that Pale Moon was the one in his vision. She was, without a doubt, the warmly delicious woman in his arms in the recurrent dream that had been such a puzzle. Maybe not so much a puzzle now, though. This event must have been foreseen and shown to him.

Now, he longed to hold and comfort her. That thought had crossed his mind many times in recent days. He could be of help in her time of trouble, offering her security.

He did not know, now, how and when to approach the subject. Probably, he decided, not until after her three days of mourning. As far as he was aware, most tribes assumed that crossing to the Other Side requires three days. He could bide his time, show sympathy but not press forward too quickly. That would be an intrusion on her grief, and he had no wish to add to her problems.

⟨⟩

It was not long after full daylight that a couple of scouts had slipped out of the cave and carefully surveyed the area. As they had suspected, the enemy had plundered their camp, stolen everything worth carrying, and burned most of the brush shelters.

There was some talk of the futility of expecting the safe haven status of the pipestone quarry to hold any meaning to the enemy. They had surely violated any such taboo.

"That is their problem, not ours!" said one of the older women.

They fell to work rebuilding and salvaging what they could.

⟨⟩

As they worked, Beaver kept his doubts and troubles to himself. He had been traveling light, had taken his blankets to the cave, and the roan mare arrived back in good shape with the other horses. He had seen no other course of action, but was greatly relieved when the horse herders returned with no problems.

As he passed back and forth during the resettling of the camp, several times he found himself glancing aside at the Lovers' Leap. Something about it seemed to call out to him, something he did not understand. Its story was a romantic bit of nonsense. In the real world, there were better ways to impress a woman than risking life and limb in a symbolic feat of daring. He wondered, even, if a smart and capable woman might laugh at a young man who would do such a stupid thing just to try to impress her.

At one point, he paused to squat on his heels and stare for a little while at the buckskin-wrapped bundle on the top of the pillar. He was missing something, and the more he tried to think about it, the more confused he became. Could it be the puzzle as to how the successful leaper would come down from the rock? He thought not. Probably any exhibitionist who would try the leap would want an audience. Probably, the girl he wished to impress. Then, if he were successful, she could toss him a rope. If not, he would land at the base of the rock, probably injured. That would be a mixed blessing. It might arouse sorrow and pity on the part of the woman he had tried to impress. On the other hand, an intelligent woman might consider the whole stunt to be a rather stupid display of incompetence. Of one thing he was certain: He had no intention of trying to take the leap. That would be for someone not as mature and understanding as himself. Besides, his potential mate, after the harsh blows that life had given her, would not be impressed by a foolish act of bragging.

He rose to return to the camp area, glancing back once at the wrapped pipe. There was still the puzzle of its meaning, and its possible curse or evil influence. Trades His Moccasins had certainly been affected by the pipe's medicine, even though he had been an innocent participant. It was good that the pipe had been returned, Beaver thought as he stared at it.

The intricate beadwork on the light-colored buckskin seemed to glow, seeming almost to move as he stared at it. He knew that could not be, yet there was something different here. Something *wrong*. Why was he so powerfully drawn to the object? And, had not Trades His Moccasins, had not Cactus Flower, all three of them been convinced that by returning the pipe, the curse had been lifted?

He stopped still, and turned to stare again. What if it had *not*?

Surely there would not have been a transfer of such a curse to an entirely different party of impoverished refugees.

Beaver moved on, still uncomfortable over the things about this which he did not understand. Why did he continue to have these questions about the red stone pipe?

⟨⟩

He avoided contact with Pale Moon. It was her time of mourning, and he was not certain of the customs of her people. He could be patient; let her finish her grieving. Then he could attempt to approach her in courtship. The customs of her people were still a mystery to him, but her family had seemed to look with favor on him.

Once, in the course of coming and going in the camp, their eyes met. Beaver's heart jumped, and he tried to convey sympathy and concern as best he could without speaking. His spirit reached out to comfort hers. In her eyes, he could read gratitude for his understanding.

At least, he thought so. Better, though, to wait until the presumed days of mourning were over before making any overt moves. He nodded a greeting and moved on.

⟨ ⟩

He decided to take the mare and try for another kill. The little camp would need meat, and his first, though a successful hunt, had come to nothing through circumstances. He might find game again, but even if not, this hunt would remove him from the uncomfortable period of mourning.

In the back of his mind as he rode out came the old question: Could it be that these continuing misfortunes had some connection? Were they somehow related to each other, or to a common cause?

Beaver could think of none, but he saw no game larger than a rabbit, and had no clear shot at that. He returned to camp empty handed. He would try again tomorrow.

⟨ ⟩

He dreamed that night, beginning with a fruitless hunt that was indistinguishable from his real hunt of the day. He saw no game, and returned to sleep on an empty belly. At this point he was again unsure . . . Dream or reality.

Now, he dreamed that he slept, and again experienced the sensation and warmth of a woman in his arms. Again, it was not anyone whom he could identify, but it was a very pleasant interlude, soul-satisfying and comfortable. He was now ready to concede, however, that the woman of his dreams must be Pale Moon.

As he turned in his blankets to waken and change positions, he had a strange thought. This was not *quite* the same dream as before. As his dream journey carried him over familiar territory, he felt that another factor had been inserted in the dream. It was an odd thing. Somehow, he felt he had overlooked something. When he searched for the missing ingredient, his thoughts kept slipping back to the oddest thing: The red stone pipe in its buckskin wrap, perched on Lovers' Leap.

As he came completely awake, he heard again the soft laughter that he had come to associate with the Little People.

◁▷40

He decided to try another hunt on the following day. Still, in the back of his mind was the thought of staying away until the time of mourning was past for Pale Moon.

Yet, aside from this, there were other factors to consider. Who has not, at some time or other, harbored the wish to return to the safety of childhood? The world was simpler then, with others making the decisions. But, it becomes a responsibility that, after a certain point, cannot be avoided.

Beaver was being tested by a combination of events, some of which were still only partly understood. As he rode, he considered some of the puzzling events that had come into his life.

There was, of course, the immediate need for meat for the small band to which he had attached himself. He was not quite sure how *that* had happened, but it was real and unavoidable now. He felt a responsibility there.

He was pleased, and a little proud, that he had been able to find a way to save the entire band to which the young widow belonged. That had been a great triumph, and had greatly increased his prestige with the girl's people. He could tell that he was regarded with increasing respect.

Yet, at this point in his thinking, he repeatedly encountered a problem that he was unable to answer. He had tried to brush it aside, to ignore it, to deny it as a problem, but it was always there. In simplest terms, it kept resurfacing as a question in his mind:

Can I live with a woman who has killed her own child?

Time after time, he went through the pattern of reasoning: There was no other way, he told himself. If Pale Moon had done otherwise, had not silenced the infant's involuntary cries, they would have been heard by the war party. In that case, everyone in the refugee camp would now be dead. That, he recalled again and again, would include himself. If it were not for Pale Moon's courage and sacrifice, he too would be dead.

Each time his thinking reached this point, it came back at him again, in the same way. Could he live with such a woman? He did not know. He often thought how much better it would have been if he had never met this young woman and her people. Then he would try to think of something else to occupy his mind.

That was not entirely successful. Even without the threat of the militant war party bent on destruction, there were other festering doubts in Beaver's life. There was still the mystery of the pipestone, which had originally brought him on this pilgrim quest. He had to admit, he was no nearer to an answer for his doubts and questions than when he started. He had no answers at all, and in addition, there was still the mystical pull of the eagle pipe that lay on the top of the stone pillar in the canyon. Its return should have answered problems, but seemed only to produce more. He was still drawn to the object in a way he did not understand. Several times he had spent a while on the cliff opposite the Lovers' Leap, staring at the wrapped pipe. He could not have explained his fascination with the object, but its spirit seemed to reach out to him. It was calling, he sometimes felt, as if it carried a message of some sort. But, had not that been solved when it was returned to its source? They had assumed so, but now he had increasing doubt.

Overlying all of these puzzling doubts were his recurrent dreams. These included the visits from the mysterious "Giggles." He was never sure whether contact with her occurred during sleep or as a vision. Still, there was an unmistakable quality in those dreams which let him distinguish the ones with special meaning. He had begun to be able to accept the help she offered him without question, though he did not understand it.

There was also the repetitious dreamlike sensation of a woman's love, the comfort and safety that they found in each other's arms. This still seemed to be not entirely sexual in nature, although that might be a factor. It was more of a mutual protection, a security that he felt. That *both* felt, he assumed, and he had come to feel that it pertained to Pale Moon. If so, however, why would he have these doubts about how she had been able to smother her baby? How could he question his own ability to accept her sacrifice?

There was one moment that day in which he felt the urge to simply turn the roan mare to the south and ride back toward his own people in the rolling tallgrass prairie. But it was only a passing thought. He realized that he had accepted the responsibilities with his coming of age. He only wished to be able to fulfill them. For now, he only hoped to be able to *identify* them.

<>

He had ridden some distance from the quarry, and considered returning, even though empty-handed. It would not be wise to travel after dark in unfamiliar country.

One more look to the northwest from the crest of the rolling hill just ahead, he decided. He dismounted and topped the hill on foot for the last few steps to present a low profile. It was not unheard of to startle and drive off buffalo with a sudden unexpected appearance.

Even so, as he topped the rise, Beaver was surprised. He ducked behind a bush and quickly tried to evaluate what he saw . . . A band of people on the trail. Their advance scouts and outriders indicated that this must be a band of families on the move. Yes, he could see the dragging lodgepoles, the travois and the band's horse herd, driven on the downwind side of the main column by the young men. He had served that function himself a few years earlier.

Lakotas, probably, he decided. The thought crossed his mind to wonder how far out from the pipestone quarry the safe haven zone might extend. Still, he was not greatly concerned. The risk in this area would be largely from the outsiders who had been harassing the fugitives of Hungry Hawk's party.

One of the leaders of the front of the column seemed familiar . . . Yes, Bull's Horn! Beaver was pleased. It would be good to let the chieftain know of the violation of the safe haven at the quarry.

Beaver mounted and rode over the crest, his right arm lifted in the peace gesture. There was no change in the direction or speed of the travelers. A pair of riders detached from the party of leaders at the head of the column, and loped forward at an easy pace.

The scouts drew up as they neared the rise where Beaver sat, and returned his hand-sign.

Bull's Horn? Beaver signed, pointing to the approaching column.

It is so, signed one of the riders.

Good!

How are you called? queried the scout.

I am Beaver.

Yes! You were with the Trader?

That is true, Beaver agreed.

Trader is with us.

He is here?

Yes. That is true. He is injured.

Trader is hurt?

Yes. Bad wound, answered the scout.

This was quite frustrating, but it would take a little time to find what had occurred, even with hand signs to help.

Trader's woman? The child? he signed.

The scout nodded assent, and pointed toward the advancing column.

Hurt, he signed again.

Wounded? Who? The Woman? Beaver asked.

No! The Trader.

Beaver kicked the mare into a lope and hurried toward the approaching column. He paused briefly to make the expected amenities to Bull's Horn as leader of the band, then hurried on toward the rear of the procession. The wounded man would be transported by travois, which would place him near the end of the train.

He expected a serious injury to Trades His Moccasins, but was totally unprepared for what he now confronted. Cactus Flower rode one of the horses, her baby tucked in the traditional backpack used by her people. On a lead rope behind them was another horse, which Beaver recognized as one of the pack animals. It pulled a pole-drag travois, which carried a couple of tattered packs, and a man whom Beaver could scarcely recognize.

He jumped from the mare and approached, as Cactus Flower drew her horse to a stop.

"Beaver!" she cried. "Trades His Moccasins needs you."

He paused only a moment.

"I am here, now," he told the girl as he passed. He saw tears on her usually cheerful face.

The trader's eyes were closed, but opened slowly as the bumping of the travois ceased. Cactus Flower had come to a stop. The rest of the procession moved on, but that was no matter for concern. They would stop for the night.

"Beaver!" he said weakly, but with a great sense of urgency. "I need . . . Pipe!"

"Yes, my friend, we did that," Beaver reminded. "You returned it to its place."

A look of great concern distorted the face of the injured man.

"No, no . . . Its spirit . . . Trapped."

This made no sense to Beaver, and he was increasingly concerned for his friend's life.

"We will talk of this," agreed Beaver. "Let me help you to a place where you can rest. I will stay with you."

He tried to speak with a lot more confidence than he felt. Maybe he should talk to Cactus Flower to learn what had occurred and the nature of her husband's injuries.

Trades His Moccasins had drifted off again. There was much Beaver did not know about all this, but so far, he saw nothing good.

◄ ►41

The story poured out in a rush, accompanied by the tears of Cactus Flower, while her husband slept from exhaustion.

Almost from the time they had left the pipestone quarry, she related, nothing had gone well. Trades His Moccasins had been confident that the curse of the eagle-head pipe had been removed by returning it to its place of origin. Minor problems could be accounted for by chance. Within a short while, however, the same problems began to plague them again. A lame horse, a pack's ties loosening, another spilling of valuable goods into a stream through an unexplained rent in the pack cover. There must be something they had overlooked, the trader had theorized. Something involving the pipe.

Why had restoration to its place not been successful?

Then had come the event that had placed the trader in his present condition. It was not much of a story. Trades His Moccasins had been setting up camp for the night, and was gathering sticks for the fire. A party of riders approached, armed to hunt or for war, though not painted as a war party might be. The trader had welcomed them as potential customers, but they were rude and pushy. They seemed to have little experience with this country, and were limited in language, even hand signs. The description seemed familiar.

"They were outlanders? Maybe from the east?" Beaver asked.

"Yes, those are the ones," agreed Flower quickly.

"I saw them," Beaver nodded. "They are the same as those who killed the men of Hungry Hawk's people."

"Yes, my husband thought so, too. Trades tried to befriend them, but they were very rude. They started to open our packs, and some looked at me . . . Well, in a wrong way."

Beaver felt his temper start to rise.

"Did they . . ."

"No, no, Beaver, let me finish! There was a scuffle, and somebody stuck a knife in my husband, here."

She pointed to her own chest, on the right side, just below the breast.

"*Aiee*! A lung?"

Flower nodded solemnly. This was a bad thing. There was seldom recovery from a punctured lung, but the dying was prolonged.

"But," Beaver asked, "how did you escape?"

"Oh, we didn't! At about that time came Bull's Horn and his band. They knew us, of course. Bull's Horn was offended at their treatment of us. Those outsiders did not even understand respect or courtesy. They tried to run. That was foolish."

"Bull's Horn took offense to this?"

"Of course! His warriors chased them."

"Where did they go? They violated the safe haven at the quarry, tried to hunt down Hungry Hawk's people."

"That is no matter now, Beaver. Bull's Horn's warriors took many horses, many scalps. There are none left."

This was shocking information, yet a great relief. It had been so to Cactus Flower, too, but was overshadowed by her husband's condition.

"We were still trying to solve the problem of the pipe," she went on. "The old warrior who owned it had wanted to take it with him to the Other Side when he crossed over. Trades His Moccasins thought that something interfered. Maybe the son wanted it, we don't know. Maybe its value was involved."

Beaver was still puzzled. "So, whatever the cause," he reasoned, "the pipe was not on the burial scaffold. But, Trades did return it."

"Ah, yes, but to its origin, not to the Other Side," she reminded. "To some of the tribes, you know, things that are to accompany the dead on the crossing over must have *their* spirits released, too."

Beaver had not thought of this, since it was not a custom among his own people. In either case, there would be on the burial scaffold enough dried meat or other food for the journey to the Other Side, as well as weapons and blankets. The bow and arrows and the lance of the dead warrior must be ceremonially broken, his blanket slashed, the waterskin perforated, so that the spirits of these objects might be released to cross over with the spirit of the deceased.

It was not unheard of that a horse might be killed beneath the scaffold, so that the dead might have transportation to the Other Side.

"Are these the ways of the old woman's people?" asked Beaver.

"We don't know," admitted Cactus Flower. "But, Trades His Moccasins is made to think so."

"Then . . . What does he want to do?"

"My husband wants you to find a way to break the pipe to release its spirit."

"But, he knows where the pipe rests. He put it there."

"That is true. And you were there to help him."

"Yes . . ."

"So, Trades His Moccasins is sure that you will find a way to recover it and break it, freeing its spirit to join the old man on the Other Side."

He has more confidence in me than I do, thought Beaver. It was an overwhelming task that faced him. But, how could he refuse?

"I will do what I can, Flower," he promised.

The expression of gratitude in the eyes of Cactus Flower seemed to give him strength. He could not fail his friends.

But, where to start?

⟨⟩

They traveled on, following Bull's Horn and his band back in the general direction of the quarry. Trades His Moccasins seemed to sleep, but it was not the relaxing sleep that would bring the rest which he needed so badly.

Beaver now faced a tremendous responsibility, possibly the most important of his life. His feelings wavered, between the honor and trust that his friends had shown in him, and the absolute impossibility of recovering the pipe from the top of the Lovers' Leap pillar. There was no way to evade the request of the man who had done so much for him. Or, to know how to bring Cactus Flower the satisfaction that he had done all he could for her dying husband.

Maybe it would be possible to break the pipe by throwing stones or shooting at it from the cliff's rim. He pondered that possibility for a little while, certain that it would be possible, but wondering whether it would be appropriate.

Meanwhile, he and Cactus Flower made ready to move on toward the quarry, following Bull's Horn and his band.

Trades His Moccasins woke as they prepared to travel. His face was pale. It was heart-breaking to see the trader's efforts to talk. He could manage only a few words before it was necessary to pause and gasp for a breath.

"Beaver . . . The pipe . . . It must be . . . Broken . . ."

"Yes, Flower has told me of this. Try to rest, now. We will take you back to the quarry."

"Must be . . . Broken . . . Spirit . . . Cross over . . ."

"Yes, I understand, friend. I will do as you wish."

To himself, Beaver wondered if he could live up to his promise.

⟨⟩

It was nearly dark when they arrived back at the quarry. Bull's Horn had already made the customary contact with the refugees camped there, and satisfied himself that things were going as well as could be expected. His own camp, that of his entire band, would be some distance away, for reasons of water, grass, and sanitation. They would move on quickly toward their chosen area for the autumn hunt, now approaching, with the Moon of Hunting.

He was concerned about the refugees, but had been more than generous with his help. There was little more that could be done to help them. They would succeed or fail, and he was unsure which it might be. No matter . . .

Bull's Horn was more concerned about the trader. It was a bad thing that had happened, unacceptable on the plains. A trader should be immune to attack such as these outsiders had carried out. He was still offended when he thought of it. Well, it was behind them now. There was no danger from those outsiders to threaten the trader's wife and his partner. The threat had been eliminated quickly and efficiently. Too bad, though, about the chest wound, a prolonged, miserable way to go . . .

⟨⟩

Beaver and Cactus Flower set up a camp away from the others, and away from Hungry Hawk and his refugees. It seemed only right that the dying man should have some privacy.

They went through the usual lighting of the fire with the customary ritual, and Beaver helped to make the trader as comfortable as possible.

"These packs are all you have left?" he asked Flower as he unloaded the bundles from the pack horse.

"Yes . . . There has been no chance to trade, and much was lost or stolen."

This was not so much a complaint as an explanation. Sometimes good things happen, sometimes bad.

Just before darkness fell, Beaver decided to go for another look at the bundled pipe that had come to have so much meaning in their lives. He excused himself and walked to the spot opposite the pillar. He could see the buckskin pouch, and its intricate beadwork, in plain sight, so near and yet so far. He squatted on his heels again and stared at this object which seemed to have taken over his life. How could this be approached?

It might be possible, he theorized, to find a long stick or pole with which he could knock or push the bundle off of the rock. But no, such a pole would be too heavy to extend that far over empty space.

Maybe a heavy club or a stone tossed across the intervening space to crush the stone pipe. No, it would not be possible to toss an object heavy enough to do that across the required distance with much accuracy.

Darkness was thickening rapidly now, and he must return to his friends. Just as he started to rise, he thought he heard the familiar chuckle. It may have been only a whisper of evening breeze in the leaves of the giant oak near by, but . . . It could have been a voice. It was possible, also, that he only imagined that the thought which now came to him had originated not in his own mind, but from that same whisper.

It won't work. You'll have to jump!

"What?" he asked, startled, glancing around quickly.

He saw nothing, but there was that definite, familiar feeling . . .

"Are you there, Giggles?"

There was no answer, but a new thought was forming in his mind as if it had been placed there.

You can do it. Others have.

‹·›42

When Beaver returned to the campfire, Trades His Moccasins was awake and appeared stronger. It must have been terribly hard, as well as painful, to bump along all day on the travois. But now, in the cool of evening, in a more secure setting, he seemed to have gained considerably more strength.

Cactus Flower was cooking something in a tin cup from the trade packs. Beaver assumed it to be a broth, probably made from jerky or pemmican, heated with water. It would be easy to swallow.

The trader looked at him expectantly, a question in his eyes.

What could Beaver say? He must at least try to answer this unspoken question.

"I . . . I have a plan," he said lamely.

It was not exactly true, but he did have a start, given him in the same mysterious manner as some of his other recent ideas. He did not want to discuss *how*. It might have come too close to admitting that he believed he had seen the Little People. That, he was unprepared to do.

"There are those who have jumped the Lovers' Leap," he found himself saying. "If they could, then I can."

There was a gasp from Flower, and the trader looked at him in disbelief.

"Are you sure?" asked Trades His Moccasins.

"Of course. Others have."

"How do you know? Maybe that is only a story."

"I think not. But, surely, I can knock the pouch off the rock. Then it can be retrieved and the pipe broken."

"But, Beaver," interrupted Flower, "if you fall . . ."

"It is not a very long fall," Beaver insisted. "I have looked at it. There are bushes below to break the fall. It would not be dangerous."

He lied, and all three knew it.

"How would you get down, if you *don't* fall?" asked the trader.

"Flower will throw me a rope," said Beaver quickly.

None of them spoke for the space of a few heartbeats. Then, Cactus Flower spoke.

"I can do that."

⟨ ⟩

The next morning Beaver decided that it might be a good thing if he could practice a little. He went back to the Lovers' Leap and studied the width of the space he would have to clear, and the size of the top of the rock. Then he took a couple of ropes, and laid out on level ground a replica of the jump he must make.

Time after time he made the jump, testing his muscles, planning the foot from which to push off, and on which to land. Finally, he decided that he was ready. As ready as possible, anyway. He had determined in his own mind that if he fell, he would try his best to grab or kick the bundled pipe off the rock, so that it could be retrieved and broken. He hoped that would not be necessary.

"I want to be there," insisted Trades His Moccasins.

It seemed only fair that it should be so. Cactus Flower prepared the travois and Beaver brought the horse. The trader was placed on the drag, and the strange procession headed to the Lovers' Leap. The injured man was placed where he could see the attempt. There could be only one . . .

Beaver carefully paced off the distance to conform to that he had practiced. The try could be postponed no longer.

He took three deep breaths, filled his lungs and sprinted toward the canyon's rim. Pushing off, he soared across the space he had measured so carefully, toward the flat top of the stone pillar. In midair, he wondered whether he had paid enough attention to his ability to stop without plummeting on over the farther edge.

It seemed a long time that he hovered, hanging over the rock and the all-important object below him. *Too far* . . . In midair, he realized that the momentum of his jump was going to carry him on, over the edge. Frantically, he twisted, tried to stop his forward motion . . .

He was never certain afterward exactly what had happened. He may have closed his eyes, or maybe not. He did seem to recall that he *had* gone over the edge. Cactus Flower did verify that he had dropped from sight behind the pillar for a moment. At least, she *thought* so. She did describe his appearance as he climbed *back* up and over the edge, stood up and stepped over to pick up the pipe.

He stuffed it inside his shirt.

"Throw me the rope!" he called.

Flower quickly complied, and Beaver looped it around a projection of the rock to lower himself to the canyon floor.

On the way around and back up the path, he found himself confused. *He seemed to have a foggy memory of clawing at a projection of the rock, regaining his balance, and turning. Had he been boosted back up?* Or did he merely find the strength to do what seemed impossible? He would certainly not mention it to the others, and he was uncertain whether they had heard the half-whisper:

"There! Now go on up!"

Or maybe that, too, had been in his imagination as he struggled for survival.

<>

That evening around the fire, the three friends discussed their next move, while the infant cooed softly on a blanket near by. Beaver had handed the pipe, still intact and in its case, to Trades His Moccasins. The trader seemed to be the one who had, through no mistake of his own, inherited the bad luck curse. He must decide how to proceed. And, after all, he had been the leader of the little trading party.

The events of the day, however, had sucked most of the strength from the trader's body. Even the short trip from their camp to the Lovers' Leap and back had been difficult. His labored breathing made a whistling sound, and it was apparent that it required more effort with every breath.

"Would it not be good," Flower suggested, "to break the pipe, loose its spirit? Then it could cross over."

Trades His Moccasins took a breath or two before mustering strength to answer.

"No . . . No one to . . . show the way . . . I will . . . take it . . . with me."

Beaver felt a chill, which enfolded his heart and made his own breath come hard.

"No!" he protested. "You get some rest, and it will be better."

Trades His Moccasins smiled a dry smile for a moment, took a breath, and spoke, again with difficulty.

"You know better . . . A chest wound, Beaver . . . lungs. But . . . stay with me . . . you break . . . the pipe."

"Now?" asked the distraught Beaver.

"No . . . When I start . . . across."

His breath was coming harder, but he still had something to say.

"Flower . . . It has been . . . good . . . now . . . you stay . . . with Beaver."

There was a long pause, during which neither of them could look at each other.

Then the trader spoke again.

"Beaver . . . Take care of her . . . of *them*."

"I will," said Beaver, through his tears.

"It is . . . good . . . now . . ."

Weakly, Trades His Moccasins extended his hand, the one that held the buckskin pipe case. His face was ashen, but there was a sense of peace as he tried to smile.

"Now . . . Break the pipe!"

◁▷Afterword

There were the prescribed three days of mourning, with songs from each of the tribes. Those of the trader's people, those of Cactus Flower, and Beaver added those of his own. Flower gashed her forearms to shed blood in her grief, as was the custom of her own tribe.

With the help of Hungry Hawk's people, they erected a scaffold at a place acceptable to Bull's Horn and his Lakotas. The body of Trades His Moccasins was ceremonially wrapped, and accompanied by appropriate food and water for the journey. The eagle pipe, smashed by the blow of a stone in Beaver's hand, was placed by the trader's side, still in its buckskin pouch.

When the ceremonies of mourning were complete, Flower bathed and purified herself. Finally, they could no longer avoid the conversation prescribed by her dying husband.

"We must talk," she began.

"Yes . . . I . . ."

"Stop," said the girl. "Beaver, it was too much for my husband to ask. I will understand, if you . . ."

Beaver held up his hand to interrupt her.

"No, it is not that. I was made to think that you should say 'no' if you wish. It was not his to choose, but yours."

Flower dropped her eyes.

"But," she said cautiously, "my husband was mostly right in his decisions, no?"

Beaver's face flushed with embarrassment.

"That is true," he mumbled.

"Then," Flower continued, "maybe we should follow his wishes."

"It is good," said Beaver. "But . . . Is there a time of mourning before . . ."

"Before I take another man?"

"Well, yes," he mumbled awkwardly. "Is there?"

She nodded.

"Yes, a moon or so. When it is time, I will tell you."

Beaver did not answer immediately, but in his heart he felt that he was now certain of the identity of the woman in his arms in the odd, recurring dream. It could be no one else.

And it was good.